TYRANTS

ALSO BY MARSHALL N. KLIMASEWISKI

The Cottagers

TYRANTS

STORIES

MARSHALL N. KLIMASEWISKI

W. W. Norton & Company

New York • London

Excerpt from *Strindberg's Letters, Vol. 2: 1892–1912*. Edited and translated by Michael Robinson. Copyright ©1992 University of Chicago Press. Used with permission. By kind permission of Continuum International Publishing in the United Kingdom.

For information about permission to reproduce selections from this book, write to Permissions, W.W. Norton & Company, Inc.
500 Fifth Avenue, New York, NY 10110

For information about special discounts for bulk purchases, please contact W.W. Norton Special Sales at specialsales@wwnorton.com or 800-233-4830

Manufacturing by RR Donnelley, Bloomsburg
Book design by Judith Stagnitto Abbate / Abbate Design
Production manager: Devon Zahn

Library of Congress Cataloging-in-Publication Data

Klimasewiski, Marshall N.
Tyrants : stories / Marshall N. Klimasewiski. — 1st ed.
p. cm.
ISBN 978-0-393-33096-0 (pbk.)
I. Title.
PS3611.L557T98 2008
813'.6—dc22
            2007036233

W.W. Norton & Company, Inc.
500 Fifth Avenue, New York, N.Y. 10110
www.wwnorton.com

W.W. Norton & Company Ltd.
Castle House, 75/76 Wells Street, London W1T 3QT

1 2 3 4 5 6 7 8 9 0

For my mother, Marilyn Turner,
with gratitude and love

CONTENTS

ACKNOWLEDGMENTS

THESE STORIES have appeared previously, sometimes in different form, in the following publications: "Nobile's Airship" in *The Yale Review*, "The Third House" in *Tin House Magazine* and *Best of Tin House: Stories*, "Some Thrills" in *TriQuarterly*, "The Last Time I Saw Richard" in *The Missouri Review*, "Tyrants" in *The Atlantic Monthly*, "Tanner and Jun Hee" in *Ploughshares*, "Tanner" in *The Antioch Review*, "Jun Hee" in *The New Yorker* and *Best American Short Stories*, and "Aëronauts" in *Subtropics*. I'm very grateful to the editors of those publications.

Some of these stories were written with the generous support of the National Endowment for the Arts, Emory University, the Fine Arts Work Center in Provincetown, and Yaddo. In addition, they have all benefited from the guidance, insight, and patience of the people who saw them first. I have been extremely fortunate in my teachers—Hilary Masters, Margot Livesey, Jim Daniels, Gerald Costanzo, Richard Messer, Robert Early, Phil O'Connor, Aharon Appelfeld, Joan Silber, Leslie Epstein, and Elie Wiesel—and also in my agents, Elaine Markson and Gary Johnson, and my editor, Jill Bialosky. I'm very grateful to all of them. And to my fellow fiction writers (plus a few poets) in the workshops at Carnegie Mellon University, Bowling Green State University, and Boston University. For several years now, Washington University in St. Louis has been an invaluable source of sanctuary and support. And I'm particularly indebted to the readers I lean on most heavily: Peter Ho Davies, Lynne Raughley, Zachary Lazar, Anna Keesey, and most of all, Saher. Thank you!

TYRANTS

NOBILE'S AIRSHIP

NOBILE TOOK the morning train from Milan to Parma and Parma to Bologna. He changed for Florence while a shower fell on the tin of the train shed, and rode through rain all the way to Rome. At his appointment with Mussolini he would ask for a rescue plane and a pilot—a precaution to wait in reserve on the support ship. His family was with him. It was a last vacation before his flight to the Pole. The bald hills outside Siena pitched and fell into olive groves but the General's mind drifted over the white quiet of the frozen sea. His daughter wandered from berth to berth, bursting through doors without knocking. His wife had sent back three cappuccini—this one too bitter, the last shy of foam. You'll be changed, she said to him now, and he turned to her. It was a long time since she had addressed him with anything other than an imperative. It was a long time before the other war still and this train they rode was still blameless and remarkable and the airships he built were said to be superior to planes. His wife was young still, but sheathed already in the resignations of an older woman. Nonsense, he told her. Nothing will change. He turned back to the window and coughed.

Bettina took a ride from a neighbor to Agrigento and the slow train to Palermo; from Palermo she took the ferry to Naples and the train from Naples up the coast to Rome. Ugo Lago met her at the station. He was afraid the sight of her would disappoint him, having lived among the women of the city for months now, and initially it did; but he tried to hide it. He brought her to the offices of the *Popolo d'Italia*, where his friends pretended, as prearranged, that Il Duce had been looking for him. They begged him to stay—said he couldn't be spared. He waved them off and swept her back into the sunlight and took her to every cafe in the city where the waiters knew his name. It was a warm, clear day with an inland breeze; he had a motorcar that belonged to his landlord, away in Anzio. But Bettina was strangely unimpressed. Her boredom—her composure in the face of so much urban charm—rekindled Ugo's desire. He brought her to the apartment and pressed his case, tried romance, teasing, a pinch of force. Yet still Bettina was resistant. She had undressed as soon as he closed the door, but placidly, as if alone. He had grappled with her until they were both slick and bruised. But Ugo Lago had nothing to show for it. They lay side by side with swollen lips and stared into the landscape of the plaster ceiling while an argument broke out in the street below. Bettina went to the window.

You've lost weight in Rome, she said, the dear droop of her ass before him. She was as sad and lovely as ever while framed by the window and set against the urban facades.

You smell wrong, she continued, I don't think you're eating well. And your shoes are smudged. Also, you never notice when you've been insulted—did you know that? It's sickening.

She slouched and stared into the street, scratched beneath one breast.

It's loud in Rome, she said. I prefer the country.

So in the morning he drove her out the Via Flaminia all the way to Bolsena, where she swam in the lake while he sucked on olives. He had never learned to swim; he distrusted water when it gathered into a body. On the drive to Orvieto they found a lamb who had wandered astray—it walked with apparent purpose along the gravel fringe of the road. Ugo stopped and picked the lamb up and placed it in Bettina's lap, kicking, and she smiled at him as she once had for the first time since stepping off the train. Shortly they came to a farm with a herd of clean, mild sheep and a goat; a high stone wall, and a pond where geese swam. There was a fragrant olive grove behind the stone wall and no door on the front of the house. Bettina held the bleating lamb in her lap and Ugo beeped his horn. They saw the farmer's head first, then he leapt up onto the wall and stood above them, looking down with a smile fouled by conspicuous charm. He was too young to be a farmer it seemed to Ugo, too tall, as dark as any Sicilian—darker than Ugo himself. How fast will it go? the farmer asked, nodding at the car.

Since Bettina seemed to have lost her voice, Ugo Lago explained about finding the lamb. But the farmer said, Keep it. The lamb for a ride.

No, said Ugo, they were in a hurry; they had to get back to Rome; he was a journalist for the *Popolo d'Italia*—why was he rambling on this way? And what was he supposed to do with a lamb?

Suit yourself, the farmer said. He stood on the wall with his hands in his pockets. The goat stared and chewed and the geese paraded haughtily toward the near shore of the pond. Ugo poked Bettina until she opened the car door and set down the lamb. It began to sniff among the mint that grew by the road. Then she closed the door and they drove away while the farmer waved.

In a moment Bettina asked, Where are we now?

Her voice was weak. She had to repeat the question to overcome the sound of the engine.

We're nowhere, said Ugo. Close to Orvieto. We'll be in Rome before dark.

·

SHE WAS WARM and uncritical, if distracted, through the remainder of the week. That she never let him have his way only served to reinforce his affection for her. He took her to the station and kissed her with tears in his eyes and promised he would send for her again—to stay—just as soon as he had his promotion. It was said that his stories had caught the eye of Mussolini himself. She must be patient.

Fine, she said, impatiently. Now go back to work.

She touched his chest.

They need you there.

When he was gone she watched the train for Naples pull away, then waited for the train to Viterbo. From Viterbo she changed for Orvieto. No one heard a word from her for more than a month. Ugo Lago's fears ran from the improbable to the fantastic—kidnapping, drowning, unaccountable detainment or unwitnessed death—and the tragic, remote possibilities fanned his passion. When the police coarsely suggested she might be unharmed and not so much missing as elsewhere, he told them, bravely, that he could live with that so long as he knew she was alive and safe.

In April she married and sent a letter to Ugo and he cursed her in every cafe in the city where they knew his name. The next morning he begged his editor to give him the airship—begged for the story as fiercely as he had begged out of it the week before—and that evening he caught the last train to Milan.

It was a good story, but not a big story—a small story. Still, he would ride in the airship *Italia* the breadth of Europe and north to the Arctic, as far from Italy as it was possible to be. This was an Italian airship, an Italian commander, General Nobile, an Italian crew save a Czech and a Swede, and they meant to fly over the Pole and west to uncharted regions of Nicholas II Land. All heady material. But on the other hand, Nobile and half the crew had been to the Pole already, with Amundsen in '26, and before Nobile had been Byrd and before Byrd, Peary. The Pole was not the destination it used to be, nobody had heard of Nicholas II Land, and Commander Balbo had largely convinced Il Duce that airplanes were the future—that the time of airships was over already. The rest of the world was so certain that Italy didn't belong in the Arctic without Nordic leadership that even the king hedged his endorsement in case of disaster. And coverage would be limited by the fact that Nobile could afford to carry the weight of only two journalists. It would be Ugo Lago, of Mussolini's *Popolo d'Italia*, and the Venetian Tomaselli, special correspondent for *Corriere della Sera*.

Still, there was a good band and half of Milan to see them off. The ground crew were dressed in folk costumes and aviator caps. At the General's signal they let the ropes slip through their hands and the band broke into "Giovinezza." The airship rose and circled the city, then paraded, with its typical ponderous majesty, through the valley of Po. They flew east across the Gulf of Venice, over Trieste and north to Vienna. They threaded the valleys between the mountains of Sudetenland, flying dangerously low beneath storm clouds. The rain beat against the hull above them, competing with the strain of the engines, while headwinds coerced the nose of the ship into a drunken duck and lunge. Everyone had something to do except Ugo and Tomaselli—there was no chance to file a report as Biagi monopolized the wireless for navigation. Ugo stood at the back of the cramped control cabin and watched the mysterious bulk of the mountains around them, dangerously abbreviated by the cover of fog. He wished for a fiery crash: a terrible, fantastic death for them all. Infamy. He would settle for nothing less than catastrophe.

But the General flew his ship safely through and the sky cleared enough to see the lights of unknown towns among the dark trees below. He was an odd source of authority, this General: mild and trim, he lacked the Fascist assurance one expected in an officer. His salute was self-conscious. But he was an engineer first, had drawn the pencil lines that marked the *Italia*'s conception and watched over her construction, and he piloted the ship with the proud confidence of a father. He took them into Poland and landed, finally, at a hangar in Jesseritz near Stolp on the Baltic Sea.

Jesseritz was cold and bleak, as far from Rome as another century, yet barely halfway to the Pole. Ugo had a dinner of salted escolar and a hunk of *pane* that was stale already. He went to bed early, where he shivered with the cold and his miserable loneliness and what sleep he gained was permeated by terrifying dreams. In the morning he sent two hundred words to Tomaselli's thousand. He stood his colleague up for dinner.

The second night in Jesseritz he still couldn't sleep. He got out of bed and without bothering to dress walked through the empty streets of the town in his nightshirt like a wayward Mediterranean ghost. He kept to the road. An old woman who drove by on a cart full of cabbage passed him without a glance, and he wondered if, in addition to Italy and the weave of his life, he hadn't managed to float clear of whatever essential volume it was that rendered him substantial and distinct in the world. He came to the bridge over the Stupia and climbed up onto the low stone railing and stared into the water below. It was sleek and black, menacing and inscrutable like water everywhere. But the fear it inspired was the only familiar aspect at hand. He heard birds in the trees along the bank—it was that close to morning—and their song was unlike the song of any bird he had ever heard in Sicily. The smell of the river and of the forest beside it was entirely wrong as well, and even the moonlight, diffuse through clouds, seemed alien, worthless and dim. There was nothing to hold him here, nothing to cling to, but then the sight of his own hairy feet on the sandstone rail of the bridge distracted him, and he had a clear and terrible picture of himself, as if looking down from above.

He was a small man, not yet thirty, not strong or agile, with dark hair already receding and sad, unconvincing eyes. He was not without advantages—he had a portion of his youth still—but his jaw hung open slightly, by habit, in a manner that made him appear half stunned and eternally braced for disappointment. It's possible the impression was the result of his thus-far desultory life—had nothing to do with his mouth—but the fact remained that he was a swarthy Sicilian perched in his nightshirt on an unnamed bridge in the north of Poland. He was deeply embarrassed. It would never do. He climbed back down—careful now, suddenly shy—and snuck back to town off the edge of the road. The breakfast fires were lit at the inn. The keeper chopped wood in the dark. He crept into his room and fell asleep, but his dreams remained restless and severe.

The airship traversed the Baltic Sea to Stockholm, where a fleet of silver pursuit planes escorted them briefly. Then north to Tromsø, from Tromsø to Vadsø, from Vadsø to Spitzbergen. Over King's Bay they saw the red and black roofs of Ny-Ålesund and the fragile settlement only served to accentuate the emptiness of the kingdom surrounding it. The sight of such a forsaken and hostile landscape warmed Ugo's weary heart. How wonderfully unforgiving it seemed—how predisposed to cataclysm. He welcomed frozen Spitzbergen as if it were the vineyards of San Cataldo. Their support ship, the *Città di Milano*, was moored in the wedge of open water in the harbor. Farther inland, apart from the houses, the wooden ribs of the hangar that Amundsen had built for the *Norge* in '26 seemed a blanched omen in the midnight sun. They landed, and the Arctic expedition began.

But the weather, foul the length of Europe and promising no foreseeable clemency, delayed the flight to Nicholas II Land. Ugo had been without a restful hour of sleep since the day he received the letter from Bettina. Exhaustion, combined with the disconcerting effects of the never-setting sun, began to impair his sensibilities. There was little to report on while they waited, his time was largely unoccupied, and with the sun circling the sky as if bewildered, the hours of daytime and night became unmoored and strangely intractable. Ny-Ålesund amounted to a jumble of nearly identical clapboard houses. A narrow-gauge rail ran from the quay to the mine. There were no roads or landmarks, the paths from point to point shifting according to the swell of impenetrable drifts, and if the snow was not falling into your eyes, the glare from the sun was likely blinding. As a result, Ugo was nearly always lost. The problem was exacerbated by the bundled sameness of the Norwegian miners who lived in the settlement: all men of course, almost always alone, stepping briskly with their hooded heads hung and rendered shapeless by layers of wool and fur. The Italian crew seemed clumsy and coarse among them, their gestures superfluous. Only the General was at ease. His smile had been entrenched since the moment they lifted from Milan, and his serenity had swelled the farther north they flew.

One clear night with the sun beating up from the snow in a glory of white, Ugo found himself dully following the boot heels, then the footprints as he fell behind, of a stranger whom he took to be heading toward the *Città di Milano*. He was thinking of the Bettina of San Cataldo. In the mundane, frequent memory that had transfixed him, she peeled potatoes into a zinc pail on the floor between her legs, her skirt hiked up past her knees. She was entirely removed from the work of her hands—thoughtful and composed, her eyes sad with longing—while the pail filled with peels. He thought he had known the nature of her longing, but he had never asked; nor had she volunteered her confidence. Now it was clear that he had been absent from her aspirations—that they had likely flourished in the broad, vague terrain of life after Ugo Lago.

It was the whistle of the coal train that distracted him from his thoughts. Looking up, he found himself alone. The footprints he had followed extended across an enormous field of unbroken snow toward the mountains of West Spitzbergen, but there was no one ahead of him to fill the prints, no form to impinge upon the monotony of white. The huddled rooftops of the settlement lay perhaps a mile behind him—thin dark lines half lost in the glare. He was alone in the midst of nothing at all. The light of the midnight sun had a splintered quality that lent shadows where there was no substance to cast them. The smoke from the crawling train recoiled in low white pillows over the coal cars and the mechanical wheeze of the engine merged with the mortal chuff of his breath through the muffle of the fur on his hood. He turned forward and back again. It seemed at first a dream, as terrible as those that were haunting him, if less violent. But then he was overtaken—slowly, and in the midst of a sensible calm that sank his lungs against his ribs—by the certainty of his own impending death. He would never see Italy or Bettina again—it was more than a wish now, more than an unspecified foreboding. For hadn't he made his way already into a realm beyond the reach of the living?

·

WHEN THE WEATHER finally allowed for the departure to Nicholas II Land, the General decided he could afford the weight of only one journalist. The crew would be trimmed to fourteen. Ugo Lago and Tomaselli agreed to abide by the flip of a coin, with the loser gaining, as compensation, the later flight to the Pole. But when the toss fell to Ugo, the General intervened. Tomaselli was the senior man; he had been a captain in the Alpini. Ugo could not ski or swim—on this, the longest, most critical and dangerous flight, it would be Tomaselli instead.

Forgive me, the General said, clutching Ugo's arm. But you understand.

Ugo had hardly managed to summon a care for the expedition beyond its means as his own demise, but he was outraged by the injustice of this decision. He retired to the dismal saloon of the *Città di Milano* to wait for news from the airship and complain to what meager company he could find. A pair of trappers skied in with the skins of polar bears and foxes, both white and blue, which the sailors wore across their shoulders like stoles. Every hour the crew of the *Italia* reported their progress over the wireless, and one of the journalists who had arrived by ship—the Norwegian or the German—would return from the bridge with the news. When Ugo sat down to dinner, the airship was entering the stretch of sea where nautical maps had boldly placed the island of Giles Land since a Dutch sea captain thought he had glimpsed its peaks in 1707. When he stood from the table, Giles Land had been erased from the maps. The ship had met with milder weather; it seemed the flight might be a historic success.

Ugo had heard enough. He staggered above deck and rode to shore with a pair of sailors. He wandered until he chanced upon the one-room hut where he was boarded, nearly buried by a drift that hadn't existed that morning. The fire was dead in the stove, the water frozen in the sink, and the cabin dark with all but one window covered by snow. He fell onto the cot fully dressed.

They chase you beneath the olive branches, the reach of withered limbs, and you're out of breath when they catch you. They turn you on your back and hold you down while the sheep crowd in, and they have the lamb— you can see its terrified eyes pass by—but down your throat it goes. You can't breath with the head of the lamb in your throat, the gauze of its wool on your teeth and tongue, and you want to bite down, to be able to breath, just to close your mouth before they shove the front legs in, but you can feel the lamb bleating into the flesh of your throat and who could bite through a bleating lamb?

The cold woke him. He felt he had been asleep for hours, but who could tell? Outside the clear skies had given way to snowfall again. He shoveled coal into the stove and resuscitated the fire, longing for the smell of burning wood, for something recently alive to touch. Then he walked to the docks, where the dingy he came in on was gone. There was no one on the quay, and the moored ship appeared vacant from shore. Even the smoke from its stacks was thin. He struggled through drifts to the railway line and followed it back into empty Ny-Ålesund. He found the store, but the door was locked and the lights out. The yellow post office was likewise abandoned. Then he remembered the airship, and he guessed it must be disaster: some terrible, compelling news that had drawn them all to the wireless on the ship. The General's whim had denied him his fate.

Just at that moment, in the distance between two buildings, he saw a figure hurry by. He stumbled after, but when he rounded the corner the figure was some distance ahead. He was up on the rise of the tracks, walking toward the mine through the wind and snow. His shoulders were hunched and his chin tucked, as if he was holding his heavy coat closed.

Hello! Ugo called. He spoke in English, as near to a common tongue as the settlement could afford. What is happened?

The figure turned and watched him without a reply. Ugo struggled through the deep snow along the edge of the tracks. Wait, please, for me, he called when he was up on the rails. Then he waved, perhaps frantically, relieved to find he was not alone.

The stranger responded by turning away and hurrying up the line. Wait, please, Ugo called again, then slipped into Italian: I'm a journalist from Rome! For Christ's sake, tell me what's happened!

The man began to run—a shuffling, shy run, his narrow shoulders swinging beneath the anorak. Ugo was so surprised that for a moment he stood still watching. What's wrong with you? he shouted, though he was thinking, What's wrong with me? He couldn't imagine what might draw the stranger to the mine in such a hurry, and ridiculous as it was, he had the impression that the man believed Ugo was chasing him. He hadn't been, of course, but now he did. He ran after, as best he could in his layers and boots, not bothering to call out again. He felt he might do some liberating harm to this stranger—might resort to a simpler vocabulary until it seemed he was being properly understood.

There was a low wooden structure built against the side of the coal tip with an archway for the trains. The figure disappeared into the black mouth of the mine and Ugo was alone again in the snowfall, sweating and out of breath. Approaching the dark, he heard the pound of machinery and the rattle of chains, the chilly tonk of metal striking rock, but he had no idea what was past the archway. He half expected the train to come screaming forth, but he ran until he was swallowed by the mine, surrounded by the sounds of geological violence with the sear of coal dust in his nostrils. It was as dark—yes, he remembered, though it was a thing of his past now—as night. A moonless night among the stand of pines at the far end of the cove, where you can meet her when her family is asleep and no one will see you. He didn't dare move while his eyes adjusted. When they had, he found he was facing a narrow corridor by the side of the tracks. At the end of the corridor was a room, the sappy light of a filthy lamp hung above a table, and before the table, a woman. There she stood. Her hood was off, her shoulders wet with snow still, and he could see her eyes in the lamplight. She was watching him. She was alone. She stood stiffly with her hands braced against the table behind her—clearly frightened, prepared to step aside if he pounced. Her name came to his lips. He didn't pounce, though, so much as capitulate—he may have spoken her name aloud—and when he passed through the doorway he was knocked on the head, and he pitched to his knees and his vision collapsed.

He came to in a prone position on a bench in the same room. He lay still a long time, not entirely convinced he was alive. Then he turned toward the purr of a strange and quiet engine. There was a sort of angel standing in a doorway with the brilliant snowlight surrounding him. He wore a foil candle-lantern. His face was black and turned up toward the sky.

Ugo grunted unexpectedly when he swung his feet to the floor, and the angel turned to him, surprised. He was only a boy. He came for Ugo, shaking his head and saying, No no no, from within the hollow of a Norwegian inflection. Ugo's forehead felt massive and still expanding. He tipped it toward the doorway and followed through with the rest of his body—screamed, and the boy got out of his way. He stumbled into the sunlight, squinting terribly, and fell onto his knees in the snow outside the mine. Above him, hovering impossibly and slow with menace, the gray hull of the *Italia* hung in the empty sky like a massive, looming moon.

•

AFTER THE PEAKS of Spitzbergen receded down the slope of the horizon and there was nothing to see beneath the cover of clouds but the dull white of the pack ice and the gray of open channels of sea, it was obvious to Ugo that the airship had found its proper element. It was a landscape apart from the world, so alien here past the last comfort of land that it seemed isolated by more than latitude and climate, by some less tangible amplitude as well. It would require a vehicle as ingenious and unlikely as an airship to reach such a place. And now that the ship was here, it was difficult to imagine it ever existing elsewhere. You could stick your head out a porthole of the pilot's cabin and the dark gray girth of the hull above you was a close cousin to the family of shades that had settled the landscape. If the wind was in your favor, as it was on the route to the Pole, the engines were quiet and unimpressive and your speed across the pack seemed effortless, almost nebular. Ugo watched a pair of birds—murres or auks, who could tell?—change their course to accommodate the airship, but there was nothing startled in their evasion. Just east of Cape Bridgman someone spotted a polar bear, who stayed by his seal hole while they passed overhead.

Ugo was in the way no matter where he went on the ship, the object of constant frustration. He knew enough to take it personally. He was on board this time instead of Tomaselli, the Alpini journalist with the medals and the military bearing, and some stories had circulated about the woman he was said to have chased into the mine. He knew the General would have left him behind again if he could have afforded the slight to Mussolini and his newspaper, and where the General leaned, his crew lunged.

He was shooed from the pilot's cabin down the dark corridor of the gangway above the keel. Under the belly of the ship the motor gondolas hung like sidecars at the end of catwalks. There was a mechanic crammed into each—Ciocca and Caratti—with the loneliest jobs on board. Ugo lingered in the rigging for a time while the airship spent the favorable wind on a wealth of clear skies north of Greenland, but eventually the cold chased him back inside. The gangway was cluttered with tents and packs and cans of petrol, crates of pemmican and inflatable rafts, chocolate—pounds of chocolate in foil bricks—and a phonograph with three sleeved disks. There was hardly space left to walk, but the rigger Arduino came busting through on his rounds.

They had strong tailwinds and tremendous visibility through

the region of previously uncharted sea, though there was nothing to chart except the tessellated landscape of ice. The wind would be brutal when they turned for home; the crew was pleased, but anxious. With less than a hundred kilometers to the Pole, they approached the towering battlements of a dark cloud bank and rose to a thousand feet to be sure of an accurate bearing. Then they were there, and the General took them down through the tiers of cloud and fog in a slow, descending spiral. The pack ice materialized below like the innermost layer of sky. It was utterly identical to the ice they had flown over for hours—white and gray and articulate and empty in just the same way, profoundly mundane to Ugo's eyes—yet they dropped the oversized flag (plunk into a wet heap), and the Milanese coat-of-arms, and the medallion of the Virgin of Fire from the town of Forlì, and lastly the six-foot wooden cross that the Pope had blessed and warned was heavy. As soon as these mementos landed, smudges on the skin of the sea, each began to float from the top of the world as if rolling off the slope of the globe. Nothing remained at the Pole for long. Where was the flag that Nobile had dropped with the *Norge* in '26? Ugo wanted to ask. *What did they think they had claimed?* He stood by through the crew's celebration and felt fond of them and ashamed. Over the wireless, the General informed Mussolini that the flag of Italy flew again above the ice at the Pole, and it seemed indicative to Ugo that for this man the noun had only one verb. He felt his faith in even the simplest fundamentals of nation and claim and the empty profits of endeavor slip from his possession as silently as it had accrued. What could you tell men like these? No ...

He climbed into the gangway and fished out the phonograph from under the jumble of survival gear. He brought it to the cabin—no one was paying any attention to him—and with a few cranks it stuttered into the stiff strut and bounce of "Giovinezza," the Fascist battle hymn. There were blackshirt salutes all around, and everyone was surprised to see Lago behind the gesture—relieved, even. The General smiled and nodded with pride and a touch of embarrassment. Ugo followed with "The Bells of St. Giusto" and "Beautiful Italy, With All My Heart," and lord in heaven it was almost criminal.

Then all at once, as if by silent consensus, the men of the crew turned their attention to the difficult business of the return trip, setting a course along the twenty-fifth meridian east of Greenwich. And though headwinds immediately began to whistle through the canvas frame of the cabin and the drone of the engines doubled in pitch with the strain, the faces bustling around Ugo remained endowed with the grinning satisfaction of accomplishment. He was forgotten again. He was happy, without reason. He watched them for perhaps an hour until a cool reserve of sleepiness—a sensation unlike anything he had felt in weeks—gathered through the length of his body. He climbed into the gangway, found a sleeping bag and a patch of floor space toward the prow of the ship. And though he could have fallen asleep at once, though he knew he had access tonight to the dull, commodious reaches past the last inkling of consciousness or dreams, he lay awake to savor the anticipation of the emptiness.

•

THEY WERE DEAD into the wind, so much so that the General considered capitulating: crossing the Pole and continuing on to North America instead of returning to Kings Bay. He had maps on board of the McKenzie River basin. But the weather reports on the wireless suggested they might slip ahead of the storm, and Spitzbergen had begun to feel like home. In a little while they were sandwiched between a cover of clouds above and the lay of ground fog below, the two meeting in a gauzy horizon. There were flurries on and off, and when they dipped into the fog to test their speed and drift, the whole of the ship was immediately encased in a thin glaze of ice. The struggle of the engines was punctuated occasionally by the crack of ice shards flung from a propeller into the surface of the hull. Their progress was achingly slow. The General ordered those he could spare to sleep in brief shifts, and though Lago had claimed the only spot on the ship truly out of harm's way, no one was anxious to wake him. He was a grim presence somehow, a walking blow to morale—it was evidently agreed among them, if unspoken. Let him sleep.

Somewhere perhaps a hundred kilometers north of the coast of Foyn Island, the elevator wheel inexplicably jammed and the ship became locked in a nose-down position. The General ordered the engines cut, but their forward momentum carried them near enough to see the ice in perilous detail. Finally they began to rise—the ship was light, having spent so much fuel—and they drifted up through the clouds until they broke into sunlight for a navigational reading. It was eerie, the silence, and the sense of being carried back toward the Pole by the wind—as if they weren't to be relinquished. Cecioni took the elevator wheel apart and cleared the ice, and when he put it back together it seemed to work. Heated by the sun, the hydrogen in the hull began to valve off, so the General took them back down into the gloom.

There were glass balls filled with a red dye—he had devised them himself—that could be dropped and timed to determine the airship's speed over the ice. While the General was watching one of these fall, Cecioni said, We're heavy. He spoke so calmly, with such matter-of-fact delivery, that everyone hesitated a moment. It didn't seem possible. The General looked at Cecioni, then at the gauges—it was true, they were losing altitude. They had been flying low already to take the reading. He ordered the nose of the ship tipped skyward and the motors brought to full throttle, hoping to maneuver out of the fall with dynamic lift, but they only fell faster. Then he ordered the engines cut and the heavy ballast chain dropped, but a measure of panic had broken out and nothing happened quickly enough. There was a knot in the rope that held the ballast chain, and Caratti's motor, on the starboard side, was running still. The General put his head out the porthole to shout at Caratti, but when he glanced down at the approach of the pack ice—its surface splintering from the illusion of monotony afforded by altitude into a broken landscape of crevasses and erupting plates—he knew it was too late. He pulled his head in, braced himself, and wondered, briefly, if the hull would burst into flames or bear down and crush them, one and all.

They struck stern first, and those in the control cabin were thrown through the collapsing frame to the ice. The General felt his limbs snap—or did he only hear this?—and found time to antici-pate being smothered by the weight of the ship. But following an instant of blindness, which he expected to be his last, he had the impression of a flood of light—like waking from a nap in the dark, curtained parlor to step outdoors into the daylight of the courtyard. He lingered among the scent of the mimosa and he could hear the tap of his daughter's shoes, chasing the cat across the paving stones, but his eyes were open and he lay on his back and when his vision was returned to him, placing him on the pack ice again, he saw the creased and partly deflated hull of the airship *Italia* rising above him and drifting away.

Where the cabin had sheared from the keel, ropes and wooden girders and strips of canvas were hanging down, and though the port and starboard gondolas were intact still—with Ciocca and Caratti still in them—the motors were silent. Everything was silent—every-thing was motionless, except the rise and drift of the ship. A man stood on the bridgework to the port gondola—he was near enough that the General recognized him as Arduino—and he seemed stunned by the sight of the ice and the wreckage and the scattered survivors receding. At the hole in the keel where the ladder from the gangway to the cabin had been, two other men were visible: Professor Pontremoli and the journalist, Ugo Lago, who had both been asleep at the moment of impact. The ship was adrift now, car-ried eastward by the gale, nose up and listing. It would simply float away. The General watched until the gray of the hull merged with the gray of the fog around it and only the creased black letters, *I-T-A-L-I-A*, remained visible.

Then those vanished as well. It didn't take long, a matter of minutes.

•

HE WAS LEFT on the ice with seven crew members and the wireless unit remarkably intact. Only he and Cecioni had broken bones—each a leg, the General an arm as well. They had a single tent, some water and a good deal of pemmican. Malmgren shot a polar bear who lingered by the camp, and when they opened its stomach they found it contained the pulped pages of one of their navigational books and little else. There was enough meat to last for weeks. But in a few days, when their signal over the wireless failed to elicit a response, the group split into two. The most restless and able among them—three men—set out by foot toward the low tops of Foyn and Broch islands, visible to the south. But the pack ice was so slick and jumbled that Viglieri was able to watch them through field glasses for two days. It was difficult to tell if they were moving at all.

When they were finally out of sight, the five who remained behind settled into the quiet boredom of their isolation. Cecioni and the General never left the tent—they could barely crawl—and the cool blue of its silk lining, lit through the night by the sun; the snap and ripple it made when the wind blew, or the sounds of dripping and melting outside it when the wind was calm; the humid, stale quality of the air and the sad smell of pemmican: these were the limits of a world. The others kept an eye out to the north for a signal flare or a wisp of smoke from the crew who had been carried with the airship. They had the bulk of the supplies with them on board the ship still, a sufficient store of food. How far could the lame hull have drifted? But there was no sign. And there was no response to the messages the General sent over the wireless, though they were receiving clearly. Each night they listened to the wild reports of miners turned special correspondents in Ny-Ålesund—their disappearance and presumed deaths had become a story of worldwide interest—and to the time check from the Eiffel Tower at 8:00 p.m.

Greenwich and even to the news reports on San Paolo, the station out of Rome. The batteries were weakening, but they listened through the whole of that chilling toccata from the Bach Partita in E minor on a station in Hamburg one evening, and the General lay in pain and miserable reverence and thought of his ship merged with the fog, of the faces staring down.

It was a Soviet farmer who heard them first, a lonely man with a wireless for family, and that seemed appropriate to the General. But soon they were in touch with the *Città di Milano* and the airplanes began to cover the ice like migrating seabirds: the Junkers and the Maake floatplanes, a Heinkel floatplane and a Cirrus Moth, the Fokker ski-plane, the Dornier Wal, the Italian Savoia-Marchetti and the French Latham 47 that Amundsen went down in, never to be seen again. One didn't know how quiet it had been until the buzz of airplane engines became a regular interruption, but for three days the pilots flew nearby without seeing the camp. When Major Maddalena in the Savoia-Marchetti finally spotted them and circled low for a drop, there was a man in the cockpit behind him turning the crank of a cine camera. That night they had cigarettes and whiskey and oranges, and the tent filled with the smells of rescue, but the General thought of their image on film—dirty and wet and unshaven men, two of them crippled and crawling, the snow around them filthy with bear meat, tins, and debris—and it seemed to him that nothing would get any better now, that he had been a fool to think it would. It would get worse instead. Their rescue would be the beginning of the end. It was momentous to be rendered in film—it meant glory or disgrace, no in-between; what good could come of their rescue?

In a few days a Swedish pilot in a Fokker ski-plane succeeded in landing on a strip of melting ice nearby. Despite the General's protests—he had drawn up a list of the order in which they were to be rescued, himself last of all—the pilot insisted on taking him first. His injuries were the worst, he was lighter than Cecioni, and his guidance and level-headedness would be welcome back at the base ship. The pilot had his orders. So they carried him to the plane (it took the bulk of the afternoon, though the Fokker was only a stone's throw from the camp) and strapped him in. He was sweating and exhausted, still anxious about leaving the others behind, even if for only a few hours. When they lifted away and circled low over the tent, he cried at the sight of it there on the ice, so small and uncouth, and at the memory of Arduino and Pontremoli and Ugo Lago, who had suffered this view before him.

The next day, the Fokker toppled tail over nose when she came in to land by the tent, and the Swedish pilot was stranded in place of the General. Of the twenty-two airplanes devoted to the rescue, not another could land on the short strip of ice. There was a joke that made the rounds in Rome saying the General had broken his leg in his hurry to be the first man saved; he was hushed and ignored on the *Città di Milano*. Three weeks later the Russian ice breaker *Krassin* came upon Zappi and Mariano, two of the three who had set out to walk for land. They were stranded on a shrinking ice floe, having drifted as far from Foyn Island each night as they had managed to march in the day. The Swede, Malmgren, had been left to die a month before. Then the *Krassin* shoved on to the tent, and the rescue was finally complete.

•

BUT THERE was no sighting—there never had been a sighting, despite all the flights over the vicinity and the sweep the *Krassin* made—of the crippled airship. No trace of its passengers.

In July of 1930, a Captain Theodor Grödahl went ashore at White Island, where he found heaps of brushwood, clearly gathered, and the rusted remnants of an iron box. He was looking for the crew of the *Italia*, but this was thin evidence: it likely signaled the brief stay of a passing trapper, or even the occupation of some earlier castaway. In August of that year Dr. Adolf Hoel discovered, on the same White Island, the lid of an aluminum pot and a canvas boat and a crude sledge, along with several other artifacts all labeled "Andrée's Polar Expedition 1896." The log of their balloon trip was largely preserved. There was exposed film from which printable negatives were developed. And there were human remains—still so intact that the cause of death could be traced: trichinosis, gained from eating under-boiled bear meat.

Almost every year new remains were discovered in the Arctic. Most dated back to the wooden sailing ships. But the massive hull of the *Italia*, the keel as long as a whaler and the wide nose-cone, the fuel cells and gasbags and any impression of the crew, who had been so well supplied, were never found. In 1930 the R101, the last of the British rigid airships—twice the size of the *Italia*—flew into a hillside near Beauvais and burned with forty-eight men inside. In '33 the *Akron* fell into the sea and seventy-four of the seventy-seven on board were lost. Then the flames of the *Hindenburg* were filmed in '37, and the airships were finished, once and for all.

The crash of an airman in pursuit of his latest exploit—even the wholesale death of entire squads of airmen—was stomached by the general public as the inevitable price paid for progress. But the crash of a dirigible was hubris and catastrophe. It was a fact that never failed to sadden General Nobile, and he was among the last to relinquish the future of the airship. Upon his return to Italy he was quickly and entirely disgraced, in the manner well practiced by Mussolini and his commissions of inquiry. His ships were a threat to Commander Balbo's fleet of long-range planes, and Balbo had the ear of Mussolini. Nobile was stripped of his rank and censured, obliged to take his expertise abroad. He went to Germany, then Russia; was in Chicago when his country entered the war; then exiled in Spain until Italy was rid of Il Duce. Finally he returned to Rome, quietly and without distinction, and with the scud of decades and the death of enemies, his name and accomplishments leaked back to the surface and his reputation was largely restored. He was ninety-three when it was half a century since the *Italia* had reached the Pole. A ceremony was arranged, and though his health was poor and he would be dead in two months, he traveled with his wife to Vigna di Valle on Lake Bracciano to attend.

There were photos and historians, a commemorative stamp, and a postcard. The General summoned his strength to stand through the whole of his speech. He honored his crew, those who were saved and those who were not, and asserted that a telling measure of what the world had lost or had cast aside in the span of fifty years was marked in the demise of the airship. Then he sank into his wheelchair, smiling and damp. In the evening his wife took him down by the lakeside, where they threw bread at the ducks and were silently, uncustomarily pleasant to one another. She took him to the room. She tucked him into bed.

His pride wore off and he was sad again—short of breath, unable to sleep. He longed for a breeze from the porch, but the warm night was still around him. Then he wondered as he always had: would he ever be rid of these three men looking down on him? They were above him now in the dark room, as vivid as they had been that day, when he was burdened with the last sight of them on earth. There was Arduino on the bridgework: he was stunned and still. The professor squinted and knelt and leaned, as if judging whether it was too late to jump. And Ugo Lago stood beside the professor, Ugo the strangest and most haunting of the three because he looked down on the General with a salacious calm. He stood with the cocksure port of a man whose circumstance has proven felicitous; it seemed he was sailing into the midst of his element. He was the mutinous captain of a last flight for this ship the General had made, but looking back it seemed his withdrawal was fashioned with a grace that the indignity of Mussolini's reign and the horror of the war and even the advance of air travel into ordinary boredom had rendered obsolete. He was reconciled, and safe already.

It was Ugo then, most of all, who had wedged like a shim between the General and these handsome latitudes south of the Arctic. It was he who inspired the envy that had enfeebled the General's life.

THE THIRD HOUSE

ANGELA'S FAMILY owned three houses. Henry fell quickly in love with her. Her father was well funded, inheritably and otherwise, and engaged in writing a book. These were Angela's self-conscious phrases; she referred to her father as "Mr. Jones." "What does he do?" Henry had asked, and she had said, "Mr. Jones is engaged in writing a book, Henry." Henry heard the irony but chose to overlook it.

Mrs. Jones was a lawyer who couldn't work due to illness and Angela's two elder brothers had died in a sailing accident. It was too much, really—too picturesque and romantically misfortunate—yet all apparently true. "Drowned, but not forgotten," Angela said of her brothers. Henry had no idea how to interpret her tone there.

She was twenty, six years younger than Henry, but it didn't show. She attended the college where Henry, sadly, cut the grass. He was sitting in on classes also, through the film department, and he worked for an ad agency in the city but it didn't pay. She rowed for the crew team and wore her sleeveless jerseys on her way back from the river or to class or the library and then to bed with him too when he asked. The muscles of her upper arms were long and glossy. Her habitual expression was a willing and absorbed smile which seemed at first to soften the bite of her irony but was in fact its most articulate feature. Henry had been in love before—you could say continuously, since adolescence—but never so decisively, or with so little encouragement. She accepted his romantic attentions without especially answering them; she seemed, he thought, hesitant to decline what she was due, although she might have been just as happy to leave these pennies in the till. One weekend she took him home to her family, apparently for the lark in it. "Mr. Jones will be fascinated," she said. "Be sure to wear this shirt."

The first house was in the woods in the best part of the state, with the trees bare much of the year and beautiful nonetheless. Even the trunks and crowns of Connecticut were not created equal: they were knobbed creatures, congested and dismal, to the north and east, hung with clothes or composed in clumps and rags between highways, but as one traveled south and west toward the shore and the city they gained balance, solemnity, and a winter sophistication which might evoke (or, in Henry's case, install) childhood memories in black and gray punched up by a touch of limbed menace. Angela's father had had this house built to his specifications. It was low and horizontal, discreet in front, with deep eaves; in back there were tall windows conveying panels of landscape. It was fitted to the slope, unless the hillside had been sloped to fit. The leaves from the trees had recently fallen and were still bright. In the room where Angela's father sat—whichever it might be—there was a fire laid and moaning. The books had exploded from the shelves and settled on every surface like a pollen—they were damp on the edge of the tub and redolent beside the coffeemaker; hardbacks in drab cloth or older paperbacks with out-of-fashion covers, well handled but cared for, not shabby yet. Incredibly inviting. All weekend they slipped into Henry's hands. He flipped the pages, read a line or a paragraph, and everything he read seemed apt—appropriate to the Joneses or their house or both. *The large, low rooms, with brown ceilings and dusky corners,*—this was James—*the deep embrasures and curious casements, the quiet light on dark, polished panels, the deep greenness outside, that seemed always peeping in, the sense of well-ordered privacy in the centre of a 'property'*—They smelled good, these books. Or not good in the right way.

Mr. Jones' book would be a study of James: a broad perusal through some narrow linguistic aperture which he politely declined to explain. It was a dilettante's occupation, he said, a way to pass the time. He said so with a quick and clipped delivery that served modesty with beautiful rigor. He had taught once, at the same college that Angela attended, but he didn't any longer. He didn't work. He was engaged in writing a book. In the mornings he bustled forth from the mysterious back of the house—the region where Angela's mother lay (Henry had yet to be introduced)—to prepare the first stages of a breakfast that would linger until noon. Black coffee for his wife (and for Henry), tea for himself, pills and vitamins, oranges cut for the juicer. The table was laid with newsprint: *The Times* and *The New York Review of Books* and *The Guardian* a day late from London. Angela was studying in her room. Mr. Jones took coffee back to his wife. Then he sat with Henry and they read together. He had halved lenses and his thinned hair was as the bed had left it. He was solicitous to Henry, but abstracted. He didn't seem to dislike him, or to be fascinated. He seemed not the slightest bit altered or disturbed by the company, which made Henry feel comfortable and welcomed, even if it was merely negligence. His small talk was professorial, to Henry's ear, gracious and well crafted, though his flat and dampened voice may have been most responsible for the effect—it leveled sentences into thick, sad slabs. He said, "I'm making toast here, Henry, and we have some apple butter—will you join me?" but it was as if he had said, "My sons died young, Henry, and my wife is an invalid—can you imagine?"

Around noon he always sat back and sighed and said, "Well." There was a breathy "h" sound coupled to the "w." He clapped his palms flat on his pants—a wonderfully decisive, preparatory gesture. Then he returned to the back of the house. Angela would emerge, sour and sharpened from concentration. She wanted to know how breakfast had gone. She wanted to know what they'd discussed. "Don't imagine he likes you," she said, and ate a crust of toast from her father's plate.

"He does, though," Henry told her. "He says he digs me."

She rubbed at one eye behind her glasses and scanned the articles her father had left exposed. "You think so?"

" 'Henry,' he said, 'I'll speak plainly. I dig you. I'd like you to have my daughter.' "

She said, "We'll see," grinning only a little. She seemed truly disappointed, as if she'd left them alone together hoping for the worst. Despite her remorselessly lovely face, Angela's hair was kinky and unruly—she failed to wash it or comb it as often as most other girls her age, and she napped at the drop of a hat—so that it often trailed her like someone else's prank. She was cynical about even cynics, and could never be surprised, yet it was a comfort to feel that she should probably consult a mirror more often than she did. Henry wondered how long his novelty might last. He said, "Anyway, we don't need you, Mr. Jones and I. We don't need your approval, you know. We'll elope if we have to." When she ignored the joke he unsuccessfully resolved never to tell her another again.

•

FOR THE WEEK surrounding Thanksgiving she invited him to house number two. It was a cottage in Maine. There were as many books here, predominantly about sea voyages or polar expeditions—with maps inside the covers. There were fires burning in two rooms. A fire here was to dry the damp from your clothes and bake the salt into your skin. The pages of the books were often salty. The floors had warped so that they creaked or groaned in poignant, leathery phrases. Angela spent the better part of each day upstairs with her studies while Henry was downstairs with Mr. Jones. She had chosen chemical engineering—a discipline of great mystery without the slightest intrigue for Henry, as it was for her father—and though she could seldom get through half a chapter of a novel before falling asleep, she never dozed in front of her glossy, congested pages on thermodynamics and the principles of mass transport. Had Henry been invited to the house to keep her father company? Maybe the invitation had been his idea. Henry listened to Angela's pacing from the room below and sometimes he heard her mother as well, coughing or moving about, at the farther end of the house. He still hadn't been introduced to Mrs. Jones—hadn't set eyes on her, in fact—and neither Angela nor her father had bothered to apologize for this, or make an excuse. Mr. Jones would stop reading when they heard his wife stir, though he kept his head still and you could only tell by the way the focus drained from his eyes.

Mr. Jones didn't fish himself, but he would walk down the hill before dark—in no hurry, though it was always raining on this visit to Maine—to buy a good fish from the boats coming back. Angela would undress Henry while they watched Mr. Jones through the window and listened for her mother. They left their shirts on but took the time to remove shoes. It was too disgraceful to stumble about with your pants bunched at your ankles. At least to Henry it was. Probably not to Angela. He stood behind her and they watched her father's orange parka slip down through the break in the hedge, and then, in the reflection on the surface of the window, he saw her close her eyes and smile. She was a person who smiled when she was angry, Henry had learned. What he had taken for lust, initially, he recognized as anger now, though he didn't know exactly who or what she was angry at and in certain ways he never would. When they were tired of standing they lay on the warmed floor near the fire. The person on top watched for her father. She said he watched impatiently but it wasn't quite true. It was enough, when he was alone with her, to know that her father would be there later as compensation, when Angela had retreated again.

Mr. Jones brought back a cod or a flounder. Lunches were haphazard (a crate of mangoes had been delivered through the mail, or there was soft cheese to spread; a ripe avocado without instructions) but Mr. Jones prepared elaborate dinners, Henry as his sous-chef.

Garlic and clarified butter and capers—ingredients unfamiliar to Henry, or translated into unfamiliar states, or simply handled with an unfamiliar reverence that rendered even the garlic exotic. Some evenings Angela joined them, but never Mrs. Jones. There wasn't a Thanksgiving turkey or a mention of turkey or anything that could possibly be mistaken for a trimming. Henry lied about this to his parents on the telephone that evening. It would have further damaged the poor impression they had somehow formed already, although they hadn't met Angela or her parents. "Did they feed you?" his father asked first. "Your mother cooked enough for a small army," he said. And "What did they feed you?" his mother wanted to know. *Who are these people?* was what they meant, of course. *Can we trust them?* There was the sound of machinery beside his mother, and the television turned up to overcome it. She was vacuuming while she talked—there had been an accident involving a cousin and cranberry sauce. "Put Mr. Jones on for a sec, Henry," she shouted. Henry told her, "No, he's out chopping wood," which was true—it was why he had chosen this moment to call. He stood in the far corner of the dining room, facing the windows, the spot in the house farthest from Mrs. Jones' room. But he had to shout and the house was silent—he would certainly be heard. He wondered now just how quiet he and Angela had been, together in this same room earlier that afternoon. He watched Mr. Jones swing an axe sadly in the majestic drizzle. "I'll tell him you said thanks," he said, and had to repeat himself. "I got to go," his mother said. "But listen, get Angela to come here for Christmas, okay? I'll make a nice meal."

Angela had taken Cream of Wheat and a Rusty Nail upstairs to her mother after dinner. Her father carried wood in before Henry could help, and together they rebuilt the fire in the parlor. He said, "Play some music if you like?" when he and Henry were alone together. The neighbor's cat had followed him in, and leapt up as soon as he formed a lap. The records were all of orchestras and their components—formal men not unlike Mr. Jones on the covers, involved in passionate or contemplative gestures or bent over instruments that were strangely cluttered for the sounds they produced; also women caught open-mouthed in song. They were people who lived in houses like these, whose evenings sounded this way and lingered like so—Henry knew it. They belonged. Everything in this house belonged. The characters in the books Henry took down from Mr. Jones' shelves belonged, too. It was a life from the right kind of book, the kind Henry had always loved, and by now he realized this was what had made it feel familiar despite the total lack of resemblance to his own life or to any household he'd ever visited. In the books he loved it was usually raining, or it was snowing, and precipitation was a virtue. It was poorly lit, and there was a chill to burn off and a fire to do it by. There was an overlay of loneliness, or someone ill upstairs in a bed; there was a quiet history of disappointment or tragedy behind each scene. But attractive tragedy. There were affairs as well, of course. *Her father's life,* Henry read, in one of these novels, *her sister's, her own, that of her two lost brothers—the whole history of their house had the effect of some fine florid voluminous phrase, say even a musical, that dropped first into words and notes without sense and then, hanging unfinished, into no words or any notes at all. Why should a set of people have been put in motion, on such a scale and with such an air of being equipped for a profitable journey, only to break down without an accident, to stretch themselves in the wayside dust without a reason?*

When the music began, Mr. Jones said slyly, "You're a Bach fan," as though Henry had been holding out on him.

"Who isn't?" Henry ventured.

·

HIS ROOM upstairs was at one end of the hall. The damp cold bled readily through the old window casings. Angela never came to him at night, though he would listen for her and sometimes walk to the bathroom, hoping she was listening too and might be provoked. He wondered what she wore to bed here: what did the daughter in such a haunted family sleep in at the house in Maine? There were photos of the dead brothers downstairs. They looked both fragile and imposing: forthright tending toward hostile, though slim and small-shouldered. Except that one was fair-haired and the other dark, they looked very much alike—matching expressions. Henry assumed their mother's illness was a product of their deaths—a very literary grief—but no one had said so. "Oh, don't ask," Angela had told him, offhandedly at first, but then her eyes had miraculously softened. She said, "See? If I start to *care* for you at all then maybe I have to worry about what you'll think of my family. When we both know you're just not worth it."

"Try to resist me better," Henry said.

They had been on the beach—it was made of black and rounded rocks in Maine. The wind and salt made her skin feel tight when he touched her. Sometimes Henry remembered that there was a third house yet to come and could hardly believe his good fortune. It was in Baltimore, where Mrs. Jones had grown up. Angela said it was her favorite—almost the last thing she and her mother still agreed on.

The last night in Maine, he dreamt he was asleep in this room, just as he was, then heard Angela's knock at his door. When he rolled over she stood in the doorway in the short, filmy nightgown she wore at school, and with the light behind her he could see through both the gown and her flesh, her torso just a shade less translucent. She would relent, sooner than either of them expected. They would marry but without a ceremony, disappointing both families equally, if differently. She would be pregnant before she meant to be too, and leave college, and he would get a paying job at a television station in Boston, setting them sufficiently apart from their families and the other accoutrements of what had seemed like unfolding lives and a desired, attainable future that even when they moved back to Connecticut, a few years further on, there weren't many binding expectations left to resist, or friends who had missed them, or familiar, promising roles available to be played still. They were happy enough for a long time, though they never resembled what they'd wished to become.

But when he woke, the knocking had turned into coughing, coming from the bathroom. It must be Angela's mother. Outside, the rain was blowing. Her breathing stuttered, and she seemed to be choking. Henry got up and went as far as the door to his room, but he couldn't bring himself to open it. Surely her daughter and husband were awake. No one could sleep through that, could they? Her cough had a wet catch to it, a gluey stop. What would Henry say when he got to her? That morning he had finally met her—or had spoken to her, at least. He had taken her coffee up. Angela was in town; the phone had rung at just the wrong moment. "I can take it," Henry had said, and Mr. Jones had hesitated, considering, while the phone kept ringing. Mrs. Jones hadn't spoken when Henry had knocked at her half-open door. She had been standing by the window, smoking and examining her fingernails. When she saw him she had turned away, obviously surprised, and said something quietly, to herself. Henry had prepared an elaborate, nervous introduction—*at last* and so forth, *a real pleasure, finally* . . . "Ah . . . shit," she had said, exhaling. She had a wide, soft face made pale by a frame of dark hair very much like her daughter's. She was younger than he'd expected—quite a bit younger than her husband, he guessed—and nice looking. Not ravaged at all. Henry had set her coffee down on the bed table. "Pardon me."

She said, "Yup. Thanks," turning her face away further, fluttering a few dismissive fingers in his direction. She'd produced a cough to cover his exit.

Now he kept his hand on the door latch and listened. There was a last, decisive hack from the bathroom, then she spat. A single sob. Her breathing was heavy but regular again. She spat once more, then became very quiet. He intended to stay put until she had walked back down the hall to her room because he was afraid she would hear him if he moved. But he was freezing, and she might have fallen asleep. He stepped carefully and the floorboards creaked that much more. The bed creaked getting into it. He lay still and listened for her, with the rain falling against the window. It was hard to place the soft, intelligent face he had seen that afternoon (not as striking as her daughter's, but prettier) with such an obnoxious cough. Eventually, he fell asleep.

In the morning there was nothing amiss in the bathroom. In the kitchen Angela's father was pouring Henry's coffee already and brewing a second cup of tea for himself. He poked a finger at the folded paper. "Snow they're telling me, Henry," he said. "If you can believe it. How did you sleep?" He stared—perhaps a challenge, as it seemed. Henry said, "Just fine."

•

THEIR SHARED BREAKFASTS had become too comfortable and routine for the sour note to linger in the air long. Mr. Jones had been to the beach already to collect mussels. He gave the last lesson in what had been a week-long course on the preparation of shellfish. The mussels that closed to the touch (never eat the others) would be debearded and scrubbed and then sautéed with garlic and parsley stems and bay leaf and thyme. Served with the cooking liquid strained through a cheesecloth. Where did he learn all these recipes? Henry wanted to know, and Mr. Jones smiled and pointed approvingly—good question, yes, he had an answer for that. He said, "Now here's the thing. You're going to have to come back, you understand, and next visit I'm going to steal you away from Angela and you and I will walk down to the docks together one afternoon. You'll see.

"Listen," he said, resting his hand on Henry's back, "if you don't come away from there with a better idea than crab cakes, it's your own fault."

A joke. Henry laughed with him. Evidently Mr. Jones didn't want to share Henry at all. Would Angela be impressed or disgusted? he wondered.

A bit later that morning there were footsteps in the hallway—someone was coming down the stairs. Angela's father regarded the ceiling and folded his paper in anticipation. They were measured steps on the staircase, but then brisk enough rounding the corner. "Surprise," Mrs. Jones said, quietly, and carried it with a smile and shrug. "Don't get up."

Her husband had begun to, but he sat back down. "How are you?" he asked, with the floating indulgence that habit must have made of the question, and she said, "Good," in such a way as to close the topic. She poured herself coffee.

Mr. Jones watched her for a moment, then looked out the window, as if checking for snow. But the rain had stopped, and if anything it looked like the day might clear. He seemed to remember his tea next, and turned all his attention to it.

Mrs. Jones sat down beside Henry and swept the cat from the table with a backhand. She took a deep breath when she was seated—tired out from her journey, but satisfied with the destination. She wasn't quite as young as he had thought at first sight, but she *was* a pale and softened version of her daughter. The same dark hair, although hers was straighter and not as long as her daughter's, more orderly. There were soulful bags under her eyes—not unattractive, somehow. And her robe, which was a dark blue and draping satin, seemed inappropriately intimate.

She took up a portion of the newspaper. Across the table her husband made a momentary attempt to return to his own. A corner of her section had poked into the butter. It swung toward Henry's forehead when she turned the pages, and she didn't seem to notice, but Mr. Jones did. He fidgeted with his tea some more, then chose a mango from the crate. He didn't peel it though—it sat on a magazine in front of him. There was a clock above the stove behind Henry that kept a loud, labored time. Henry wondered if he was expected to initiate a conversation. He wondered if Mrs. Jones knew his name. She turned her pages and sipped her coffee so comfortably that he might have assumed this was a customary morning, despite her absence the past week, except that Mr. Jones was so unmistakably disturbed. He was stealing sad glances at the pages laid on the table in front of Henry, but when Henry finally broke the silence, offering his section—"I'm done with it"—Mr. Jones was momentarily confused, then shook his head sternly.

The exchange seemed to provoke Mrs. Jones. She said, "I'm going to make French toast," and pushed back from the table. "Beat some eggs for me, Henry?"

"Right," he said, and followed her.

She asked him what they all had had for Thanksgiving dinner. Her husband let the cat out, then went into the parlor without a word, leaving Henry alone with her. Now, had he missed his turkey? she asked—perhaps to let him know that she had overheard the lie to his parents, although nothing in her manner seemed meaningful or sly. She kept sitting down as if to let him do the work, then remembering something else—she was never seated for more than an instant. "What did your mother cook?" she wanted to know. But she didn't pay attention to his reply. He kept his description as brief as possible, yet she still cut him off. "Here," she said, "dash of vanilla."

Then she said, "Oh no." Henry had been pouring. "Too much milk," she told him.

"Mm. Sorry."

She took the bowl away and dumped the eggs and milk down the drain.

"We'll start over," she said, but not unhappily.

Music began in the other room, and Angela's father came back. "May I help?" he asked.

She said, "Here." She was rinsing the bowl. "You do this, how 'bout?" To Henry she asked, "Can you set the table, do you think?"

There was a note of doubt to the question, or else he had imagined it. But sure enough, he managed to put the wrong forks out. She said, "Well I guess it's *like* dessert—French toast. Let's call it breakfast, though." She laid the correct forks herself while Henry stood aside. He had set four places but she took one away.

Then she made "the boys" sit down at the table—out of her way, she said. Her whole mood seemed to brighten further, but her husband remained nervous. She said, "I have a bone to pick with you, Henry. You might as well know. It's not fair at all that you're leaving today, just when I'm feeling better. Angela and Mr. Jones get a whole week of you" (even she called him "Mr. Jones") "while I laid in bed and had to hear all about your charms second-hand. Who wants juice?"

She wielded the pitcher, one hand on the back of his chair. The bread was frying and the syrup was warming and fragrant. The music was something sweet and delicate with a violin and piano. She said, "Talk to Angela," while she poured. Where *was* Angela? Henry wondered. "Tell her we can have you one more day, Henry. You could convince her if you wanted to, I'll bet." She just finished the sentence before a string of escalating coughs caught up with her.

Mr. Jones couldn't seem to contain himself any longer. The coughing set him free, and he took his napkin from his lap and stood. "Dear—" he said. "What are we doing, dear? This is . . . here." He reached across Henry's shoulder and tried, unsuccessfully, to take the juice pitcher from her hand. "Let me help you, please," he said, while she cleared the last of her cough. "This is, ah . . ." He laughed. "Come on now."

He had been tugging on the pitcher, but she wouldn't let go. She looked at him squarely and mildly—there was something impressive about it—while their four hands remained on the juice pitcher, suspending it above Henry's shoulder. Her smile had been expanding, slowly, and when she made a face—raising her eyebrows and crossing her eyes—Mr. Jones let go. She said, "No juice for Mr. Jones."

She turned back to the stove, and her husband sat down again. He picked his cloth napkin up from the table and refolded it in his lap. Henry thought they might share a look, but Mr. Jones returned to studying the window instead. He was a different man. Looking back on the morning later, that would be obvious as something available for Henry to take caution from, but he wasn't paying the proper attention as the events unfolded.

She served the French toast to the two of them, refilled her coffee, and sat down in front of her own empty plate. She moved now in the loose-jointed way that some people do when they've drunk too much; she fished a pack of cigarettes out of her robe and lit one. She smiled across the table at her husband—it was a perfect imitation of warmth—but he succeeded in never looking up at her. When she caught Henry watching the performance, her expression shifted and she leaned toward him, her chin turned away, and spoke out of the side of her mouth in a stage whisper. "Tell me *everything* you told Mr. Jones," she said. "The short version. I mean it, Henry. Catch me up on *you*."

There was a great deal of sly indulgence in her smile and in her lean. She ashed into her plate. And Henry smiled right back at her—in fact, he found he wanted to wink. This was the moment to pull away and recognize he was in the middle of a dynamic that had long preceded him; it was the right moment to be satisfied with having seduced Angela's father and consider her mother a negotiable obstacle. But something in the look she gave him suggested an acknowledgment of his success thus far—*I think you know me*, her eyes conceded; there was a touch of admiration, Henry imagined—as well as an invitation to one last challenge. She seemed to be saying, *My husband was easy, of course, but I want to be charmed too, Henry*. And Henry might have resisted her if the resemblance to her daughter wasn't so present or the comparison, finally, he decided, so clearly in Mrs. Jones' favor. This was one thought he had, anyway, later on. This was one excuse. Another was that whatever he did next, it wouldn't have particularly made a difference in the long run. We like to imagine the single step in some other direction would have been the first to a far different destination, but of course we make the same mistakes wherever we find ourselves, and our tendencies and weaknesses aren't subject to single decisions. It may be that any path we would have instinctively been drawn to, or inclined to trust (there would have been fewer than we'd envision from the safe expanses of reconsideration), would have fed into a more or less identical landscape. This morning would always be his introduction to his wife's mother—as he got older, the implied ceremony of the occasion seemed more meaningful to Henry—and he would have to remind himself, looking back, that there had been a few moments once, before he knew Mrs. Jones at all, when he'd imagined he could impress her. Sometimes he told himself that if he had seen the third house before meeting her— the house in Baltimore that she'd bought on her own, where she'd lived alone before she met Mr. Jones; the house she'd return to when her husband was unexpectedly dead before her, selling the two she'd never cared for at contemptuously low prices—he might not have misjudged her so. It was an ordinary lump in an uncertain neighborhood, rendered dark by overhanging trees, with a sagging roof and clogged gutters and a tacked-on porch. It was the middle of three nearly identical houses at the end of a street roamed by busy, inconsiderate children. Mrs. Jones sat almost cheerfully by the windows or on the porch of this house, disobeying her nurse, treating her daughter with the same polite indifference as ever—as if they were amiably agreed-upon enemies, or old friends who'd never cared for one another. But she was particularly talkative and vain with Henry at this house. *My charmer,* she called him. *Sit down here,* she said, *close to me.* "Ah Henry," she sometimes said, when he told a story or carried a joke, "if only I had met you first. I'll bet all the girls tell you that." Flattery was the vehicle in which she preferred to convey her disapproval and mistrust.

On his initial visit there, not long after Mr. Jones had died, at a moment when Angela was out of the room, Mrs. Jones had asked him what he thought of "the first house" now that he had finally seen it. She smiled kindly and mildly, sincerely interested in his opinion, and proud. She was almost ten years past the day he'd met her but still pretty in a way that suggested vulnerability— it was still a persuasive disguise. By then he knew that her sons had been twenty-one and nineteen when they died; Angela had been thirteen. They weren't good people, these sons, according to Angela—they were self-involved and manipulative in the same ways their mother was, quick with a slight, suspicious of women. But their mother had been a different person when they were alive, Angela said. She had loved them so forcefully that Angela herself, and her father too, had enjoyed a dose of surplus affection—as if the boys couldn't contain all she hoped to pour into them and some had spilled over onto her daughter and husband. She wasn't an invalid before they died. She had liked her job and been good at it. She had kept an ambitious garden at each house. Since their deaths she'd never stepped on a boat or stood on a dock, and beaches—in Maine or anywhere else—had entirely lost their appeal for her. She didn't like to see her grandson in a bathtub.

Henry didn't know what to tell her. The house was not quite ugly, but he couldn't see that it had any particular strengths either— he could hardly imagine what to falsely praise—and what he found most discouraging about it was its mundane, upholstered resemblance to the ones he had grown up in. "It's homey," he told her, finally, then had an inspiration and added, "I can see why Angela liked it, growing up."

Mrs. Jones had smiled—still kindly, it seemed, if indulgently, though how would he ever know? How to know what instincts she acted on, cruel or protective, and who could say what she had recognized and properly identified in Henry before anyone else had, or what affinities they might have shared under different circumstances? "You think it's ugly," she said, patting his hand—consolingly, perhaps. "You and Mr. Jones."

·

BUT IN MAINE, he was young. He had his heart's desire in sight and it included them all—the parents along with the daughter, all the houses. "Tell me everything," she had said, and smiled memorably. And he didn't hesitate: he returned her smile, and Mrs. Jones leaned a little closer still, and Henry said, "Well," with Mr. Jones'"h" in it, and slapped his knees in imitation. He found himself doing these things without meaning to.

He said, "We've gone through Bach, and ... Rachmaninoff." He was whispering. "We've given Henry James a good once-over, naturally." Her grin narrowed, as if to a point; *this is perfect,* she seemed to be saying to him, in that moment. *Oh, you're sharp.* "And, ah ... we've covered flounder two different ways," he said. "A great deal on garlic. Mussels, of course. Then there was my trip to Martha's Vineyard when I was ten. Skinned the elbow," he said—he did wink, and flashed his elbow. "And then the family sailing over from Poland, and Ellis Island. The house in Torrington. The plumbing fortune. All leading up to our shared affection for your daughter, I guess. That's ..." But she was smiling differently now. "That's pretty much the short version." And she was looking at Mr. Jones instead. When Henry looked too, his own smile staled. He had half forgotten that Mr. Jones was in the room.

Mrs. Jones laughed a little—sweetly. She had made the game end before Henry realized it. She coughed once briefly and sipped her coffee, watching her husband through both. The record ended in the other room and they heard the needle swing back into place. Mr. Jones put his silverware down on his plate and finished chewing. "Henry ...," Mrs. Jones said, then turned back to him. "If you stay—Henry—you know ... maybe you and Mr. Jones could dust off the skiff. He hasn't had anyone to sail with since he killed the boys, I'm afraid."

Mr. Jones sighed. He appeared tired and possibly disgusted, but not surprised. Henry began to feel sick to his stomach.

Mrs. Jones continued, ostensibly speaking to Henry but watching her husband. "Wear a life vest is all I'm suggesting, darling." Mr. Jones pushed back from the table. "That's my advice. Going somewhere, dear?"

Her husband closed his eyes and sighed and said, "Pardon me."

"Oh, you lost him, Henry," his wife said, watching him turn away. "You *had* him," she said, her eyes still on her husband. "I could tell you had him."

Mr. Jones collected his parka from the peg by the door and

pulled his boots on in no particular hurry. Henry needed to offer something, or take something back, but he couldn't imagine where to begin. "You were getting to be just like a son," Mrs. Jones was saying, "Henry. Except not dead. Will you be gone long, dear? I was hoping you'd do the dishes." As he crossed to the door, ignoring her, she said, loudly, "It's noble, Henry, to just walk away." She was actually looking at him now—at Henry—and he was so stupid that in that moment he still felt she was speaking to him, and that he might be expected to formulate a reply. "Silence is best, you know," she said. "Never give in." When Mr. Jones slammed the door behind himself, she began to cough.

．

ANGELA HAD OVERSLEPT, she claimed. She said she woke to the sound of her mother shouting and then coughing, and she had slipped into the room and started the kettle going while Mrs. Jones was coughing still, Henry still sitting dumb at the table. She offered small spoon and china sounds into the silence when her mother was finally quiet, then she sat down with them and took up a section of the paper. In a little while she asked her mother, "Want your shawl from upstairs?" though she read while she spoke, disinterested. Mrs. Jones' gaze drifted just above the table, and she tapped at her lips, absently, with one finger. "Water's boiling," she replied at last.

Henry thought it was over—everything with Angela must be—and that he'd never had a chance. He should have known that. He'd gotten in over his head—anyone else in his position would have recognized it. In the car, driving home, Angela appeared to him in a different light now: more or less mild and defeated, and not so mysterious or fierce as simply depressed, when compared to her mother. He'd often been surprised to find a trick door in the back wall of his love affairs, and when one day he stepped or stumbled through it he would invariably be disappointed by the view from outside. He didn't dare tell her what had happened over breakfast, incorrectly assuming that she'd hear about it from her parents—or that she *hadn't* been asleep upstairs, of course, and had heard it all for herself. Wasn't that, in fact, the secret to life in that house? Hadn't it been the case all week? Half of him never stopped suspecting she had listened from her bedroom and left him to his fate, even when the next trip to her parents was proposed and, when he told her he couldn't go back there, could never face them again, she truly seemed not to understand. "They *love* you," she said. "For some reason. They wear me out, asking about you."

And a little later, when she wanted to elope (he'd known her indifference to their relationship was a pose—why did it surprise him when she dropped it?), she was convincingly mystified when he told her he didn't like the idea that half her attraction to him depended upon her parents' disapproval. She said, "No, that's *your* fantasy, dear. Not mine." And anyway, she wondered why he imagined she would ever have taken her parents' opinion into consideration.

·

IN HER last years Mrs. Jones practiced the invalid's art of ill-timed imposition. She could be counted on to require an emergency visit (usually following the firing of a nurse) at any worst possible moment, and when she invited herself back up to Connecticut she liked to buy the plane tickets before proposing the trip to her hosts. Angela would pretend to be determined to make her stay in a hotel, or to say that that sounded like a lovely trip but unfortunately they wouldn't be available to see her those dates, yet she also depended upon Henry to object to such measures and act as her mother's apologist. It was a banal marital dance they performed, like any other.

On what turned out to be both her last and her longest trip to Connecticut—all four endless weeks of December—Mrs. Jones' previously uncanny ability to sniff out the lies and arrangements devoted to Henry's affairs had blossomed into a broad and sloppy suspicion. "I'll just come for the ride," she kept saying, or "Why don't we all go?" She was wrong this time: a particularly lasting diversion had in fact just come to a premature end at the hands of a younger and unmarried rival, and Henry was desperately volunteering to shuttle his son between the busy appointments of a seven-year-old—not to free himself for other stops but to be alone long enough to indulge his anger and continue the pressing and solitary debate he'd been having with his lover. "Who's he talking to?" Mrs. Jones asked Angela, whenever Henry was on the telephone. She devised petty reasons for Angela to call him at work, and when her daughter ran out of patience she began calling herself, giving the secretary a false name, then hanging up as soon as she heard Henry's voice. None of this satisfied her though, and when the chilly air turned arctic, up and down the coast, two weeks into her stay, she claimed she'd forgotten to leave the water running in her house and required Henry to drive down and check on it. There was nothing he wanted more than two days alone, and he almost agreed too readily, sending her suspicion off with him to Baltimore as well.

He spent the first third of his drive on thoughts of his lover (a production assistant on the last commercial he'd shot—a girl with excessively long legs and no patience and a brilliance for schedules and details; perhaps he'd never properly kept up with her), the second third on thoughts of his mother-in-law (what had sent her into this frenzy? In the past, her suspicions and little jokes had been coy and discreet, as if she'd never wanted to alert her daughter, only to let Henry know he could merely fool one of them), and the last third on a scheme that came to him. A few years back, on a visit to Maine, while Henry and Mr. Jones sat in lovely, distressed Adirondack chairs and watched Angela keep Brian from stuffing pine needles in his mouth, Mr. Jones had suddenly turned and broken the habitual, uneasy silence between them to say, "I've finished my book."

He had whispered the news, and that fact combined with the gleam of pride in his eyes almost broke Henry's heart. "Is that right?" Henry had said. "Congratulations! My goodness—I'd love to read it."

"Oh no," Mr. Jones had said, gaining control of his expression again. "No, it wouldn't interest you." But when Henry pressed, he was willing to supply the title: "The Tragic in James: Its Syntactic Delay." Henry received this with nothing more or less than incomprehension, but to Mr. Jones his expression must have looked like disdain, or something worse. "Well, that's only the working title," he'd added. "Anyway, it doesn't matter. No one will ever read it." And when Henry insisted they should all celebrate, at the very least, Mr. Jones had retreated entirely again to the high ground of failed eye contact and shadowy smiles from which he generally regarded his son-in-law. "In all honesty," he said, "it isn't perfectly finished. I suppose I'd appreciate it if you'd keep this under your hat. I only meant to tell you, after all."

Then he never mentioned the book again—not to his wife, so far as Henry knew, and certainly not to his daughter. Either he never approached a publisher, or when he did he was rejected, and when he died, Henry tried to urge Angela and her mother to search for a manuscript but neither believed he'd ever really written anything.

So Henry would search. And in fact, who could say what he might find answers to in some drawer or closet of that stuffed house, cluttered as it was by too much of the furniture and debris and too many of the books and paintings from three houses?

Henry was so diverted by the idea of finally ransacking the Jones' past that he didn't quite process the sound he was hearing as he unlocked the front door, though it was clearly the sound of water. He found it streaming and foraging—it seemed sentient and even intent, a kind of infestation. It cascaded in thin falls down the wallpaper and dripped through the fixtures. It rippled in thick, dull syllables on the carpeted staircase. He took all day just to mop and drain the standing water and find workmen to join him for the heavy work tomorrow. He would have to telephone Mrs. Jones and get her permission to pull up the carpeting and throw away most of the furniture. Under the carpeting the floorboards might be warped. In the basement a small lake settled darkly, smelling of mothballs and mold. He wondered if anything would be salvaged in the end.

That evening he halfheartedly poked into the crammed closets, where the sagging boxes peeled away in his hands, but the damp and the smells it brought forth made the familiarity of this house—of its fixtures and pull-shaded windows, its slipcovers and patterns of repeating stagecoaches and stenciled flowers—more potent than ever. It felt as if he'd be unpacking his own past.

"The Tragic in James: Its Syntactic Delay"—how could such a topic possibly be interesting, anyway? Mrs. Jones and Angela were probably right—there probably wasn't a book at all, and of course Mr. Jones would have reserved the lie for Henry. No one else would have believed it. No one else would have wanted to as much as he had. But even if such a book existed, how could it turn out to be revealing in the way that Henry hoped? Would he give up even a glance at his lover, much less a few words from her ineloquent lips or the merest brush of her fingers, for the chance to read such a book? Henry had wished for the wrong things, he decided. He'd been granted his role in the wrong family and novel. He couldn't face the phone call to Mrs. Jones. He couldn't stay in the house, but a hotel room alone was out of the question too. He lay the seat back in his car, in the driveway, with the heater running, on this street full of revving engines and strange calls in the night that might as well have been the one he grew up on, and he comforted himself with the thought that he was still young: there was still plenty of time for catastrophe and misfortune, for everything he'd misguidedly chosen to fall out of his reach again.

SOME THRILLS

☐ FF TO the football game, that was the story. They waved to mother—father and son—then got into the car and pulled away still waving. The road was empty and the neighborhood dark as they drove down the neck of the causeway and along the rim of the bay. It was one of those small towns on the shores of a small lake in the northwest corner of Connecticut where the pine trees and dirt lanes, the Colonials with dates blocked in a forefathers' font and the steeples tucked between hills, attracted a seasonal corps of wealthy New Yorkers. This was October though, and the summer battalions had retreated to the city. An aspect of the town that Brian found appealing, his father less so, would emerge again: the casserole cheer that had been embarrassed into seclusion while the summer people (with their sweat and linen and the sharp edges of an accent) were among them. Now there were whole streets and beaches left dark, shores of closed-up cottages—particularly here on the south side of the lake where the drone of ski boats and the wedded smells of bar- becue and algae bloom had fattened the summer months. The year- rounders who remained behind, among the pulled curtains and the docks stacked in turned-over gardens, seemed to Henry like the unfortunate survivors of a devastation.

"Settle in," he told his son, when they had left his wife behind. "Buckle, please."

The tone of his voice suggested a change of plans, which should have surprised Brian but didn't. His father had never taken him to a football game before or, for that matter, ever betrayed an interest in the sport. When was the last time he had gone anywhere alone with his father? There was a thrill in picturing his mother still there by the window, her small shiver and frown while she watched the car pull away, without her son in the room beside her this time.

"Listen," Henry said, "tonight we're thick as thieves. Huh?" He reached over and took the hat from his son's head. He stole glances while he drove. "Do you need the sweater?" he asked. "What do you have on underneath?"

"My green shirt." Brian pulled up the sweater to show.

"That's fine. Lose the sweater."

Brian took it off and tossed it in back with his hat. Henry smoothed the hair on his head. "Tonight it's you and me," he said, "and that's as far as it goes. It never happened. You understand?"

His son nodded.

"You and me? We went to the football game."

Henry wrote and amended television commercials. It was hard to say whether too much time spent in thirty-second cells had lent him his concision and impatience or whether the traits had been his to begin with and brought to the trade. He was the sort of father who addressed his son with jokes meant for the other adults in the room, and Brian had developed the habit, here in ado-lescence, of pretending he understood and laughing along, even when he suspected he might be the brunt. It was spying, in a way, though if you thought about it from the other end then it was get-ting noticed, his eyes on you for a moment, the indulgence of his wry smile. The trick was to take things for granted. *Don't ask where we're going.*

Henry drove them south out of the disheartening darkness. There was an occasional streetlight in Thomaston and then the fellowship of traffic on the highway, and he welcomed even the billboards of Waterbury. They passed the bright stadium where the game would be contested without them and continued toward the long corner of Connecticut. The car was an Austin Healey of the pewter shade particular to roadsters and the bullet race cars of the early sixties: flecked and textured, a color as vivid in black-and-white film. Sexy hip gills, and a grill suggesting the oval, toothy smile of Truman. The leavening effect it usually had on Henry—the sense of weightlessness, sunk into the curled bucket joints of its fist—was burdened tonight by the presence of his son in the passenger seat. Instinct told Henry he was making a stupid mistake. But who could say what this son of his—so agreeable and opaque, with the cagey innocence that ran in his mother's blue blood—might be willing to know? Who could say what he hadn't guessed already?

In New Canaan they left the highway for a back road and wound past the orchards and the empty lawns and the distant houses that glowed from a safe remove. They turned in at a pair of stone pillars topped by lanterns, a driveway overhung with leafless linden trees. A broad house full of lit windows hunched before them, with a row of cars in front.

"A party," Henry said. "Do you suppose we're invited?" he whispered, feigning amusement. He parked the car and sat back to survey the house. "I have no love for parties," he said. He and Brian exchanged a glance of understanding. "Your father spares . . . ," he trailed off. They watched the silhouettes that moved behind the curtains. "I don't know," he said, then got out of the car.

They snuck across the lawn by the tennis court, past a rowboat overturned there, through a garden where the wings of a wooden goose spun in the chilly breeze. They circled the house. Their view into the windows was obscured by curtains, but they heard a man arguing with a foreign woman—a heavy accent, difficult to place—then someone yelling while another man laughed, then music playing, as faint as could be. They came to a window where the curtains were drawn aside and in the room a woman sat before a dresser and a mirror. Henry watched her for a moment: her reflected face, which was critical and distracted. It seemed she might sit before the mirror, trying smiles and fingering the lines that formed, indefinitely.

Henry rapped against the frame of the window until it loosened. The woman was startled but didn't shout. He slid the window open and climbed in through, and Brian followed.

"Well," the woman said, watching them in the mirror before she turned to face them. "If it isn't Henry." She spoke as if pleased and surprised. "And he brought the kid," she said.

While she was speaking, Brian's father crossed to where she sat. He was smiling, but not convincingly. "I thought we had a date, Chicken Little." He leaned down, squinting with mock affection, and touched the tip of her nose. She smiled back—squinted, mimicking—and said, "You should speak to your secretary more often."

"Hal!" she yelled.

Brian's father straightened. "You're drunk?" he asked.

A man appeared in the open doorway across the room. He was short, tanned and handsome, and prematurely gray. "Ah," he said, lazily. "Now what?"

"Look who's *here*," Chicken Little told him, brightly. "This is *Henry*—he's the one with the car—and that's Henry's kid." She spoke quickly, with enthusiasm. "Probably they drink beer. Have we any beer in the house?"

Hal laughed, quietly and through his nose. "Goodness," he said. He held his hands together before him, one clasping the other, in a composed, almost clerical manner. He gestured with an open hand to Henry—"One more"—then clasped them together again. "Why not? Bringing your son though," he said, smiling at Brian and nodding slightly.

"Get them some beer, Hal," Chicken Little interrupted. She flicked her fingers: *away with you.* "We'll be out in a flash."

Hal's grin fell, and he stared for a moment at Henry. Then he smiled, then he left.

The woman turned her own smile from the doorway to Brian's father. She mooned up at him beside her. Quietly, she said, "How are you, love? Did you hurt your hand?"

"Come on," he said. He took hold of her arm, but when she wouldn't budge he lifted her from her seat. Her smile dissolved and she struggled—"Let *go*"—then fell slack and slid to her knees.

He held her up by the arm—she was dead weight. She grimaced, and when he let her go, she fell into a heap. "Asshole," she said quietly, rubbing her arm.

Then she straightened her legs out and smoothed her skirt. She bent down toward her toes, stretching athletically, as if this had been her plan from the start. She said, as if to herself, "What in the world could be keeping him?" and scrambled to her feet and left the room through the door where Hal had been.

Brian's father was grinning the grin that meant he was enraged. He didn't move, but his eyes turned to Brian by the window. He stared expectantly, as if hoping for guidance, then sadly, as if disappointed by what he saw, or failed to see. He began to speak, but stopped.

"Wait in the car, I think, " he said finally. "We'll be along in a minute." He left by the same door as those before him.

•

HE WAS in a long dark hallway lit by bright slivers beneath the several doors. Someone was in the kitchen with Hal—a woman's voice was audible. Someone played the piano. There was a mirror at the end of the hall, reflecting the rise of stairs. Henry saw her heels ascending. He followed her as quickly as he could without being heard. At the newel he saw the flutter of her skirt as she topped the stairs and made the turn. *Here we go*, he thought. He climbed along the edge by the wall where the steps creaked less. A door opened in the hallway, letting a spike of light through, and Henry froze and watched between the rails of the balustrade. The bald spot lit at the crown of Hal's head was still for a moment, listening. Then he turned back into the kitchen.

At the top of the stairs Henry caught her halfway through the door to the guest room—waiting for him, as he knew she would be, though she shook her head no and said aloud (timidly), "Don't," before she closed the door.

And truth be told, he would have preferred not to. He wished, for once, that there might be another way to get her attention, or that they might spend a single evening together without lapsing into performance. He put his hand in his pants to hurry things along, but he was better prepared than he would have liked to admit, and there you had it—who was digging his grave? He wondered what had gone wrong tonight, or if this surprise had been her plan from the start. He wondered if Brian would do as he was told.

She was by the dresser with her back to the door, bent down over a low drawer and riffling through folded clothes. Her skirt and stockings were pooled on the floor around her feet, and the architectural composition of her backside from this angle—the flare of the arch that topped the columns of her legs, the pale facade of skin—was engaging enough, though the effect was diminished by his certainty that it was a studied pose, practiced in mirrors.

Yet she peered at him past a black-clad shoulder with what seemed sincere surprise. She straightened, struck embarrassment, and spun around. She said, "I mean it, Henry, not tonight," with what he imagined (he had never seen it in her face before) must be sadness. But then, possibly aware of his hesitation and concerned that she had performed too well, or more likely because she always overacted in the end, she added, "Don't fuck me tonight."

As simply as that, she got him into his part. He fetched her from the dresser and bent her over the bed, where she sighed, happily, and reached a finger back for him to suck while he fumbled with his pants. They banged and tugged, wasting no time, both of them quiet and not wanting to be interrupted. But in the midst of things his mind drifted away and he looked out the windows to where the car was parked beneath the trees. It was empty. He'd suspected it might be.

•

As an increasingly practiced spy, Brian never considered obeying his father's instructions. He did wonder if he should follow his father, but the moment had passed him by. He was lagging behind. He stood alone in the bedroom now, under a high ceiling. There were two doors out of the room, and the two tall windows. On the dresser, among a bright clutter of glass and metal objects, were several photos: of Hal and Chicken Little together, of Hal alone, and of Chicken Little with a girl. They had the same fair hair and the same tight smile, girl and woman—both sharply dressed in solid colors. Fibbing eyes.

The door that had not been used up to now opened, tentatively, and from behind it appeared the girl from the photo. She looked at the open window first, then at the dresser and Brian. She shivered and stared. "Weren't you supposed to wait in the car?" she asked.

"Uh huh."

They stared a bit longer.

"What are you going to do?"

He shrugged, hoping to appear accustomed.

"Does your father always take you along when he visits his girlfriends?"

She looked younger than Brian—twelve? he guessed. Maybe thirteen? "How old are you?" he asked.

She frowned. She said, "You can follow me if you want to."

She left the door ajar, and he did follow her. She was at the next door, at the far end of the room, her hand on the handle while she looked back, waiting. "Close the window though," she said. He returned to the bedroom and let the cold billow in against him for a moment.

He followed the opened doors (she was gone) through three spacious rooms, each filled with heavy furniture in neat arrangements and large, patterned rugs. A single lamp was lit in each. Adult voices battled in distant parts of the house, but these rooms were empty and felt little-used. He came to a foyer that connected the house to the dark garage. "Up here," he heard from above, and stepping into the garage he found a narrow stairwell to one side. There was the oddly comforting smell of motor oil, and at the top of the stairs stood the girl in a rectangle of light. She walked away as he followed.

It was another bedroom, with a dipping roofline. The girl sat on the narrow bed, watching Brian and swinging her feet. Beside her was an open suitcase and a woman filling it with hastily folded clothes—the woman was short and solid with a round face and cropped black hair and green, astounding eyes, which she turned on Brian momentarily, thereby striking him dumb. She was quite beautiful, and furious.

"Come on in," the girl said. He advanced cautiously upon the girl and the bed and the remarkable woman. "Rose is packing to leave and Mother thinks she's going with her but Rose says she's not. What's your name?"

He turned his attention from the woman to the girl. "Brian," he said.

"Claire, Brian." She held her hand out and he took it, shook. "Rose is going back to Cork even though my mother's desperately in love with her and I am too. She couldn't care less about us."

"Christ save us," said Rose, with mellifluous venom. She continued to pack, folding clothes against her bosom and slamming shut empty drawers.

"Your father's Henry," said Claire.

Was it a question? Brian said, "Uh huh."

"What I know about Henry is he has a sexy car and a not very good sense of humor and he's married. My mother and I are very open with one another. What's your mother's name?"

Brian had gotten hung up on the part about his father's sense of humor. If true, it seemed like a detail with far-reaching implications. "Angela," he said, eventually.

"Angela," Claire repeated. "I'll bet she doesn't know a thing about my mother, whose name is Elizabeth by the way, as you probably know. I'll bet you don't tell your mother anything and that's why your father brings you along."

Rose had just stormed into the bathroom attached to the bedroom when the sound of broken glass came from there. "Ah for fuck's sake," she said, then seemed to stomp on whatever she had dropped: there were three crackling thuds. Claire had half turned on the bed to listen, but now she directed her attention back to Brian above her, who lingered in the no-man's-land before the bed.

"It's been my experience that boys are closer to their fathers and girls to their mothers, and I can say that I never let word one slip to Hal—you met him. Mother probably always thought I would tell about her and Rose but I never did. He just sniffed it out on his own. He's smarter than any of us thinks, you know."

Now a steady succession of tinkling smashes came from the bathroom, as if Rose was tossing the contents of a medicine cabinet against a wall. Claire signaled with one finger for Brian to come closer. She cupped a hand beside her lips and whispered into his ear, "She's out of her gourd," as the last smash expired. The sound of the woman crying filled in the silence that followed.

Claire had been watching Brian with rapt, greedy attention. She stood up next to him now and, half turned away, in profile, she said, "I have excellent posture because I ride in shows. Feel my back."

"Yeah," Brian assented, without feeling. He worried about the crying woman.

"I have a fierce teacher—she's brutal—and what she says is I have a fine seat, she has to admit. You're probably afraid to touch me."

He shrugged. He sat down on the bed where she had been sitting. The furniture up here was entirely different from the furniture in the house below: it was light and a little shabby, mostly wicker.

The room smelled slightly musty, like a cottage. He listened to the quiet crying of the woman in the bathroom and glanced into her suitcase. Among the less interesting items he spotted undergarments in red and black—licorice shades—and Claire, noting his attention, picked one of them up and pressed it to her nose. She leaned, lightly, against his knees and held the panties out for him. "Smell," she whispered. "It's sweet." Lord how he wanted to, but not in her presence. Instead he lay back, feigning boredom.

She said, "What you're thinking is I'm younger than you and who can be bothered, but girls ordinarily develop faster than boys as everybody knows." She pushed his knees apart and fell onto her own on the carpet before the bed, between his legs. She leaned across his stomach and stared at him. He was afraid his surprise showed. She said, "The only reason I care about you is you have red hair." She reached and touched his hair. "Does your mother have red hair?"

Then Rose came into the room and said, "Well what in the name of Jesus . . . ? Take it elsewhere, then."

"Get!" she said, when they hesitated. She stepped toward them and swung her arms. "Get! Shoo! Out of my sight, you—" She didn't finish. Claire had stood and pulled Brian up, and she kept his hand and said, "Come on," leading him back toward the stairs. He stole a glance at Rose from the top step and found that she was watching him—her eyes still astounding, furious and wet. "Come *on*," said Claire, who had lost his hand, but Rose held his gaze and shook her head no—sadly, he thought, though in a way that seemed mysteriously meant for him.

"You're in love with her too," Claire said below, in the foyer, leading him back into the house. "Everybody is, with eyes like that. Everybody except Hal, who doesn't know *how* to love."

She led him toward the front of the house, where he hadn't been yet. He hated being led by the hand but her flesh itself, inside his palm, was not bad. "Now what?" he risked, though he tried not to put much enthusiasm behind it.

"How much exactly do you know?" she asked him, quietly, passing through a dark hallway. Without waiting for an answer, she said, "Do you know who exactly is here tonight?"

"Why don't you tell me."

"In other words, you don't know anything."

They came to a door and she listened at it, holding his hand still, then turned to face him. Leaning against the door, in the dark hallway, she whispered, "Everybody's here. Not just your father." She listened again, then continued. "Nobody was supposed to be and everybody is. Hal was meant to be in the city and Rose up in Allston—it's her night off—and me gone too, though I won't say where. Mother's Henry comes over with his kid, that being you, and Mother makes dinner and you all play house together or something, which is what I'm not supposed to know but do, don't you dare ask me how. Anyways, here's the catch though. Last night she sneaks up to see Rose—Mother this is—and Hal catches wind and finds them together doing me and thee," she pointed, "can only guess what. And the sky falls in. Follow?"

"How *do* you know all this?"

She stared—offended? "You have the prettiest lashes," she said, finally. "They're next to invisible, but now that I see them . . ."

He sighed.

She said, "The thing about you is you should have been a girl, I think."

"Tell me again how old you are?" he asked.

"Anyways," she said, "do you want the rest or do you want to kiss me while you have the chance?"

He began to say . . . what? There was nothing there. *Kiss her, then*, he thought, but his body, it seemed—the whole upper half that would need to lean and bend down toward her, much less his lips—wouldn't take the message.

"Okay, okay, okay," she said, as if she had been watching these thoughts and gaps play across his face. "Just come closer and I'll tell. I have to whisper so no one will hear."

He eliminated the half step of distance between them and stood waiting. "Closer," she breathed. "No kisses—I promise." He shrugged, and leaned a shoulder against the door beside her and slouched. She turned in to him so that their noses were nearly touching, closed her eyes, and inhaled. When she opened them again, she smiled. "That's nice," she whispered. He heard adult voices and a trickle of music in the distance past the door.

"In that room right there," she said at last, canting her head, "if I'm not very much mistaken, are one Hal and one Mother and your father and also Robert, who is mother's other lover—not at all the equal to your father, Brian." She touched his chest as a sign of assurance. "And also Robert's wife named Lauren, whom I have never met, and *also*, also, father's sister and her husband, Aunt Jean and Uncle Mac, who showed up just completely on their own, uninvited, which they always do. Everyone else is invited—your father first and then Robert this afternoon when Mother decided she was running off to Cork with Rose, her one true love. Which she isn't. Got it?"

"Sure," Brian said.

"You're bright," she said—sincerely, it seemed.

"You're precocious," he replied.

Which made her smile and hunch her shoulders with shy delight and touch his nose with her fingertip. "What a word! If I hadn't promised, I would kiss you now, you sweet boy."

So he did kiss her. It was easier than he'd expected, and pleasant too, though her lips were still and parted.

"Well," she said, registering surprise. Then she said, "Hold that thought. First we should make an unexpected appearance."

She took his hand again. With her free hand she flung the door open upon a long, largely empty, dimly lit room with sofas and a piano, leaded-glass windows, and a fireplace in which a mild fire muttered. A man sat at the piano, playing, but there was no one else in sight. Claire was disappointed. There was a long delay before the man turned his attention toward the commotion she had made of the door, and his playing never faltered while he watched them across the flat rim of his halved glasses. He was roughly as thick as wide, with a back that declined sharply in contrast to a gently sloping front; his gray-bearded head perched on his shoulders like a chimney. Past him, at the opposite end of the room, there was a paneled door on runners, left ajar, and from behind it came a bustle of voices in an indeterminate mood. Ignoring the man at the piano, ignoring the music (as all three of them seemed to), Claire dragged Brian to this second door. The man watched their approach over one shoulder, their departure over the other. Brian could not help meeting the man's stare. He loosened his hand from Claire's and managed to fall a step behind as she repeated her violent entrance.

"Ah," said Hal, immediately, "the children! Just what we need! Come in, Claire, come in. Bring your little friend."

Though the door still rattled in its casing, Claire said, "Oh, don't mind us. We don't want to disturb the grown-ups."

This room was as large as the last, and similarly laid out. Another piano, smaller, was crowded into a corner as if it had been disciplined. There was no fire in the fireplace though, and a long table at which no one was seated occupied the center breadth of the room.

Hal seemed to have been on his way out, but his path was blocked by a disheveled woman. Her attention turned to Claire and Brian, and she asked, "Whose children are those?"

"Where's Mummy?" Claire asked her father.

"These are *your* children?" the woman said to Hal. "Good Lord, Robert, what are we *doing* here? Someone just tell me what we're doing here."

Brian guessed that Robert must be the tall man who stood by the fireplace and leaned his head, with poor posture, on an elbow supported by the mantel. He stood beside an armchair in which an older woman with a grandmotherly grin sat stiff and straight, her legs dangling above the floor. This man had turned to the desperate woman in the doorway, and in response to her question he grinned and shook his head, as if politely acknowledging a joke he'd heard before.

"Claire, dear," Hal answered, "you've struck upon the thousand-dollar question. Where's Mummy indeed—you've hit the proverbial nail, Sweetums."

Claire smiled at her father, and holding the smile, she shifted her attention to the woman beside him. "I'm Claire," she said, crossing the room now (abandoning Brian), leading with her outstretched hand. "Elizabeth and Hal's daughter, Claire. You must be Lauren."

The woman shrank from her. "Don't speak to *me* that way, little girl."

"We're looking for Mummy and Henry," Claire said to her father, her smile intact. "Brian and I are." Her voice had acquired a British curl. "We've been to see Rose just now and we're charged with a secret."

"Of course you are," Hal said.

"What *is* the problem with all of you?" Lauren had backed up a step—she was in the next room more than this one now. She stamped her foot for emphasis. "Why is she *talking* that way? Are all of you *completely* out of your minds?"

Claire said, "She interrupted me, Papa."

He frowned.

"You don't even know how ridiculous you are," Lauren said. "This whole thing is ridiculous, this whole evening." She was speaking to Hal. "You invited us to a dinner party, in case you've forgotten . . ."

"No," Hal said. "That wouldn't have been me. The invitation, I mean."

"It most certainly *was* you."

"That would have been Liz, I think."

"And it's your house! And she's your wife!"

"Do you think so?"

" 'Scuse me," said a voice behind Lauren, from the other room, and when she stepped aside, surprised, there was Chicken Little. With raised eyebrows, she pointed at Claire and gestured with one finger: *follow me*. Then she walked away quickly while Claire ran to catch up. A beat passed before Hal set out in pursuit. But Lauren took hold of his shoulder, propelling herself past him. She called, "Hey! Hel-lo . . . ," receding already.

While Brian tried and failed to raise enough courage to follow, all four of them quickly disappeared from view.

The old woman was clapping and smiling. "Bravo," she said, still watching the door through which they had vanished. "Oh goodness!"

"You approve?" Robert asked her.

"Oh I certainly do. Wasn't that wonderful?"

He turned away, and wandered toward a chair at the table.

"Oh, I'm so glad we came," the woman said. "I can smell these things, you know—I said to Mac this morning, 'They're due, I think. They're overdue,' I said."

·

HENRY WAS UPSTAIRS in the studio, waiting. All the canvases were turned, with their mundane backs to the room. He had stood still staring out the windows that faced toward the lindens and the Austin Healey for what seemed a long time, but now he began searching in his pockets until he found the plastic container with the proper label. He managed the cap and poured the little red pills into his palm. There were mugs and plastic yogurt cups full of liquids on the work table, and he found the one that was nearest to clear, then tossed back the pills and washed them down. There was a terrible flavor that trailed late, though—tannic and sharp, vaguely chemical.

The door opened and Elizabeth swung into the room, pulling Claire behind her. She shut the door quickly, and they both stood still, listening. "I'm leaving now," Henry said, evenly. It was what he had decided while looking out the window. But Elizabeth and her daughter were intent on the door and the hallway behind it. A commotion of feet ran past, and a woman whose voice he didn't recognize was speaking. When the commotion moved on, he resumed. "I'm taking you with me. Claire can come too, I don't care." He crossed the room with a determined stride. "We'll find Brian on the way. Here we go!"

She wheeled and leapt from his touch, stumbled backward into the room. Then she straightened, grinned upon him, and said, "No."

"Hello Henry Korbusieski," Claire said, speaking slowly, flirting.

"Claire." His eyes remained on her mother, who had turned away from them to stroll toward the windows. "Do me a favor, would you, Claire? Get lost?"

"Tell him," Elizabeth said.

"Tell him what?" Henry asked.

She turned now. "Claire is here for a reason, dear. Tell him please, Claire."

"It's sad," Claire said. She sounded pleased. "You won't like it. I'm here to tell you that it's true, Henry—what Mummy said. It's all very true and tragic. Mummy is—will you look at me, please?"

"We are leaving," Henry said, facing Elizabeth still. "We just need to get out of this house."

"*Mummy*, Mr. Henry," Claire said, "*is*, if you must know, very much in love with Rose. She loves Rose! *Finis!* If it makes you feel any better . . ."

"Thank you, darling," Elizabeth interrupted. "Thank you, dear, that's fine." To Henry she said, "Now do you believe me? It's all true. We leave for Cork tonight. I think you're sweet, dear—I always have. But I'm through trifling."

Henry began to respond, but he found he had nothing available to say. He stared instead, without much affection, at this lover who had often astonished him. She *was* lovely—yes—but not startling any longer. Not extraordinary. The force of her beauty was quickly becoming implied, an event in her past that had left visible traces. There were small deltas forming at the corners of her eyes, and her forehead creased at the provocation of almost any emotion. It was possible her hair was colored. Henry felt unwell, and his vision seemed to be blurring, probably from whatever had been in the cup he drank from, yet he thought he could trust this clarification as it formed. She was crazy—she was a little unwell, and quite steadily if just beyond reach, as a matter of fact—and she was pampered, and fairly inept at practicalities of any kind—at conversation, for instance. She had no sensible skills, that he knew of. She'd never learned to drive. She wasn't even a particularly good actress. She wouldn't last a week outside the tristate area, much less in Cork with Rose the nanny. What was he doing here? What had propelled him—what had seemed worthwhile?

Henry himself was past forty, though his fair complexion and his surplus of energy might still suggest a younger man. There had been an afternoon, not long ago, while driving the hour home from work and from a rendezvous with Elizabeth, when he had thought, I can't keep doing this. I'm becoming foolish—isn't there something I'm squandering? The lake at home was desolate, as usual, but the light upon it—the reflection of so many fallen leaves—was beautiful in its way, if you took a second look. The air smelled of what must be snow. It usually depressed him to drive home in winter, when his town was stripped to its core of dull farms and failing ventures, but this particular evening he was reminded that there were a lot of people in the city—most of his clients, in fact—who would kill to stay out here all year. Or who thought they would, at least, before trying it—shouldn't their jealousy be enough for him? Angela had greeted him with a kiss and her dry enthusiasm, and with her pleasant lack of curiosity. There had always been something sly and irresponsible about her and it seemed to invite the worst from him with a permissive irony that he appreciated. She herself had been his prize once, of course, abducted from Elizabeth's end of the state. She had worn sleeveless shirts and rowed crew for Yale. She'd impressed him the first night they met with her batch of gimlets in a pitcher (though unintentionally—she hadn't cared to impress him then). A gimlet was something he'd heard of somewhere, and craved in ignorance. Now, on this particular evening, just a week or two ago, Angela had made the season's first wassail. The house was saturated with a fragrance that his own mother might have purchased in the form of a candle. Henry was disappointed to discover two friends in the living room—two women who socialized without their husbands, and who must be disappointed to see him too—but there was a fire in the fireplace, and the women politely smiled. He sat with them and chatted and drank his wassail, trying to lay low but contributing when he could, and they were solicitous and laughed at his jokes. And he found himself taking what he hoped was an honest accounting of the measure of allure still left to him. His jowls, he knew, were the jowls of an older man. He had a menacing brow (it had served him well), and small eyes, and fleshy lips, and sometimes these elements together in a mirror coalesced into the impression of a dangerous petty bureaucrat, here at the threshold of middle age. But in addition he believed he had some sex appeal left. He was tall and still fit, possibly strapping. He had the broad shoulders and large, pale hands of a good, solid Polack. Among the last things in a lifetime, he sometimes thought, there were few sadder to anticipate than the last beauty who would bare her surprising breasts for you, though on other days he recognized that the man who had such a thought was already, probably, sad and doomed. But that evening, sitting in his living room with these lovely, local women all stranded better than two hours from the island of Manhattan and looking none the worse for the loss, he had thought that Elizabeth wasn't necessarily the end of indulgence—that it was a concession he could put off a little longer—and also that the end, when it did come for him, would arrive with greater compensations than he generally allowed.

Yet only a few days later, sitting on the fender of a van on Greene Street and watching Elizabeth act in his commercial—watching her call her single line up to a window while the rain machine sent two intersecting circles of downpour into her face and the cameraman dollied and swooped on his crane, moving in to catch the wet strands of hair curled along her temples and the oiled, beading cleavage at her neckline—Henry had thought, No, he was kidding himself. He was *in love* with this woman. It was a term that had never before come to hand, regarding Elizabeth, and it might be only a gaudy costume in which he disguised more mundane emotions. What he felt for her was related to the thrill she got from slumming, shagging the dropout from the farm village of back-state Connecticut; his attraction to her had begun as the other side of that coin. But the attachment had quietly grown, he thought, or perhaps mutated—had goitered into vanity and a wish to save or reform Elizabeth, which was silly, not to mention out of character. He didn't have a reformer's patience, or a savior's innocence.

Today, right now, a new layer of clarity opened before him: he was only bored, not in love; he'd been pleasantly challenged, not in love; he was not in love so much as in haste, in decline, and insecure. Next, he'd be insipid. He could hear himself explaining to Angela one day: I never intended . . . I'm only making myself miserable. Awful.

"Are you listening, Henry?" she said to him now. "You look ill, dear, are you ill? He looks ill, Claire."

"Not to me."

"Get him a washcloth. Get a bucket. Do you want to sit?" she asked Henry.

"We should go," he persisted, even though he didn't mean it any longer. "Please, Elizabeth."

"Yes, but sit down first, love." She had a hold of his arm. She was leading him to the butterfly chair. And she was right, he felt nauseous. The chair proved no help though—it folded his stomach in half.

"Claire, dear . . . ," Elizabeth said.

"Coming," Claire called, from the bathroom that joined the studio to the bedroom. Pass through that bedroom and you came to another, Henry knew: the guest room with the canopy bed and an iron spiral staircase that led to a widow's walk. A dogleg left through that and you were back in the foyer at the head of the stairs with the stained-glass windows brilliant before you and the balustrade that had been lifted from a church in Umbria. One more, he thought. Soon I'll be ready for the compensations, but not yet.

He tried to focus his diminishing energy. He reached and took hold of Elizabeth's blouse where she leaned before him, and pulled her toward his lap. "Listen," he whispered. His voice sounded dull and his tongue felt thick. "We're making a mistake here—both of us. It's this house. If you would let me get you out of here . . ."

She tsked. "You're sweet." She patted his crotch. "Look at you— sick as a dog, and your tail still wagging. *Let* go, please."

Claire returned with an empty wastebasket and a hand towel in a basin of steaming water. "Can I wash him?" she asked her mother.

The hallway door opened and Hal stepped into the room. "Ah," he said. "The party we've been searching for."

"Hal," Elizabeth replied, pleased and surprised, still crouching beside Henry. "Where have you been, I wonder? You're just in time, darling—we're about to strip Henry down and wash him clean."

"Really?" Claire asked.

Then Lauren came through the door behind Hal. She bumped him out of the way and turned and saw Elizabeth, and her eyes widened. "You!" She pointed.

"My," Elizabeth said.

There really was something bloodthirsty in her eyes by now. "Come here," Lauren said.

Elizabeth lost her smile. She stood up from her crouch swiftly, then turned and fled through the bathroom door.

"Hey!"

Lauren pushed past Hal, who moved aside. Even Claire stepped out of her way. But there was something that rose in Henry—to his distorted sensibilities, it seemed a noble and protective impulse, a sacrifice almost. He had his fleeing lover in mind. As Lauren passed he reached out from where he sat in the butterfly chair and caught hold of her ankle—he had aimed for the left but ended up with the right. She toppled over and landed, then picked her face up from the paint-splattered floor and looked at him with surprise—with an evident sense of betrayal even, as if she had counted on his support. She struggled to stand, but he had her ankle in his fist still and he slouched back in his chair without letting go, so that she slipped again. Claire laughed, then covered her mouth. Lauren looked at Henry with disgust. "*What's the matter with you?*" she asked, the tears just beginning to break from the corners of her eyes.

•

BRIAN STOOD in the doorway where Claire had left him. He took a deep breath, not at all sure of what to do with himself. He wondered where his father was, and it occurred to him that he was supposed to be waiting outside, in the car. The old woman had gotten up and was busy turning her armchair to face the man who must be Robert—he slouched and stared at the cigarette he was lighting. Brian backed out quietly and slid the door closed.

At the leaded windows in the adjoining room he cupped his hands against the glass to see out past his reflection. The Austin Healey was there still, across the lawn, at the head of the row of trees. There was a moon out, flashing momentarily between the clouds, and the wind blew the wooden wings of the goose. Only when he heard this clacking sound through the window did the music still quietly spilling from the piano in the room register in his mind. He turned around. The gray-bearded man sat playing, watching Brian over the top of his glasses. He bore a stern frown, not angry so much as disgusted. "Please," he said, his voice a pitted rumble. "Take a seat."

He gestured, with the shift of his eyes, to a sofa not far from the window, facing the piano. Brian sat down. For the first time all evening, he half wished that the mistake which had somehow taken him this far would be discovered: that he might be shut out again, left in a running car or at home with his mother—considered unworthy and returned to comfortable ignorance.

"I wonder, Brian, if you're familiar with the classical piano repertoire." The man's eyes shifted to the keys. The notes he played were an utter mystery.

"No," Brian told him. The man glanced up at him, as if for further confirmation, so Brian shook his head no.

"Lessons?"

"No."

"When you were younger, perhaps?"

He shook his head again.

"The"—he paused—"*radio*," the man pronounced, or asserted.

"Not really."

The man took his hands from the keys and inhaled a massive breath that swelled his chest and rolled his shoulders back. He ran one hand through his beard while his elbow rested in the other. Then he looked at Brian and opened his lips to speak. Instead, he held a finger aloft—*here*—and began to play a melody that Brian was astonished to find familiar. Brian smiled, despite himself, and when the man looked up across the rim of his glasses, he smiled too. "Yes?" he asked.

"Uh huh," Brian said.

"Good boy. The Rondo Alla Turca, Brian. Mozart. None other."

When the piece was done he immediately began to play it a second time. But he stopped paying attention to what he was doing. He said, "I know your name is Brian. I heard our Claire say as much. My name is Mac, but if you were my student, heaven forbid, you would refer to me as Mr. Carlyle."

He played the piece to its vigorous end and started into it a third time. Brian's smile faded and he thought of the football game being played without him in Waterbury, and then of his mother at home on the island. He imagined her lit by the fire with a book in her lap. She would be squinting with the particular impatience that she reserved for evenings with his father away. But when he and his father returned home later that night she would be carefully busy and distracted, as if she hadn't noticed their absence.

The door opened and Chicken Little walked into the room. Her face was composed, as if relaxed, but she closed the door with stealth and scanned the windows while strolling to the sofa by the fire. She was certainly beautiful. She was his father's lover, an identity Brian found deeply suggestive and largely opaque. She sat down heavily, sighed, and let her head tip back. She closed her eyes. But then, almost immediately, her eyes snapped open and she glared at the man who played the piano. "Mac!" she said. "Are you torturing the boy?"

"Quite the contrary. I'm playing through his favorites from the classical repertoire."

She laughed. "You lousy bastard," she said. "You lousy snob." She squinched her nose and grinned at Brian.

Then she lay her head back again and closed her eyes as if to nap. In a moment she opened her eyes, and with her head tipped back still, resting on the sofa, she stretched her lips and jaw into a range of distortions, as if testing their limits.

She snapped to attention. "You shitty old tyrant," she said, which had no appreciable effect on the man's playing or expression.

Then she caught sight of the paneled door and frowned, as if disappointed by its presence. Springing from the couch, she crossed the room on stockinged tiptoes. His lover, Brian thought again, less and less pleased with the notion.

There was an old-fashioned keyhole in the door, and she crouched to look through it first, then put her ear to it. With her profile to the door, she was facing Brian. She raised her eyebrows, then motioned for him to come and listen. Which he did, though he really didn't want to.

There were voices there, but the words were indistinct. Chicken Little—close beside him and vaguely fragrant—gestured with absolute disgust at the man playing the piano, who was just then falling through the last notes of the Mozart. To Brian's surprise, he followed with something quiet and gentle, and now they could hear the voices in the next room. The old woman was speaking—not quite clearly—and then came Robert's voice. "Do you have a strong faith, then?" he asked.

"Well," the woman answered, hesitating, "for me it comes and it goes."

"Yes."

"I believe in God, but I have my doubts about the Holy Spirit."

"Yes. Tell me, do you believe in redemption?"

"Redemption."

"Yes."

"I don't talk religion all that much, is the thing. Most people I talk to don't talk religion."

"Naturally."

"Sin and be forgiven—I believe in that. To a point."

"*Noc*-turne," the man at the piano intoned.

"Poor Robert," Chicken Little whispered.

She turned her ear from the door and said to Brian, whispering, "Do you want to know something about your father, dear? Do you want the absolute bottom line on your father—as I see him, anyway? The be-all, end-all bottom line?"

He did and he didn't. It was terrible to believe she could know. He said "Yes."

But she said, "My goodness," distracted again, "Claire's right. You do have lovely lashes."

Brian shrugged—disappointed, now that the opportunity had passed.

"You've seen my Rose, I guess?" she asked. "Well then you know a thing or two about eyes. I don't think I can let her go, Brian, I really don't." She tsked, and shook her head. "What would you have me do? I wonder. I'd be interested to hear your advice on this mess."

For an instant he considered the question seriously, but then it was really too much. All at once it was too much: he knew when he was being patronized by a disinterested adult. It might take him a minute, but he could figure it out. And though it was the last thing he wanted to do, Brian thought he might cry. He sighed. In an

effort to keep his composure he turned away from her and slipped
down from the crouch he was in to sit on the floor, his back against
the door frame. Boredom: he aimed again for boredom. She tsked
and touched his hair. She said, "Relax, sweetie. I was only kidding. I
don't really want your advice." Against all odds, this made him feel
better. "There's nothing to be done, anyway," she said. "Never was.
Now if I could find a nice young man with a dashing young sister—
it doesn't seem impossible, does it? But short of that . . .

"I have to say," she continued, after a pause, "I always wanted
to know what Angela looked like. I'm dying to know, really. Is she
a mouse, your mother?" She was watching him as if waiting for an
answer, but it was clear she didn't require one, and it troubled Brian
that she was something his father had chosen, and had driven him
here to see.

She said, "I doubt it," answering her own question. "I'll bet she's
stunning. Here, I'll tell you a secret."

She leaned in very close to him and stared and smiled—whispered with a heady indulgence. "Secretly," she said, her voice full of
breath and the wet click of the "c," "if you want to know the truth,
I always suspected that Angela was black. Some exotic black thing—
dark dark dark. With breasts"—she gestured, both hands beneath her
own—"and enormous lips." He watched her, dismayed. She leaned
back, grinning. "Course the sight of you threw cold water on that.
Didn't it?"

She looked away, and seemed to drift for a moment, seated on
the floor beside him. She may have been listening to the piano.

Then she turned and regarded Brian with a new smile. Leaning
in again, she laid a hand on his shoulder and whispered into his ear.
"Tell the truth," she said, and despite the coy angle of her glance, she
seemed to mean it. "Are you Henry's boy?" She stared.

But then she sat up straight. She cocked her head to listen. "Uh
oh," she said, and scrambled to her feet. Brian snorted unhappily
and shook his head as she loped from the room. She closed the
opposite door just as the one beside him flew open. He and Claire

both jumped, surprising each other equally, but Claire recovered first. "What are you doing on the floor?" she asked, annoyed. "Why are you sitting on our floor?"

"I don't know!" he answered. "Where have you been?" He got up.

"Where have I *been*?—now there's a question. I'll just *tell* you where I've been, you lucky boy. I just will."

She looked over her shoulder at the piano and the man behind it, and frowned. "This way," she said, leading him to the sofa by the fire where her mother had sat.

But when she was seated her attention was still focused past Brian, on the man at the piano. "No," she said loudly, "on second thought, this really won't do. I think we'd better take our very private conversation elsewhere." She grabbed Brian's hand and led him, despite his resistance, to the door through which her mother had fled. As they stepped from the room the piano burst into a terrifying trample of notes, and she slammed the door on the din.

They were back in the dark hallway now. Predictably, she produced an amorous smile for Brian. While the dampened piano galloped around them, she leaned close and fingered a button on his shirt. "Miss me?" she asked.

"Have you seen my father?"

"You can't answer a question with a question, you know. No matter what they teach you in those schools up there—"

"Stop it," he said—aloud, he was sure, though she showed no sign of having heard him.

She said, "Yes, I've seen your father. In fact I think he's grand, myself, even though Mother's quite through with him." Should he say it again? He tried: "Shut up." Her voice changed—sank, took on a coy inflection—but it had nothing to do with him. "Now I would *die* for Rose," she said, "don't get me wrong. But here's the thing. The thing is, I like boys. The more I learn about them the more I like them." She rubbed her forehead against his chest and spoke into his shirt. "I can't imagine who wouldn't like boys, really. I can't see why boys waste time on girls, even. Would you like to explain that to me, Brian—why it is that boys waste their time on girls? Would you explain it slowly, so that I'll understand?"

He was out of patience. He wanted to hit something, or kick something, break something; his muscles ached for release. He wanted to shock. He took her chin into his palm and lifted her face and kissed it. He aimed for her lips but when he missed, that seemed better. She made a funny sound at first—a kind of moan—but then she kissed him back, or missed, or connected glancingly on his nose and chin. And now that he had begun, he didn't know where to go. His arms ached, so he wrapped them across her back and squeezed her—his muscles needed to be drained—then took her bottom into his hands and squeezed, his teeth clenched, kissing her, his teeth clicking against hers. He could crush her. But she was pushing away, her hands in his chest, and grunting. She was trying to speak. For how long had she been pushing away? He let go of her, instantly prepared to apologize.

She stepped back, appraising. But she grinned then, and giggled. She took hold of his hand. "You sweet, sweet boy," she said. "You devil. Not here though."

So she was leading him again. She led him through the dark hall-way, and the lit, empty rooms of the house, to the foyer by the garage and then outside into the cold. The night smells rose up, and the breeze blew around them. He felt so much better—in an instant—stepping out of the house. She shivered, leading him up the lawn toward a dark place by the tennis court, and what a pleasure it was to see her shiver—what a pleasure the cold was, his own. There was a rowboat here: this was her destination. She crouched and reached up under the seat of the overturned boat. She felt around blindly and produced a beach towel and a thick wool blanket. She unfolded these and spread them on the grass under the boat. It was tight work—not a lot of clearance. Brian scanned the lit windows of the house and it seemed that every one of them accommodated some agitation—shadows moving against the curtains. It gave the impression of a party or a heated argument raging from room to room. Voices could be heard indistinctly. The sky began to spit rain.

"You first, Romeo," said Claire beside him. She held the aluminum rowboat so that it tipped away and gestured for him to climb underneath. Which he did.

She slipped in with him and they lay together close. The seat of the boat, against his hip, made it hard to turn over or move, but there was space up here beneath the bow. There was a fat candle tucked behind the seat where the blanket had been and she lit this. Rain tapped intermittently on their roof. Claire was busy and impatient, but Brian was gaining his bearings, still. His frustration—the ache—had been drained by the night air. But Claire adjusted the blanket, pulled the ends of it over them haphazardly, then undressed, shimmying her skirt down and flopping against him, her shoulder catching his nose.

"Sorry," she whispered, distracted.

When she had her skirt and underwear at her ankles she covered her crotch with her hands. His view was shaded by the partial cover of the blanket and the seat of the boat close above her. The candlelight was yellow and brittle, reflected against the belly of the boat. She bit her lip and turned her eyes to him. She lay on her back and he on his side, facing her. The rain picked up, and the wind blew against his back, but in front he was warmed by the heat of her agitation and the rub of her skin against him. She looked sad and intent, chewing her lip. He felt he had missed a cue, and worried that he had misrepresented himself in the dark hallway. He heard the wooden clack of the goose's wings in the midst of the metal tap of the rain. "Well?" she whispered. She took his hand and put it into the mix with her own: soft and bony, alternating. "Your hand is cold," she said quietly, holding it close. She watched him. She pushed his hand in time with her own, then closed her eyes, let go of his hand, made a small sound something like a sigh, and began to breathe differently. He left his hand there, feeling the motion of her own fingers beneath his and the stranger forms beneath that. She pushed, and the back of his hand pressed against the cold of the rowboat seat. The candle tipped and their shadows lurched. He wasn't sure if he was neglecting an opportunity or being excluded from it, but he was almost certain this wasn't the full extent of his anticipated involvement. The sounds she made became urgent and muffled at once, and the rain fell harder, briefly, in a tin patter on the boat. Her breathing shortened until it stopped, and she was taut, her chin tipped, her neck fully exposed—in that moment she seemed a thing apart, more than he had ever guessed at. His own breath caught—*here I am*, he noticed.

Then she gave way, and rose up again. Soon she curled against him and put her face in his shirt.

As the beat of the rain slackened, in a calm between gusts, he heard voices coming from the house, where something further had clearly gone wrong. Claire's cheek was cool, her sweater warm, and her bare legs warmer still. She shook once more but differently now, and he realized she was crying. He reached down toward the stern of the boat and found the bundle of underwear in the waistband of her skirt. He pulled it up as well as he could along her legs—she half accommodated, responding sluggishly to his nudge. When the skirt was back to her waist, though it was turned in the wrong direction, she sighed and pulled away from him, lay on her back to wipe at her tears. "Pshhh," she said, resignedly. "*I* don't know. Am I going straight to hell? *I* don't know."

"No," he said, though now that she mentioned it, he supposed she may.

A gust blew against his back.

"You don't think? I do. I honestly do—in fact, I know it. Not that I'll be alone there. Not that I won't have Mother and Hal with me and all. Your father too, God knows. It's people like you and Rose who go to heaven. It's your compensation."

This statement conjured an immediate string of images in his mind: Claire in flames with her mother and Hal; then his father burning while Brian watched, with Rose, from a cool remove; then

Brian himself in the torture of flames, side by side with his father. He remembered the look that Rose had given him when he stood at the top of her stairs—was it meant to be complicit?

Claire said, "I never did tell you what I saw your father doing." She paused—remembering? "I don't guess he's afraid of anything, is he?"

There was a sound from out in the yard somewhere—a call or a horn—but Brian couldn't make it out clearly over the howl of the wind.

"Do you want to know a secret thing I never told anyone before?" Claire asked. "Say yes."

"Okay."

"Okay. This is important and lousy, just so you know." She sighed. "So one year which is two summers ago now, Mother sends me away to get me out of her hair. So fine, okay? So *where* she sends me is to this Aunt Mary, who everybody knows is crazy because she left Greenwich and moved to Charleston just all of a sudden. Which is in South Carolina, in case you didn't know." There was the sound again, twice. A car horn, Brian thought, though it was far away and faint. "But Aunt *Mary* doesn't want Claire around either—messing up her house and laughing at her friends' accents, which I *could* not help, I swear to God—so she sends me—get this—she packs me off to *Bible* camp. No joke. Which was terrible, and very boring, and very very inappropriate on her part. But then one day they decide we're going on this field trip to some place, some farm, except it's a long ways away so they get us all into these stupid vans and they make us play these games. The big game goes you have to try to be the first one to spot the crosses—the three crosses, you know what I'm talking about? Little one, big one, little one—have you ever seen these stupid things? They're made of pipes or something and some crazy person put them up all over the place down there. I mean, they're everywhere. And they're so *obvious*, and they look so *stupid*, stuck in the middle of somebody's farm or whatever it is—but I'm on this bus with a bunch of Bible school kids from South Carolina so they're all dumb as possible. So okay. I can go along. I spot the crosses, I *say* so. I win a *prize*. It's a box of *Cracker* Jacks, if you can believe it. So it's not like I'm looking hard—it's not like I even *care* about this stupid, stupid game—but I just keep seeing these crosses because they're practically everywhere and I'm always the first one because I don't know why—because all these other kids are blind or something. Their noses are like smudging the windows and they can't see the stupid crosses. So I keep getting these Cracker Jacks— it's a nun, mind you, a nun handing out Cracker Jacks—and she won't stop giving them to me, even though nobody else has any and I don't even want them. She won't even let me give them away." Claire began to cry again. The horn—a car horn—blew again from the dark past the boat. "Do you see what they were doing to me, just cause I didn't talk like them and I didn't like to hear about Jesus dying for my sins and stuff? I'm like piled up with these Cracker Jack boxes and there's another stupid set of crosses coming along— there they are, right there—and nobody's seeing them and nobody's seeing them—'Claire has a gift,' the nun is saying, which isn't true, and she shouldn't be allowed to say it. And I try to tap this numskull girl beside me and I point to the crosses and she goes yelling, 'The crosses, I see the crosses,' but then she says, 'Claire showed me, Claire saw them first,' and she's so proud just cause she *told* on me. *What the hell is that?*"

Her expression shifted directly from sadness to anger. She tipped the edge of the boat and peeked out across the lawn. "Who is that?" There was a car parked across the end of the driveway, down by the road, and the driver blew the horn again.

"It looks like a taxi," Brian said.

"It *is* a taxi. What's it doing here?"

A figure emerged from the foyer door: small and round, bundled in an overcoat, laboring with two massive suitcases. "It's Rose," Claire said, her tone changing from angry to wistful. "There she goes." She wiped at her cheek. Rose trudged awkwardly toward the taxi while Brian and Claire lay against one another, watching.

Then a light came on in the portico at the front door of the house, the main door that no one had used all night. Rose looked back—her face was too far away to be clear in the dark and the rain—as Chicken Little emerged, Hal close behind her. She looked wild, Chicken Little—no longer in control. "Shit," Claire whispered. She allowed the rim of the rowboat to dip down for better cover.

But her mother wasn't looking in their direction. She was shouting at Rose, who was halfway down the drive. Her words were bent and distorted by the wind, and Hal was behind her now, trying to restrain her. She struggled to get away, her elbow appeared to catch him in the chest, and he slumped back, letting her go. She ran a few steps toward Rose, then stopped and turned. She broke in the direction of the rowboat, watching Rose over her shoulder. Claire let the boat tip down further. "The candle," she hissed, motioning with her hand. Brian leaned and blew it out. For just a moment it did seem that she was coming straight for them, but she stopped at the last car parked in the row, and she climbed in and started it with a belt of gas. She threw the car into gear and the wheels spun, then caught—she drove toward the boat. The headlamps popped on and flashed into Brian's eyes.

Then the car veered away, carving through the lawn, and accelerated down the driveway. She flew past the house, where Hal charged as if he would leap into her path, but he arrived too late—or possibly stopped at the last moment. Rose was running, attempting to run, laboring with her suitcases down the center of the driveway beneath the trees. Claire tipped the edge of the boat back up so that she and Brian had a better view. There was Rose, in the light of the headlamps, tripping, turning her ankle, and past her, not far away, was the taxi driver, who had gotten out of his cab and was waving his arms as if to catch Chicken Little's attention, as if she might not be aware that she was barreling down the driveway straight into his car and the woman who had fallen between them. But Rose got up, and she left the suitcases behind. She darted, with the swiftness her brevity had suggested might be possible, into the cover beside the driveway, out of the path of the car—which veered, following her, then began to veer away again, around the trunks of the linden trees. The car skidded, braking, but too late. It slammed into a trunk, the back end carried through, and it spun in a circle before it came to a stop. The engine screamed for a moment, then quit. One of the headlamps was smashed; the other cast among the shadows it threw.

"Well," Claire said. "Geez."

After a moment, Hal broke into a sprint for the car. Robert and Lauren and the older woman—Claire's aunt—had all gathered out on the portico. Past the car, Rose emerged from a darker corner among the trees and ran to the taxi driver. She pointed, and while she climbed into the cab, he collected her suitcases from where they lay on the gravel. Hal had reached the damaged car. He was tugging at the driver's-side door, but it wouldn't budge. "I should help," Claire said, but she didn't move. The taxi driver got into the cab and pulled away with a flourish. Then the passenger-side door of the car opened and Chicken Little stepped out: shaky, but standing. Claire sighed. "Some thrills," she said, without enthusiasm.

They lay still, watching for a long time, though there was little left to watch. Claire's mother limped a few paces and appeared to be laughing, or possibly crying, then sat on the wet leaves close to the car. Hal inspected her knee with the soothing indulgence of a doctor. They were both speaking at once—he calmly and she with a touch of wilting hysteria—and though their words were lost in the breadth of the lawn and the sound the rain made, they looked intimate together, partly lit by the weak glow of the remaining headlamp, which seemed to be dimming. Even the conversation that had started among those gathered on the portico was milder now, deflated. But Brian saw his father, framed alone in a high lit window, and he didn't look well. He had something in his hand—a bucket? He slouched, leaned against the edge of something in the room. He was scanning the yard, sadly it seemed, and Brian hoped he was looking for his son.

Brian lay against Claire in an intimate posture of their own, and he watched her watching her parents and felt a shiver spin through his chest that was partly affection and partly relief. He thought to himself, *She'll come and visit. And I'll show her the lake.*

But then she rolled to face him and stared with plain disappointment, or possibly resignation. She was about to speak. But she sighed and rolled away, out from under the boat, and she stood and brushed her skirt off. She turned her back on Brian. She folded her arms across her chest and began to walk down the long slope toward her parents and the battered car. Brian watched her and waited.

He waited for her to turn back—a small acknowledgment, that was all he expected. And when she never did—when she walked just as leisurely as that down the whole of the long and mild slope without ever turning for even the briefest glance—he found himself in possession of what he immediately considered his first fully adult and ennobling thought. He was in love, he decided—perhaps he had even made love. And love was dreadful, and shameful and sad, and though it was over between he and Claire, he could hardly wait to be in love again.

THE LAST TIME
I SAW RICHARD

THEY WERE in their middle thirties, the three women—counting down, each with deep and untapped maternal stores. They were something entirely new, for Brian. They were often folding him against their bosoms and mussing his hair and licking the toothpaste from the corner of his mouth (a negligence he didn't remember being prone to earlier) until his edges were rounded and the rough pretensions of his youth had been smoothed and he couldn't always muster a full sail, an embarrassment which further provoked their kindliness and nurturing instincts.

This was the thing they had in common, but it was only revealed slowly; at first, he had thought each was nothing like the last. Grace had her winning flirtatious token—a closed-lip grin and shy squint, accented by a dip of her chin toward one shoulder—and there was an endearing space between her teeth when she did dare to part her lips. She was a painter, with Mars violet smears beneath the fingernails of her small hands. At the clubs where his band played she was often the instigator: prodding the boorish or inclined with an irony that they sometimes missed, or telling self-deprecating anecdotes in which she came off as clumsy yet undeterred, and a little prim. But at home she was quiet and surprisingly lovely, with her dark eyes suspiring and the wiry bundle of her little body inert. She lived, inexplicably, in Flushing, which was itself winsome, if inconvenient. Beneath her public efforts she was sensible and settled in a way that Brian admired and hoped to be capable of himself one day—though he might not have hoped for anything of the kind had he not met the other two women first.

Emily had preceded Grace, and though they met in Provincetown, she was unmistakably Pacific: she had the hair (blonde and unstylishly long and straight as can be, in the manner of Joni Mitchell, that Californian from Canada) as well as the nimble combination of social activism and apathy. Beneath her crepe-paper shifts and blouses exhausting the cement spectrum, her body was a vessel built for speed more than cargo. She was hipless as a boy, and her breasts were small wonders of flesh and physics: petite and assertive, with dime-sized nipples that often conspired to embarrass her. But if her body did not speak maternity, it was nevertheless the first language of her nature. She was constantly feeding him, undeterred by the limitations of her culinary repertoire, and she tended her thriving garden with coos and pets and whispered encouragement as much as with trowel, loam, and water.

But first of all there had been Andra: twice divorced, born in Poland and visiting from Frankfurt, with a lovely, clotted accent and a wardrobe devoted to silk. She was a musician—like Brian, except that while he muddled in the slums of the term she resided at its heights: a classical pianist, with a devotion to the atonal belligerence of the twentieth century and a lovely, fluent touch. And she was the first to introduce the unorthodox proposal.

Her stay in New York was only three weeks long, but the third week was the right one—strategically ovulatory—and like the other women who would follow her, she was short on time and eggs. She told him her husbands had each proven inadequate at the most basic level, and the fact was, she never really had been interested in any but the briefest relationships with grown men. Even these husbands had turned out to be children, charges more than lovers, though she blamed herself since this had been the essence of their attraction for her initially. She had determined to go it alone. She had timed this trip carefully, and she had chosen Brian the day she met him. Of course he would never see her again, nor hear from her, and he would bear no responsibility toward nor official association with his issue. It was a plan she might have carried through without his consent since he didn't appear to be curious at all about the protection she failed to employ (so American, she said; she had spied on him from the bathroom to see if he would rifle through her purse in search of the little pill wheel, as German men did). But she liked him, and hated to think of his reaction when the address and phone number she had given him proved fake. Her doctor had assured her that her own parts were in working order, as well as anyone could assess, and her thermometer indicated that this was a night for decisive action. She hoped he could help.

But despite her thermometer's indications, this particular night had thus far been distinctly short on action. In fact, the hour preceding her confession and proposal had been devoted to a series of lackluster attempts to spur his pony. It was the first time in his life he had failed to rise to the occasion (though it would not be the last—and what a prod to cruel metaphors the discussion that attended such a failure proved to be). With Andra propped on one elbow beside him, delivering her pitch while tracing notes and staves into the hair on his chest, he knew that she was divulging her plan not out of kindness or honor but only desperation, and he had an intimate sense— his first, really—of his advancing age.

From the beginning she had seemed to him a mature gesture about which he caught himself feeling a little self-congratulatory. Before Andra, he had never courted a girl past the gum-snapping stage, and his affairs had been colored by the unpredictable appetites and spontaneous fixations of young leather-leaning women who could not help wedding irony to lust. This lifestyle had offered its charms (if none that were quite surprising), but by thirty-two he had managed to wile away a dozen years like so and he'd recently discovered, a little late, that even he had ambitions. Also, he'd begun to sense that he was occasionally indulged as an oddity by girls who (and there was nothing flattering about finding this phrase at hand) could legitimately be called "nearly half his age." There was a gap in which he was alone, then Andra appeared—something different. She was protective from the start: her first words to him, on the wind-swept sidewalk outside a friend's apartment, were the concerned and accented "Vere is your coat?" She attached herself to him that night, immediately and casually, and in the days that followed she courted him in a way that seemed distinctly old-fashioned: she took him to dinner in the sorts of restaurants that still depended upon the guile of candlelight, and finagled intimate seating for him at her trio's recitals, where the gestures of her concentration and the gloomy admissions she coaxed from the beast at her fingers were distinctly provocative. That first night, she had politely visited his loft—appointed in what he thought was the prevailing Zen-Shaker vein—but from then on, at the end of an evening, she always steered them back to her motel room with the Stieglitz photographs and the somber bedspread. She had come to hear his band once, but had slipped out after a couple of songs (claiming allergies). True, their sex was something less than volatile—she hardly ever opened her eyes, and tended to hum instead of moan—but she undressed with a smug grin and her patience had a teasing edge that was catchy. The fact was, until this evening and his flaccid endeavor, he had begun to consider a move to Frankfurt and a season or two of unclut-tered monogamy. It might be fun, at least until the snow melted in Manhattan or she spotted her next man at a party.

But that humming. He was probably looking for an excuse, yet he couldn't help feeling it contributed to his fizzle. When he was young he'd had a friend whose mother hummed her way through the unending errands of a farm and a family of eight, and blind to the gulf between this woman and his own mother (who, though she was living among the farms then, hailed from the Connecticut of lampposts and tennis courts), Brian had asked her one day while she loaded the dishwasher, "Why don't you hum while you do that?"

"Because your mother can't sing," she'd replied, "but she sure can grind a tune, sweetie pie." And for years this phrase had described her boundaries in his mind: someone else would make the music, but his mother would make the most of it. She never had the knack for adventure that Brian's father had, but she made a fine sidekick, and this was the scheme of their marriage, it seemed to Brian. Why wasn't it enough? he used to wonder, though now he supposed his father wanted the same thing she did, in the end.

Tonight Andra had been humming the melody of a single tune, unfamiliar but vaguely God-fearing, in the cab and in the rising elevator while sucking on his neck. Her eyes had not quite been open all evening, it seemed. While she undressed them both, still carrying her tune, he thought, for the first time in many years, of that farm mother humming as she scrubbed the wash, birthed the calves, beheaded the chickens, and when Andra fed him her breast it seemed obscene as none of his younger antics ever had. The longer his apparatus was plainly unresponsive, the louder her humming became, as if she meant to soothe him into lust.

Now her trance had been broken and her plans revealed and her head rested on his chest. After a long silence she said, in her Polish/German lilt, "I am now thirty-seven years, Brian. I want baby like nobody's business."

He wondered, as he would again later with both Emily and Grace, why this woman should be reduced to a stopgap measure like himself? He was tempted to blame it on his generation's mistrust of the old familiar sacraments, and certainly he himself, product of the sort of nuptial failure that it took the seventies to perfect, could hardly imagine the explosive alchemy that might actually launch him past bachelorhood. But Andra had given the traditional route two passes and here she was back where she had started: in bed beside another man short on the most essential and democratically distributed talent of all. He thought of the dead-end coupling he had invested in, of his vigor and instinctive urgency pumped into rubber socks and disks and chemical vacancies, and it made him sad and ashamed to think that he could perform this simplest endeavor with any amenable stranger, without the aid of affection or even strenuous engagement, yet faced with the sweetness at the core of the act, its miraculous *raison d'être*, he lost his way. Perhaps Andra beside him had succumbed to similarly broad and destimulating thoughts, for she slipped into her mild, parted-lip sleep. He wanted to do this for her—and why shouldn't he? Although he did feel a vague, behind-the-scenes relief that it wasn't quite possible. Soon he fell asleep too.

But sometime in the night he woke to find Andra perched precariously above his dream-swollen signature, and at the sight of his opened eyes she whispered, "May I?" It was momentous and habitual like the performance, at last, of a song he had rehearsed all his life. In the morning she returned to Frankfurt. He never knew for sure if they had been lucky that night—the odds must surely be against them—but she had promised to write if the charm didn't take, and he never heard from her again.

•

WHAT A PATTERN he had set. It was partly his own fault for telling Emily about Andra ("If that was even her name," Emily had said), and there were many differences, most dramatically that his relationship with Emily lasted an unprecedented eleven months. But when the coddling and nurturing eventually led to his periodic lilt and they were sinking into the gelid folds of a long dénouement, she was ready with The Proposition, and the terms were much as they had been with Andra. Emily would return to her own coast and be lost among the surf and earthquakes, the coffee yoga enlightenment and the intermittent forest fires that he imagined extended, in roughly similar proportions, from Seattle to San Diego. He would gain no knowledge of and bear no responsibility for his issue. "Papa was a New Yorker," she would tell the child, and the child would understand, as west-coasters did, both the romantic lure inherent in courting a man afflicted with this most mysterious of the thousand natural shocks and the inevitable parting necessary for a woman bred on the curative Cascade shores.

Emily was a Jacobean scholar who had settled for a career in publishing, and these were the poles of her orbit: her grand designs and literary tastes were consistently grounded by a predilection for sensible practicality and a habit of resignation. She was his self-proclaimed soubrette, striving for the proper coquetry, but her performances were marred by the care with which she folded removed articles of clothing, or by her stubborn compulsion to answer a ringing telephone. So while she was attracted to a relatively novel brand of parenting, romantic in its off-kilter way, she approached it with more pragmatic deliberation than Andra. Brian presented an appealing prepotent complement to her own genetic portfolio: he was a grounded cynic with impractical habits, a redhead with untended lanky strength (important because, like all west-coasters, Emily was a triathlete) as well as familial longevity. She wasn't interested in the hit-and-run intrigue either. Once he had said yes to The Proposition (and what choice did he have? he did seem to love her, after all) she wasn't about to fly back home until she was traveling for two. Which, despite her relative youth—she was thirty-four—and immaculate health, required several months.

He found the life of the stud something less than advertised. Like Andra, Emily had no interest in his apartment (how impressive it had been to those brief residents of his receding youth), so he took the train to the cottage she had rented in Greenwich to spend weekends that sometimes turned into weeks. She had her garden there, and the Sound was near enough to provide a saline breeze, and the sky was always full of sun. Their relationship had been baptized in the aqueous light of Provincetown, and it seemed to him that they

were somehow predestined, by a blessing-turned-curse, for perpetually fair skies. But all the traditional ingredients—sun and salt air, sex
in a rented cottage—never quite coalesced into an appetizing meal.
What was wrong with him? Why did his loins seem to crave the
dark continents of water stains on cement walls and the dreary drip
of rain from fire-escape railing? Why did every rural image conjure
his childhood in the Berkshires and why must memories of youth
now inevitably lead him to this cloying sense of his aging failure?

His father was to blame, he supposed. How tempting to take
that cleared path, anyway. You might have last seen him half a lifetime ago, as Brian had, and yet who had you first failed to keep,
after all—whose attention had you first failed to hold? The last time
Brian had seen the man, his father had pulled up in the driveway
with Mrs. Faulk beside him in the Austin Healey. Brian's mother
was out to dinner with friends. It was raining. Brian was fifteen.
Mrs. Faulk was a summer neighbor, married as well, and she and her
family were back in the city at this time of year. Brian should have
been surprised to see her, but his parents had spent the better part
of that summer on the lawn and docks behind the Faulks' cottage,
and Brian had noted, aware by then of his father's lovers, the strange
vines full of thorns and blossoms that had grown on the trellis of
their friendship. Mr. Faulk was a handsome, teacherly man. He liked
to barbecue with his wrinkled oxford and his pleated slacks cinched
into an apron; he laughed politely at the things Brian's father had to
say. His wife was nothing like him—that had been obvious enough.
She was pale and sad-eyed and subtle. Brian had watched her watching his father once, and when she noticed Brian she smiled as if
now they shared a secret. There were the Faulk girls to account for
or not: Kate and Meredith, half Brian's age then. They were fond of
his mother. She doted on them. On the afternoon that he remembered best, early in August, she had braided their hair and quizzed
them on their French, correcting their accents. The Faulks were
going to Paris for the last week of summer. When Mr. Faulk took
his daughters for a swim, Brian's mother joined them but his father

hung back, watching from a plastic lounge chair by the water. "Are you coming?" Brian had asked, but the look his father had turned on him—critical and amused at once—made him regret the question. "I'm not," his father said. "I wouldn't dare." He regarded the swimmers: Brian's mother on her back, floating, while Mr. Faulk spoke beside her and the girls squawked and splashed. His father said, "Your mother has a high social polish. Have you noticed that, Brian?" Brian kept his eyes on his father. "To be perfectly candid," he said, "she's been known to shit rubies."

Then Mrs. Faulk appeared and handed him a drink. "What are we discussing?" she asked, and his father said, "Brian's been telling me that I'm a roughneck. Strictly cheap and dirty, he says, and I'm pleading guilty."

"Aren't you going in, dear?" Mrs. Faulk had asked Brian, gesturing toward his swim suit.

In November now, sitting in the Austin Healy, she wore her hair tied in a dark scarf—probably against the rain, although it was a certain fashion still in that day and lent her a bit of an edge. And although Brian never got to know her, really, the scarf of hers cinched his assumption, held all these years and not likely to be challenged or confirmed, that this woman his father had left him for was a characteristic mistake: fashionable but shallow, acquisitive and pampered. That his father might never admit much less correct such a mistake would be characteristic as well.

His father sat back in the driver's seat that day. She leaned and kissed him: reassurance. He looked disheveled, stepping out of the car. He was just past forty and not yet bald, but had prematurely developed a hand gesture that swept his hair across the furrows flanking his widow's peak. He came into the house and filled a suitcase. He moved so quickly from item to item, room to room, that later Brian would guess he had rehearsed the moves. At the time, though, he didn't realize what he was witnessing, although some particular gravity in the moment led him to ask, "Can I come?" "No," his father said, sadly, and added, "I guess not." A vacation, he said, though as bold as he had sometimes been with his lovers, a trip with another woman would be something quite new, and the suitcase wasn't large enough for all that he was packing—he went out to the car with an additional bundle of shirts under his arm, rolled into a ball around their hangers. He had kissed Brian as he left, on the forehead. But after he started the car and set the wipers going, he got out again and walked back to the house while Brian watched through a window. He looked determined and possibly angry—Brian thought he must have forgotten some essential item (perhaps his camera?)—but defeated too, wet as he was, and once inside he took Brian into his arms (so swiftly there was a touch of menace to the gesture) and held his head between his hands and kissed him, embarrassing them both. He was perspiring—a sharp smell, spoiled by nerves.

Hadn't Brian spent enough of his life in the insufficient company of his mother alone to know better than to aid and abet this endeavor? Despite all the lapses in the comparison between his mother and Emily, or Andra for that matter, wasn't there an element of that particular loneliness—the one shared by a single parent and an only child—that he knew would persist? It was when he had told his mother about his father's departure, later that night—*a vacation*, he had repeated, though without the semblance of conviction that his father had managed (and of course he didn't mention Mrs. Faulk—a secret of that kind was second nature to Brian already)—that he began to guess the full measure of what had taken place. She didn't say, *And you just let him go?* But then, she never had to.

As he lay in Emily's bed, staring out her window after his latest procreative effort, the last of the low-lying sun would lend a ruddy cast to the crown of a tall white pine and he would begin to feel jealous of his imminent offspring. Where would Brian be in a dozen years when these youths of his were tripping into the troubling mysteries that attended the generative instinct? Would the path to family happiness be straightened and singular again by that time, or would his children venture into arrangements even more unlikely than his own? What aspect of their father would display itself in their natures, he wondered, and was it possible that he might come into a reverse inheritance of some kind, that their presence in the world could exert a quiet, invisible force upon his own future? Did his own father think of him still?

"Maybe we should give it a go together," he said to Emily, surprising even himself. She sat up reading and biting her fingernails in the bed beside him. He said, "Not man and wife so much as mom and pop. You know what I mean?"

She smiled. Then the smile broke into a giggle, and she touched his nose with the tip of her finger. "Cutey pie," she said, dismissively, and relief flooded in so close behind the instant of disappointment that he did feel a little foolish. He laughed along with her. He may have blushed.

At least he knew for sure that she had gotten what she wanted: she sent a photo tucked into a "thank you" card made of recycled paper. But there was no name, there were no vital statistics, and he couldn't even be sure if the infant was a boy or girl, a son or daughter. Who could tell at that age, with the distinguishing anatomy swathed in the gauzy shawl she had often worn on their walks along the shaded avenues of the Connecticut coast?

·

EXCEPT FOR her single status here at the ragged edge of her childbearing years, Grace was not at all like her predecessors, and although he didn't notice it at first, Brian eventually came to believe that she was very much like himself. They were both a little older—he at the high noon of his fourth decade by now and she in its twilight—and they had both recently plied the lagoons of romance common to their ilk: the married lovers and the early divorced and the desperate ring-hunters. Brian had a new apartment (less Zen, more comfortable); he never mentioned and only lightly considered his progeny; he had found that the best way to circumvent the maternal lovers was to stick to actual mothers—a brassy set; and his sail, if less often hoisted, no longer failed to fill. Even as the cluttered nights and garish interiors of youth were closed to him, it seemed that broad, pastoral vistas extended ahead: his view was clear down the back side of the thirties, and the theoretical forties had fattened into reality, and he had even negotiated a brief, deliciously melancholy affair with a fifty-one-year-old mother of college students. So much time, really; such green landscapes still left to discover.

Grace lived in the oddest building in Queens, possibly in the whole city. It was fat, misshapen, and dingy from the street: a pudgy three stories of jaundice-blond brick that came off particularly poorly beside its neighbor, a beautifully restored brownstone given over to the care of retired priests (The Home for Unwed Fathers, Grace called it). But the foyer of this architectural lardass was lined in tongue-and-groove paneling, and a fourteen-foot hammered-tin ceiling conveyed a sense of lofty industry. Her apartment consisted of two almost square rooms connected by an open threshold. The windows were low slung and enormous, with wine-red trim and deep sills. She claimed there had once been a neat division between the rooms—studio and apartment—but a homogeneous anarchy had since asserted itself. One couldn't spit without hitting a cat or a painting, and with no closet space her clothes hung, mostly just above his head level, from the square railroad nails that ran the length of the partly exposed beams. (Exposed beams in a brick building—who was this architect? What was he thinking?) She had a library ladder on wheels, and how enchanting it was to watch her reach for a blouse from the top step in the dull light of an early morning.

Her paintings were of bathtubs. She had photographed a half-dozen models and she painted these in a broad array of tempera shades. The setting of each painting was as realistic, precise, and colorless as a black-and-white photo: the bits of wall and window, the tiles in some and in others the plumbing and fixtures cast in a damp, pewter light. But the tubs themselves, their porcelain bellies, were these solid, striking shades that lent the paintings their titles, each printed in cuneiform characters in the lower-left corners: *russet tub* and *olive tub* and *cadmium tub*, as well as many hues he would never have known how to name. The *zaffer tub* was a deep, earthy blue, the *cudbear tub* a lichen-esque purple, the *incarnadine tub* bloody. He sugared his coffee before a *verdigris tub* and talked on Grace's telephone beside the miniature *gridelin tub* and made love to her beneath the larger *damson tub*, which resembled a meaty bruise at night in the diffuse light of Flushing. Her cats would roam the floor below and prowl the furniture and countertops with their shadowy, shedding menace while Grace's cotton blouses billowed or swayed above him with the smallest breeze like quiet ghosts. He never got much sleep. When he shaved in the morning his cheeks were flanked in the mirror by the green tub called *malachite bice* and the blue tub called *azurite bice*. Yet her cramped bathroom offered no better than a moldy shower stall.

It was an influential space, and Grace was a different person in its chromatic muddle. She would shed her gap-toothed impetuosity as immediately and carelessly as her coat when she stepped through the door, and she might put a tired recording of a trumpet player on the turntable, then slouch into the pit of a canvas-and-wire-frame chair, joined immediately by a furball or two. As if an analyst more than a lover, she asked him broad questions but she seldom talked about herself, even when he tried to turn her questions back around. She skimmed into a sad elegance that was somehow reflected in all the colorful, gaping porcelain, and never failed to turn him on. But for this reason, it was in the offhand, slightly artificial context of gallery-opening chat that he discovered she was soliciting certain genetically well-endowed friends to "knock her up." Even Grace wanted a child; and true to form, without a husband.

"Even Grace" was a phrase that came to mind not because she was without maternal inclinations but because she seemed so contentedly alone. Obviously, Brian wondered why *he* had not been solicited, and worried that she judged him less well endowed than her friends (than Stuart with his sniffles and expensive neuroses, or Warren who was always clipping his fingers in automatic staplers). He expected her to raise the subject that evening when they were alone, but when she never did he decided he wouldn't mention it himself. She was not aware of the experience he could boast in this particular endeavor, of course, and he knew she was on the pill, yet he worried that she might secretly allow him to hoe the row and, alternately, that she didn't even consider him a worthy farmer.

Her friends all hesitated though—one after another when the plans advanced into details—and finally one night, while they lay uncovered after a pleasant and uneventful evening at home, she said to him, referring to the paintings, "What do you see? I don't see empty bathtubs, you know."

He knew by now that it was the sort of question you didn't safely answer unless you were also a painter. So he lay still and admired her frown and waited for her answer. Instead, she offered another question: "What would you say if I asked you to cash in our little love-scrum and get me with child?"

"I'd say, 'Translation, please.'"

She wanted to know what he saw in their future. Did he see marriage and heirs and bread-crumbing the pigeons from a park bench together? Neither did she. She liked this relationship plenty, and it would be fine with her if it just kept loping along, but all she really wanted from life was a kid and it was safe to say she wasn't getting more fruitful with age. If she could have found someone else to do the dirty work, she thought he might have made a fine uncle. But uncles required fathers first, she had neither the money nor the courage for the turkey-baster fallback, and Brian, in the end, was her best prospect. She wanted the child more than what they had in its place—it was as simple as that.

Although he ought to have been the best-prepared man alive for this proposal, it churned to the surface a silt of regret and longing that had quietly settled in his heart about Grace. Faced with the prospect of their imminent end, he realized how little they had managed to begin. She was an indulgent lover, receptive and game, but never quite thrilled by his deeds. She was liable to take his arm on icy days and lean with a welcome expectation, and she sometimes trembled and nearly purred at the simple press of his lips against her own, and more than once she had slept through a night with the warm bundle of her head and hands and her pale shoulders curled within the domain of his chest, her knees drawn up so that he nearly contained her. But he could never surprise her, he felt, and he had never quite threatened her privacy somehow; and it occurred to him now that if he could have *sent* her, really made her happy, really blown her skirt up, just once, they might have amounted to an item with some endurance. Yet he had never dared. Or was he simply incapable? At bottom, he knew, he was a person who let things go—who could too easily live without. It was part of why he'd always thought he would never marry. He was a little cold, in at the core. He could see that. He was, after all, a son who had not spoken to his father in twenty years—this man he had loved once, and really with more abandon (if also in fear) than he had loved anyone since. Brian had not been the one to leave, yes, but he had let his father go, and he could have been the one to establish contact again. He knew where to find the man, still; his mother had occasionally pressed him to take the step. The gap had widened so slowly that it took him well into adulthood before he admitted he was a son who was no longer in touch with his father. But when the designation opened before him that way, like a coat someone held by the collar, he had stepped into it, put his arms in the sleeves, and buttoned up.

Yes, he told Grace, he would do this for her, because what had he managed to do for her yet and what had she ever asked for from him? And he told her yes out of guilt as well, because he had loved her partly for the portion of her beauty that was lent by her sadness, and he had never truly tried to make her happy. Momentarily pleased, maybe; content when he was near. And the same limits had been in place with the women he had most cared about before her as well, including Emily and even Andra. And though he might have been ashamed of this newfound resemblance to his father—and was, in fact, to some degree—he couldn't help but feel pleased as well, childishly flattered still by even the least flattering likeness between them.

He and Grace decided to go along just exactly as they had until she was pregnant. After all, it could take a long time. She would let him know when that day had come, and then he would say good-bye and cross the bridge and pass through the borders and the checkpoints that separated Flushing from Chelsea. They would adopt a nimble approach to the regions of potential social overlap, though they still might meet unexpectedly—the city had its way of being least anonymous when you wished it most—but that would be fine, even pleasant. Unless he or Grace left New York (a prospect as ever present and essentially inconceivable for each of them as death itself), he would maintain a sense—maybe just the barest, maybe quite detailed—of this child's way through the world. Sometimes he hoped the conception would be delayed long enough for them to veer into something irrevocable and whole, and once in a while, in his weakest moments, he even wondered if he might be accepted as a booby prize should Grace prove infertile.

One night a few months later—this was October, unseasonably cold—they sailed through a buoyant evening that left him instinctively certain that she was pregnant. They had dinner in a Brazilian closet where the guitarist played perpetual variations on "Girl from Ipanema" and bused tables between his sets. On their way to the movie it began to snow—a dumping snowfall, the first of the season—and the air smelled of sledding hills and skating rinks.

It was not a good movie, a saccharine vehicle for an aging star, but they had chosen it for the part played by an actress that Brian's father had slept with twenty years earlier, and in her way she proved worth the price of admission. Her character provided the comic relief: she was the histrionic ex-wife whom the male lead still attended and indulged, much to the star's chagrin. She flounced and jostled and called attention, and said the wrong things with finely tuned guile—more beautiful, really, than the leading actress, though her hair was unruly and her range of expression unsettling. And Brian knew she was only acting—delivering someone else's lines— yet the role was so true to the woman he had met once, and to the various women who had engaged his father, that it was as if the man himself had been conjured as well, his outline rendered in the negative space. His father, Brian suspected, had been little more than a plaything at times—a shiny surface to reflect their heat—but a certain glamour had always been conferred to him too, and even this movie was aware of it. The ex-wife suggested colorful secrets and an unlikely daring in the otherwise sensible leading man. Our heroine's interest was piqued in Elizabeth's frenzied wake—just as Brian's had always been. And yet, strangely, by the end of the movie he found that he too was more taken with the star: an even-tempered character with depth in place of flash, and a mark of the hero's maturity.

Outside, the streets of Queens were white and nearly deserted, and the gauzy hush of snowfall had descended. They slipped and skated down the center lane of Parsons Boulevard and she took his arm. "Want to see something?" she asked, and he nodded. She breathed a thread of steam through the gap in her teeth, like a kettle. They hardly spoke at all. The power was out in pockets, and the top of her hill was dark. Inside her apartment she lit a candle by the futon and stripped, then opened a window so they could hear the wet rustle of snow. They made love beneath the purple yawn of the damson tub and fell asleep in each other's arms.

He was awakened by the howl of a cat, but it merged with an unanswered cry in his dream, and the features of the room were momentarily jumbled with those of his sleeping landscape. It was dark—the power was still out—and well into the predawn morning, judging by the silence on the streets below. There was a cat curled against his neck but this was not the one who had called. He lay still, wondering if the howl had been in his dream, until another low, throaty moan emerged—quieter than he'd expected—from the other room. Although he had been essentially aware of which apartment he was in, only now did he consciously recognize that it was not his own but Grace's. She slept still, on her back, her lips pursed as if for a kiss.

He found a T-shirt and the candle at the head of the futon. He lit the candle and the room took on a herky shift of shadows. Another cat thumped down from the dresser at the edge of the light. He followed his sense of where the howl had been and found the mottled tortoiseshell, Grace's youngest cat, fitfully asleep in the chair by the window. He picked her up and slouched into the chair, and though she was startled, she let him hold her, then resettled along his chest, her head on his shoulder. She purred into his ear. Outside, the snowfall had tapered off, but a white, unbroken cover lay across the street and along the dark rooftops down the hill. It reflected the moonlight and paled the city. Brian wondered what would become of the cats when Grace had a baby to care for. What would become of her work? A glance was enough to know there was nothing about this apartment—full of chemicals and hard surfaces—that was prepared for an infant. Did she really know what she was getting into? he wondered, and though he suspected the feeling would pass, he was suddenly, sincerely grateful that these were not his concerns in the end.

He returned the cat to her chair, where she began her kneading, presleep dance, then took the candle back into the room where Grace slept. It was cold in here. He passed the bed to the open window, and while he closed it, he saw a light come into a room in the restored brownstone directly across the alley. It was an old man in a tartan nightshirt, carrying his own candle—and so proximate, across the narrow expanse where the last flakes of snow spun down, that Brian ducked to the side of his window. He wondered what would keep an old man up at such an hour. It was a room where the shade had always been drawn. Brian blew out his candle, and in the dark he crouched before the sill to watch.

The man meticulously turned down the cover of his made bed. He hadn't been to sleep yet. He stood and stretched his back and coughed—the quick, deep rattle of a smoker, just audible through the closed windows and the quiet of the city. He made the sign of the cross and laboriously knelt down by the bed to pray—like a boy, Brian thought. He rested his elbows on the narrow mattress and his head against his hands. A priest, of course—a retired priest. His gray hair was cut bristle short. It wrapped down across his cheek and chin in a hoary stubble. After a long moment he crossed himself again and stood and leaned over the candle where he had placed it on the sill. With a hand behind the flame, he blew it out. But before he did, in the last instant of light, he looked through the alley and the dark into the window of Grace's apartment, and even with his room black and opaque again now, Brian imagined the priest held his gaze.

He made the sign of the cross himself, testing the feel of the gesture. It felt stiff, he guessed, silly. Then he turned to Grace, asleep on the futon. He crawled to the side of the low bed and knelt there watching her: the fall of her face in sleep, the white of her lidded eyes. He bent and put his ear to her belly. Through the fuzz of blanket and the dampening lamina of skin he heard the gush of blood and the thump and pull, fugacious and lean, of a heartbeat.

So he slipped. He resigned himself—in an instant. *Slipping* was the nearest metaphor, because it wasn't a leap, as he had always imagined. The nighttime light off the snow shone into the room, and the clothes above him cast their shadows. The priest's room remained dark to him, though he imagined the priest in bed, still awake. He would have to convince her—he didn't know how. And might he wake up with the idea behind him already—already in doubt, the product of this late hour? He would be levelheaded then, he supposed, compared to now. But would he be right? And what could account for this sense of permanence he felt, lying down beside her—this awareness of a happy deliverance?

And strange and unsettling as the sensation was, he felt he had been here already. He was here *again* now—eleven again, asleep, running a fever on a weekday afternoon. You can get it back, he thought, surprised and relieved—this relationship, this possessive love. You wake from a nap that has straddled dusk and you've been at home and sick all day—home from school and alone with your mother, the two of you passing time in anticipation. You fell asleep in the daylight but now it's dark, and you wake to the hush of the fire he's laid, its light on your bedroom door ajar, and nothing else in the house—no one speaking. The radio in the kitchen plays, as it always does when he's home again: there's the voice of the evening man spinning out in small tin phrases, as incidental to the firelight and this strange hush as the news he brings. Your father is all that the radio signifies—your father there in the next room. You know he's there by the fire too. In a moment you will hear something else, you know: the small clap of a lid placed with care on a soup pan or the tock of the ladle set down on the drainboard. Your mother will speak. Someone might turn the television on, quietly, or someone will turn a page. Somehow the spell will falter and the scene will dilate again and you'll be just who you know you are: a boy who was sick today—his son—who feels better now, but groggy. You'll have lost him then, and you'll push the covers away and pad out into the firelight, where he'll pronounce your name or say *Look who's up*. And then the whole of you—a child and his parents, the play for attention, this accustomed form—will coalesce again, ungainly and resilient.

But it hasn't happened yet—it hasn't yet. You're here still, now, shy of the claim, and the shuffle that the fire makes in that quiet room is all your own and meant for no one but you; and you and he are as far as it goes, a constant sum that you can wade into. And you're content here, and selfish, and in love, so that you think you'll keep wading further, deeper into this last thing, until it closes over and you're his alone.

TYRANTS

I THINK I was beautiful but I don't have pictures to prove it. Or maybe desirable if not beautiful, pale and amenable you know and only twenty in '41. I had not cut my hair yet. Sad eyes are a must among tyrants, plus my figure was not as you see it now. Like anyone in that Russia I lived two lives. Number one I am married to Sasha and he teaches at university with my father and we have our little arrangements you know as families will, but what harm? The house is all books. Mornings I lay the fire in Father's room and read under the bedclothes that are still warm where he slept. Sometimes I can lure him away from his papers. Sasha's grandmother brews a bitter tea downstairs, or slices herring with the vodka afternoons in the courtyard. I practice the piano while Father is away teaching. But then the police come to the door and Mother Andreevna shows them in, and Sasha is shot and Father dies in the mines at Karaganda. I learn that I am desirable. Number two. No books in this second life, though—to this day I cannot stand a book.

I will get to Stalin but let me explain first. With Sasha dead I was to be sent east but the secretary at the station in Novgorod spotted me along the platform. His name was Terehov. His office looked out on the trains. He had his man pluck me from the line and we sat down together with a good desk between us. Could I type? he asked. No. Could I write then? Yes. And read? "Yes, I can read. I can read German, English, . . . Latin, naturally."

"Oh," he said, sadly. "I see."

He sighed and pored over my bosom, then turned to his man by the door and shrugged. But his man said, "She can keep house."

"Can you keep house?" the secretary asked me.

"I can keep it clean."

"And cook?"

"His mother cooked."

"I see. And where is he now?"

"He's dead."

"Yes. Right. Well," he said. "Well there we are, then."

In the second life I wore uniforms. I cleaned a little—the feather duster, swish swish. Midmorning I am to go to his office, next door to the apartment. I knock. Come in please. He is seated at his desk, a very busy man you know: tablets and forms, the telephone. He is wearing his tunic as usual, buttoned to the collar, but behind the desk, no pants. I am to dust the big desk, empty the wastepaper basket—this requires him to slide the chair away. His *huy* is pink and wide, with a mole. It seems misplaced, like a spoiled sausage in his lap, yet this first day I'm not surprised to see it so that I know for sure it's a new life now.

I finish in his room and go back to my own to lay down on the cot. I try to recall every night I have spent in bed beside my husband and find five still at hand, or six—the rest gone. I never saw Father's parts, nor Sasha's in daylight. At night he wore a flannel bedgown—Sasha—and often books lay in the bed between us. I assume the secretary will want my participation next time and decide I will hurt him and let him put me back on the trains. It's a nice thought—I can sleep, you know—but I wouldn't have hurt him. And anyway I didn't have to. It was the same little show every day and no more—who can predict a man's appetite? Soon I dusted him too, swish swish.

Beria is coming to dinner in August—head of secret police, friend to Stalin. I am to serve, though I've not been trained. The secretary's wife teaches me which hand does what over which shoulder. She has a peasant dress for me to wear but no shawl. There is an apron that covers a little, not much. She catches me in the kitchen and gathers my hair in her hands. She sets these silver combs into my hair—very nice. I hadn't worn it up since I was seven. You see what sort of girl I was. "Turn," she says. "Again."

Beria is a small man with a pince-nez. He has small hands and quick little fingers. Here is his hand on my knee while I serve the borscht. Back and forth, kitchen to dining room. Here is his hand on my bottom while I clear the plates. I have been a topic of conversation apparently, for the secretary's wife concludes, "We *do* love our Katia. What a difference she's made."

"Is she ready for Moscow?" Beria asks. The way his fingers work—it's a little desperate.

Across the table, Secretary Terehov slouches and pouts. He swirls the wine in his glass. "Take what you need, Comrade," he says, then looks up, but at me not him. His eyes are so sad, you know—who had ever looked at me that way? *Poor man*, I think—just so, before I can catch myself.

I expected to see Moscow finally, but the dacha was near Krasnogorsk, a train stop short. My room was in the wing opposite the kitchen, apart from the other help. Beria was not a coy man like the secretary at Novgorod. He knocked at my door and opened it without waiting for an answer. I had been lying on the bed but I got up and smoothed my pleats. "Please," he said, closing the door with excessive care. "As you were."

He strolled toward the windows. "You've settled in?" he asked, touching what I had set out on the dresser—a hairbrush, a hat box. He opened the top drawer and touched my underthings. They were not fine things then, but he left his hand among them. Then he moved on to the other drawers.

He said, "We have work for you, Katia," crossing to the closet, glancing at the rain outside. "Don't be mistaken," he said, "you'll work hard here."

There were three dresses in the closet to poke.

"Cleaning—yes," he said. "Some cleaning."

Then the satchel where he found the photo of Father.

"Some other duties too. Nothing you aren't capable of."

He crouched with his back to me, ran his thumb along the frame. I waited as long as could be expected, but finally I stood up beside the bed. What I would do next I didn't know. But he heard me, and packed the photo back away in the satchel.

He was still smiling when he turned around. "Look at you," he said quietly. He said, "Those furious eyebrows!"

He scowled, mimicking me, then extended his hand and gestured with one finger. I didn't know what the gesture meant but he pointed at my uniform so I looked down. There was nothing out of place. He did it again, a flick of the finger, and said, "Come on, Katia. Be a good girl."

When I understood, I said, "Leave me alone?" It should have been a statement but it curled into a question.

"Are photos allowed?" he asked. "Photos of men, smuggled into my house? You'll kiss him at night—I know you. Sleep with him under your pillow while Comrade Beria is alone in his bed."

Probably he had mistaken the man in the photo for my husband—Father was handsome and not so old—but living in a university town I had heard people say there were no secrets left in Russia except the ones Beria's police kept. I worried he was familiar with even my small case.

"Come now, Katia," he said, dipping his chin and winking. "Make me forget."

The uniform was a simple shift with buttons down the front and I unbuttoned one and two. He gestured with his finger so I unbuttoned some more. I wore a girdle and a low brassiere that would not show at the neckline. He pantomimed with both hands, as if the shift was on his shoulders, and I did it, crossing my arms so that the straps hung at my elbows.

His smile soured but he said, "Good girl, Katia. Do you know how to pick a lock?" he asked, then said, "Unclip the brassiere."

"No."

His gaze shifted to my eyes momentarily. "No to which? No to both?"

I said, "Let's wait until later," and my voice sounded borrowed from some other circumstances—bottled like champagne and opened here to leaven the mood. I was impressed, but Beria wasn't.

He tucked the pince-nez into a pocket. He strolled around the bed to me, his hands clasped behind his back. He pulled the bra straps down my arms—quickly, surprising me, but also gracefully, leaving his hands spread at the end of the gesture: *voilà.* "You use a hair pin," he said. "Where are your hair pins, Katia?"

"I don't have any."

"You don't have any hair pins?" He tsked, speaking just above a whisper. "What kind of girl are you? I wonder. Dear dear. We'll get you some hair pins"—he leaned and kissed there—"and teach you how to pick a lock"—kissed the other, lightly.

He said, "You're frightened, dear, but your nipples are pleased, hm?"

I could feel that they had hardened so I began to cry. But he would have none of it. In a full voice he said, "Come come, dinnertime!" Then patted my cheek and left the room.

With me the thing to know is that Mother died when I was seven, but Father never remarried. We were not a famous catch, you know, and he could be difficult. Alone in the apartment—we seldom entertained—he discovered me instead. I said, *Sleep by me, Misha* (I wasn't allowed to say "with"). *Again tonight? Yes.* I read to him and then we kissed. *Like this? Not at all. Like this? Goodness no, try again.* I don't know if it was concern for me or fear of being caught that made him keep us to certain boundaries, but it was never my idea. When I was old enough he brought his best student home. And Sasha was good to me too, truth be told. He gave me drafts to read and trusted my translations, and kissed me and fumbled when we were alone. He was not impassive or cruel. I wanted to hand myself over to him the way I never could to Father, but Sasha would take so little at a time. I was a passionate girl but I maintain I was a good girl. I was dying for more but I never kissed first, never used my poor hands. They lay at my side or perhaps I dared to remove my own clothes, clearing the way ahead of him. *Naughty plum*, he liked to say, but I wasn't.

Now he was gone along with Father, the apartment on Semya Street, the black tea, and Father's pipe—all gone. And me still here: the same girl and nothing like her. I wasn't a good girl because good girls didn't go unpunished. They shot Sasha for defending Father (I didn't know, but I was probably right) and they might have shot me too if I hadn't answered their questions well. I had an instinct for this second life—look, I had not even been east. The ones like me will say, *Who's to judge?* but don't listen.

So I stayed four months in Beria's dacha. He teaches me how to pick a lock, how to gather information. Steam and reseal envelopes. Open and close doors without a sound—but not slowly, mind. Never sneak or someone is bound to see you. Dust the top molding to listen at a door. Keep busy at the far end of a room, Beria says. Make noise—not too much noise. When Stalin calls you the first time, don't answer. You haven't heard him. He might not bother to call again. This look is for when there are others with him: stupid and dull. Remember never to look at me. That's fine. This look is for you and he alone in the room. No no, more composed—*Don't grin*, Katia, heavens! That's better. Dust things up high so that you have to reach. Lean more, please—very good. You do that so well, Katia. Come over here. (No.) Oh come and do it again for me. (You don't deserve it.) I know, I know. Stand right here. Yes—keep reaching. Katia? Oh. What a sweet girl, Katia.

•

THE BEST he could get me was a post at the dacha called Lipki, where Stalin's visits were infrequent and brief. There was a house guard and the guard at the gate, the cook, the gardener. We had nothing to do but we did it daily, never knowing when Stalin would appear. I dusted the empty rooms, beat rugs, and changed bulbs. The cook kept elk meat and *khatchapuri* in the icebox. The gardener cut flowers for the foyer. It was as easy as could be to gather information, but there was nothing to gather. Or nothing I thought Beria would care for. The locked drawers were empty, or stuffed with Stalin's dead wife's clothes. In his daughter's room there were photos of her: a little girl playing chess with her father. She was fifteen now, Svetlana. There were letters too, written out in a blocky hand, all caps. They began, TO MY KHOZYAIKA, SETANKA, which gave me pause, since *khozyaika* meant "housekeeper." One went: YOU DON'T WRITE TO YOUR LITTLE PAPA. I THINK YOU'VE FORGOTTEN HIM. HOW IS YOUR HEALTH? YOU'RE NOT SICK, ARE YOU? WHAT ARE YOU UP TO? HAVE YOU SEEN LYOLKA? HOW ARE YOUR DOLLS? I THOUGHT I'D BE GETTING AN ORDER FROM YOU SOON, BUT NO. TOO BAD. YOU'RE HURTING YOUR LIT-TLE PAPA'S FEELINGS. NEVER MIND. I KISS YOU. I AM WAITING TO HEAR FROM YOU.

Another read: HELLO MY LITTLE SPARROW! I GOT YOUR LETTER. THANK YOU FOR THE FISH. ONLY, I BEG YOU, LITTLE HOUSEKEEPER, DON'T SEND ME ANY MORE FISH! DID YOU GET THE PEACHES AND THE POME-GRANATES? I'LL SEND SOME MORE IF YOU ORDER ME TO. TELL VASYA TO WRITE ME, WILL YOU? I GIVE YOU A BIG KISS.

It was signed, *From Setanka-Housekeeper's Wretched Secretary, the poor peasant J. STALIN.*

In a room at the other end of the house, in another locked drawer, I had already found a pistol. I had held it and moved the parts back and forth until I thought I would know how to load and fire. Here with his letters I thought maybe I would kill him. It hadn't

occurred to me until now—why, I don't know. And I had no notion
of doing good. I reasoned, in fact, that I would be accountable for
very many deaths. Mine first, perhaps by Beria. Then Beria himself,
unless he had the cook and the gardener and the house guard and
the guard at the gate all killed before they mentioned me, and the
others who knew about me as well: the staff at his house, the secretary at Novgorod and his wife. That many at least to make up for
Sasha and Father, but strange to say, not enough yet, you know.

All my life I am imagining Stalin but never once as a father. A
kidder. Someone who sent fruit home from holiday. Who said *little papa* or *I kiss you.* In the room with the letters open I had a first
full sense of how stupid I was. I would be no smarter when I killed
him, but the father who wrote these letters would be as dead as my
dead and now I knew why that was such good justice. I read the letters twice more to deepen the impression. *How are your dolls?* Then
folded them with the photos and locked the drawer. I wanted to
read them again later but the house guard developed a crush. He
snuck into rooms and grabbed me from behind—*Guess who?*—once
when I was picking a lock. But he was a poor guard, too enamored
to suspect me. How plain I had been on Semya Street, barely able
to provoke even Sasha. I wondered if grief or guilt had rendered me
so desirable.

•

ONLY IN JUNE was I transferred to the dacha at Kuntsevo. Beria
had warned me about Vlasik but he was unavoidable. My first day he
calls me in. Comrade Stalin requires clean windows, he says. Every
day, every window. Inside, outside. Comrade Stalin's bed is to be
made if he sleeps in it. If he sleeps on the sofa the cushions are to
be fluffed. If he sleeps on the cot *do not* take it down. Do not make
it like a bed. The blanket is to be folded and placed at the foot—
go there today and learn the fold. You are never to be in the same
room as Comrade Stalin. He is never to see you or hear you. You
are never to speak to him, or to anyone who comes through the

front door. This is your handcart. Take care with supplies. This is your uniform. This is your schedule. These rooms, these times, unless someone is in them. If someone is in them, what do you do? Guess. That's right—come to me.

Kuntsevo bore little resemblance to Lipki—it was modern and low and ugly, half as large—but it felt familiar, and soon I realized the furniture was the same, identical to the furniture in the other house. The pictures that hung on the walls were the same too. In the kitchen the same bread (and fruit and meat—everything) arrived with the same signed tags attached: No Poisonous Elements Found. It was always busy at Kuntsevo though. There were a dozen or more on the staff, and then these men from the politburo coming and going: Voroshilov, Molotov, Zhdanov—everyone. Beria, of course. My room I shared with Valenchka, the permanent housekeeper, an old woman devoted to Stalin who had no interest in me.

We all kept track of him through the day. Mornings the word was passed along, guard to cook to governess: *There's movement* or *There's no movement*. His dinner lasted half the night, so he didn't wake until late morning or noon. We would listen at the doors (though we weren't supposed to) and when he left a room we bustled in, whirling whirling, but attentive still so if he forgot his pipe we could bustle back out before he saw us. If you're too late, I'm told, don't hurry. Stop running before he opens the door. Turn to him, curtsey—he won't speak to you but he might nod—then leave the room calmly. This from Valenchka one night, and though I don't like her tone she is the first person other than Vlasik to speak to me at the new dacha. So I say, I see, I see. And what if he does speak to me, Valenchka? And what if we pass in a hallway, what then?

But I am there less than a week when the Germans invade, so everything changes. At four in the morning there is a call from the Kremlin to the guard on duty: *Wake him up immediately,* Zhukov says, *the Germans are bombing our cities.* By midmorning everyone has heard the story. Stalin is in Moscow the first days. At Kuntsevo there is less scurrying, more gossip. The younger guards talk of leaving their posts to go to the front. We hear good news and bad, side by side. Most of us believe the bad. Our front was caught by surprise. Our armies were captured while they slept. I gather my first and last information and pass it up through a guard named Stepan, who belongs to Beria too: a telegraph left out on Stalin's desk. There is also a letter from Svetlana: *My Dear Little Secretary: I hasten to inform you that your Housekeeper got an "excellent" on her composition! Thus, she passed the first test and has another tomorrow. I send my little papa a thousand kisses. Greetings to the secretaries.—HOUSEKEEPER.*

It might have begun with that word, but by now I thought of these notes as my own as much as Stalin's or his daughter's. Certainly not Beria's—I didn't report them. I lay in bed that night while Valenchka huffed and snored and I composed a note in my head that began addressed to Father: *I share a room but the old woman is good to me. Everyone is good to me, Misha,* I lied. *They treat me like a daughter—don't worry. We all think the Germans will take us as quickly as Poland. I kiss you*—which I never had said to him and he would not have said to me, though all we did some evenings was kiss. *I'm glad you asked about my dolls. They're not well—the croup. Send more peaches.—Your Little Sparrow.*

When Stalin returned to Kuntsevo we knew the worst was true. He came alone, and though it was midday he went directly to his rooms and would not be disturbed. Someone said he had taken his boots off and lay down in the bed—not good, since he seldom slept in the bed. We expected an entourage to follow close behind. Vlasik ordered a meal prepared, spare cots made up with the military fold. But no one came. Everyone was quiet for fear of waking him, but everyone wanted him awake. "No calls," he had said, but all day the telephones rang. The guards whispered to one another: "So long as he's sleeping I for one am not afraid." But we knew it was dire. Should I kill him still? I wondered.

Still no movement. By the afternoon of the second day everything went slack. Even Vlasik had retired to his room. I walked along the terraces in the sunshine. Birds called—the familiar calls, while the Germans marched through our fields. There was a grove of pear trees. I picked a pear but it was a terrible mistake: when I bit into it (an early pear—small and tart) I was back on Semya Street, in our yard behind the house, the shade falling under the tree there and the sound of my husband typing through the window, with music from a radio in Mother Andreevna's room. Father was lecturing but would be home soon. I was in the courtyard to wait for him.

Instantly I began to cry. I had to spit out the half-chewed pear. What was wrong with me? It wasn't even a pear tree in our courtyard but a lime. I could hear my father's voice—*Where's Sweet Pea?*—and the old cracked shuttle of Sasha's grandmother—*She's in back, waiting for you.* We would have been more careful had we realized she didn't know. Father insisted on discretion as it was. *Shush shush*, pushing me away, but here is Mother Andreevna, so quiet always in her skin slippers. *Baba, you scared me.* Walking away down the hall—was she crying? And what did she imagine they would do with her son, please? Did she think he didn't know about us? I sat under the pear tree and watched the dacha, but nothing moved and no one emerged. Then I dried my face and stood and walked back. I went inside and stepped through the main room past the table laid and through the parlor where the phonograph was, into Stalin's private apartment.

There were four rooms, all the same size, the same rug in each before the fireplace. Same desk and sofa at one end of the rug. In one was the bed, in two others bookcases. All the tall windows had thin curtains pulled closed day and night and heavier ones left aside. In the room I had entered these were drawn too, though. There were no lamps lit. I stood with my back against the door. As it happened he wasn't in this room, but he might have been. What was my plan? I needed a weapon. There was a brass lamp on the end table by the door. It was properly heavy, but the weight of it in my fist solidified the prospect: I would see Stalin from across a room and charge at him with a lamp in my hand and strike it down upon his wide, familiar head. I put the lamp down. Not just now, I thought, to console myself, though when would I get another chance? With a gun, maybe. But a lamp? I would open the door and creep back out, pray the parlor was empty still, and slouch into the rest of my life, such as it was.

But just then I heard him. He grunted—it wasn't so near, though. He was through the next room, around the corner. I knew where, in fact. I tiptoed to the short hall, expecting the door to be closed, but it was open. I should explain that the dacha at Kuntsevo, modern as it was, had flush toilets. And I will say that he flushed before he stood, then looked down into the clean bowl.

He saw me when he was buckling but I had known he would. How awful it was to see Stalin shit. To know he shat was news somehow, but to see him seated with his flank squished into a roll—not a young man anymore—was too much. The grimace on his face, pained and juvenile. He dimpled, as you know. Would this be news to Beria? I wondered. Stalin shits, I've seen it. All indications are that Stalin is constipated. Now shoot me—and Beria would have.

But Stalin didn't. When he noticed me his expression was no more or less sour than it had been the instant before. He returned his attention to his belt buckle. His forehead was pale and damp. He rinsed his hands in the sink and dried them, then shuffled toward me. I must have stood in his way because he looked into my eyes and gestured with his hand: *May I?* I stepped aside. I made some noise too—it was like a squeak, but who knows what it meant. He said, "Thank you," with a good deal of sarcasm.

He shuffled into the next room, where the bed was rumpled. The heavy curtains were drawn but a lamp burned by the desk. He exhaled a long, relaxed sigh climbing into the bed, punched his pillows, and propped them against the headboard. "Can you move yet?" he asked.

I said, "Yes, Comrade Stalin."

"Will you get me a cup of tea at least?"

"Yes." I nodded.

I began to back out the way I had come, but he said, "Go this way." He pointed. "This way to the kitchen. Remember?"

When I was through the open doorway and into the next room he called out, saying, "Keke?"

So he's mistaken me for someone else, I thought. A legitimate miracle. I turned, and he said, "The black tea from the Crimea. Ask the cook. And bring honey."

"Yes, Comrade Stalin."

In the kitchen the cook had fallen asleep with the radio by his ear. When I woke him he said, "*You spoke to him?*" Vlasik was alerted. *There's movement.* His favorite server—a fat, Georgian woman—was summoned to bring the tea. I was thinking I might want to find an explanation for what I had been doing in his private rooms, but the fat woman returned to the kitchen with the tray still in hand. She looked at me with disgust: "He wants her." Vlasik said, "Nonsense." He took the tray himself, then hesitated and handed it over. "You go," he said, then yelled, "But don't make him angry!" He lowered his voice and pointed: "You will tell me every word he speaks."

The little crowd that had gathered in the kitchen sent me off with plain hatred in their eyes, afraid I had beguiled him, but the guards I passed in the foyer ushered me with pleased and curious smirks, anticipating my quick demise. Stepan was at the door to his private rooms, and he gave me a meaningful stare meant to remind me of Beria. Then he closed the door behind me and left me alone in the dark with Stalin.

"Keke?" he called, mildly. His voice had the gravel weight you want from a man but it wasn't fierce or rude. I considered my dead waiting for me and my fate, which had been sealed the moment they were arrested and no more than postponed when the secretary at Novgorod plucked me from the ramp. I said, "*It's me,*" in Keke's voice—flirting, a guess—because I had learned that it was what I had available. Perhaps I could wrestle the gun away—there would be a gun, presumably. "I've brought you some nice tea, Comrade."

There was a bed table beside him, where I set the tray down. I would not meet his eyes but I thought he might be smiling. He shifted in his bed to make room and patted a spot on the covers by his leg. He said, "Can you sit with me?"

So I sat down, nearly, at the edge of the bed. "Of course, Comrade St—"

He put his fingers to my lips, interrupting—they smelled of pipe smoke. I met his eyes now. The fringe of his mustache was ragged. His face was marked in patches—as if he had been beaten, I thought, before I recognized the scars that smallpox leaves. He had what Beria called the Kremlin complexion. His eyes were not cruel as some have claimed. He said, "Don't don't do that Keke, please? Don't be so cold with poor Stalin." There was a gentle, teasing rise to his voice. He took his fingers away. "Be good," he said. "You'll pour?"

I nodded. But while I was fumbling with the screen he said, "No—you only brought one cup. Who is at the door?"

"Stepan."

He turned and called out (forcefully—the voice I would have anticipated), "Stepan!" Quickly I stood from the bed. When the guard leaned through, Stalin said, "Bring another teacup."

Stepan said, "*Slushaiussi* Comrade Stalin," and closed the door without a glance for me.

He pushed his covers aside. "Well," he said, swinging his feet out of the bed. He put his hand on my shoulder—lightly, only pretending to lean—and stood. He said, "Excuse me, Keke, please." Patted my cheek with his open palm. I could see now his shuffle was mostly for show, a self-deprecating joke, but one arm did hang stiff as though injured. Into the hall and then into the lavatory. He closed the door this time.

I touched my own shoulder where his hand had been. I smelled my hand (no smell). Now that I was alone I noticed the sound of a clock ticking. It was on the mantel over the fireplace in which a few coals hissed. Don't forget to kill him, I thought. And who is Keke? It was possible he had lost his mind but I doubted it. I thought, So it's *this* bad, and half expected a Nazi to crash through the window. I was wrong, I thought, he's not constipated. How will he kill me?

There was a knock at the far door but I didn't want to call out. The person waited a long time and then knocked again. From the lavatory Stalin said, "Keke!" with a good deal of impatience, so I sang, "Come in!"

Stepan opened the door and peered through. He saw me in the next room and glanced about for Stalin. He moved liked a squirrel, closing the door and slipping into the lit room, stopping and glancing around again. He had the teacup in his hand and he circled past me to place it on the tray. He studied me a moment. He was a boy still, not even my age, and mixed with confusion and fear in his eyes was plain jealousy too. So I sneered and waved him away—*shoo*. He was about to whisper something (instructions? an insult?) when the toilet flushed. He scurried from the room.

Stalin said, "So." His smile was still forced. He climbed back into bed and patted the same spot with his palm. "Our tea," he said. "It's cold by now but what do we care?"

I poured and passed him his cup and saucer. I said, "It's still warm." How *quietly* we were speaking! I poured a cup for myself. I said, "Honey?"

"Honey, yes." He was matter-of-fact, a little impatient. I spooned a dollop from the jar while he held his cup between us. The spoon clicked and clacked like so. He said, "You don't know what to call me now, do you?"

I shook my head no.

"Make something up?"

"Sir?"

"Something better than that, Keke." He said, "I gave you 'Keke,' now give me one back."

I spooned honey into my own tea and took up the saucer and sipped. He had peeled another layer of hope back—this impression of mistaken identity—but in the core beneath all the layers I was a calm girl already dead. As it happened, hopelessness was not new to me. And equally important to my calmness was the flavor of black tea with honey, which brought me back to Semya Street more forcefully than any pear. I closed my eyes and sipped again. I settled just the slightest bit further onto the edge of his bed as if reclining into the grave. I had been here before. I kept ending up here, in this same place, with different men. I said to Stalin, "Do you have a nickname?"

His smile was conspiratorial now—he had been watching me warm to the conversation. "Are you a clever girl?" he asked, in the voice you speak to a pet with.

"Mm-hm," I nodded. I held his gaze. We were moving in quickly.

"You're very clever?"

I said, "I'm clever." I put my teacup down.

"You don't like me though?"—not whispering but nearly; still with this rise, this foolish intonation. He could see through me, I knew, so I said, "No, I don't like you." I shook my head for emphasis. He wore a linen tunic with wide tan buttons. His left hand was beneath the cover and it could be he held the gun there. Or maybe he would just use his bare hands. Maybe his will alone would do? I leaned until my cheek was against his chest, and when he set his teacup down and stroked my hair, I pulled my legs up onto the bed and settled.

"You hate me, Keke." He kissed the top of my head.

There were three or four things from home: the tea, the darkness of the room and the fire, the sound of the clock on the mantel. I nodded. "I hate you," I whispered. How good it felt. He knew just what I wanted.

"Everybody hates me, Keke. Everybody loves me." He paused. I closed my eyes. "Let's say you are the new housekeeper?"

I nodded—the little rustle of my cheek against the linen. I could hear Stalin's heartbeat, which for some reason made me want to cry.

"You were cleaning when you came into my room?"

A nod. This was the voice I had heard when I read his letters: indulgent and sweet.

"You were cleaning."

Nod.

"Cleaning and what else? Were you spying on Stalin?"

He kissed me. I said no, but only because in truth I hadn't been spying—I had come into his room with no thought for Beria. If I had been spying I would have said yes.

"You weren't spying?" *No.* "You were just curious then? Girls are curious, I think—by nature, isn't that true?" *Nod.* "It's a dark room, you know—very hard to clean. You forgot to put the light on. And what's worse, you forgot to bring your handcart with you—nothing to clean with. What a poor housekeeper, my little Keke." *His voice swooned even higher—I nuzzled. There was something in his breast pocket—foil and paper, a pouch of tobacco.* "You were curious. That's all. We get curious—boys, girls—we all do. We want to know, don't we?" *Nuzzling.* "We want to see a man shit sometimes. It's true. And so? Does that make us all spies? Sometimes we want to see a man at his worst—so what?"

I had been crying ever so slightly but now it cracked a little wider and my lips pickled. Brushing the hair back from my ear he said, "What should we do with you, little girl?" but his voice was not so good either, slipping into a desperate range. I shook my head no in his chest. He said, "I don't know what to do, Keke—I don't know what to do," and my tears subsided because he was quickly slipping past me.

I lay still with my eyes open and rode the jolts in his chest and waited a little while longer through a series of deep sighs with the wiping at his cheeks, one hand and the other—a little frantic. Some sniffling, etc. A good thing men don't cry often, I think. Finally he lay still. When he leaned he held my cheek against him with his free hand so I would know he didn't want to disturb me. I watched him take hold of the knob on the small drawer in the bed table, but then I closed my eyes so I wouldn't have to see it. He said, "Shh," and touched my hair. He lifted it from the drawer and leaned back. A part of my mind was scheming—spring for his hand, knock the barrel away—but the better part was relieved to be granted such an easy death and also relieved that I would not have to kill a man, even Stalin. Then he took the pouch from his breast pocket, so I knew it was only his pipe. Everything was quite familiar. I began to relax.

When he had smoked a little he said, "Okay, up. Up up." I sat, stood. He put the pipe down and turned onto his side to sleep. He said, "Keke?"

"Hm?"

"Don't leave my rooms?" I didn't reply. He said, "They'll take you from me, is all."

Another minute or two and he was asleep.

·

I TIPTOED and listened at the door. There was a good deal of agitation in the rest of the house—footsteps back and forth, the telephone, Vlasik shouting in the distance. I returned to Stalin's bedside, where it was quiet and dark, and sat down on the sofa to watch him. *Stalin sleeping*—I was full of these phrases that first day. *Stalin chewing. Stalin smoking his pipe.* It was a Dunhill with the little white dot. In this room was another brass lamp, identical to the one I had held in my fist, and even better, an iron poker by the side of the hearth. But what was the hurry? Once I killed him, they would kill me, of course. It was nice in this room. I felt almost relaxed, enclosed within his plans for me, and this was familiar too.

He woke with a start, surprised to see me. "Oh," he said to himself, remembering. While he sat back and rubbed his eyes he said, "The least you could do is kiss me." But I sat still.

"Are you hungry?" he asked.

"Famished."

He ordered our dinner, then stripped off his tunic in the lavatory while we waited. I was in the hallway, watching him. He lathered and shaved and trimmed his mustache. "What should we do with you?" he had begun by asking and I had said, "Take me on a picnic?" He smiled dimly. "I'm still waiting for a nickname, you know," he said.

I said, "Misha, then"—because he was right: in this cave of his I would say whatever I wanted.

"*Misha?*" He frowned. "Noo." He pulled a face.

"Why not?"

"It's so *weak*, Keke. Is that how you think of me?"

"Yes."

"I see." He shook out the tunic. "Well, what can I do then? *Misha* if you like." He said the name in a high voice, imitating me.

Vlasik himself brought the dinner in and laid it at the table in the first of Stalin's rooms. We seated ourselves across from one another and Vlasik uncovered a *Tchokhom-Bili:* chicken and rice and eggplant, tomatoes, summer melon, peppers. In addition there was borscht and Baltic herring, new potatoes, baklava. Vlasik whispered into Stalin's ear and Stalin said to him (fiercely), "No!" More whispering, then, "No one." He flung his hand as if shooing a fly. "Go away. Go."

We waited until he was through the door, then he reached me his plate and I filled it for him. "They hate you now," he told me, but I shrugged. "They hate you and you hate me and here am I left smitten. What kind of picture do we make?" he asked.

I said, "Stop talking and eat—you'll feel better."

He smiled at this. I was making him happy.

In the evening he built up the fire and we sat at the desk and played rummy. I said, "How soon will the Germans be here, Misha?" He told me, "Don't ask that." "Shall I bring the acorns from the table?" I asked. "Not for me, no." "Tomorrow," I said, "let's not stay in all day." "We owe you a picnic." "That's true—with cheesecake." He said, "You'd better tell the cook now." I shrugged. "Forget it, then." He tapped out his pipe and repacked and lit it. I asked, "Will you kill me?"—the playful voice, floating. He grinned and said, "Will *you* kill *me?*" "I won't kill you if you don't kill me." He said, "No deals. No business between lovers, Keke." "But I don't love you," I said, while he counted. "Nevertheless," he said, "no deals."

In bed that night the fire was bright off the gloss-stained, wood-slat walls and he lay on his back at first, nervous, with me just beside him, then rolled to face me with his poor arm tucked under the pillow. He said, "My second wife has been dead nine years. How long for your husband?"

"Almost two," I said, wondering how he had guessed I was married—if there was evidence in my face or figure.

Something in my expression must have scared him because he said, brightly, "Well then! Enough of that—my mistake. Here, show me your breasts instead."

"I will not." I smiled, but my heart sank a little too. I had the uniform on still, by necessity, though I had taken off the girdle and stockings and bra.

He said, "Oh come now." He made a funny face like a boy. There was less than a foot between us in the bed and the covers were up across our shoulders. He said, "I won't touch, just give me a peep. I've seen them before you know."

I laughed a little. "You haven't seen mine."

"Well that's just the point, Keke. That's my point exactly."

I said, "If you promise not to kill me I'll show you my boobs." And this time *he* laughed—kindly but awful. He rolled over onto his back again and stared at the ceiling. After a little he said, "Not from Georgia I know. Certainly not from Moscow. Where did they find you, Keke?"

I was pouting still. I said, "I don't think I'm interested in this conversation anymore."

He said, "*What makes you think you can act that way?*"—very forcefully all of a sudden, an entirely different tone. He turned to me and propped himself up on an elbow. Firelight is flattering to anyone, but it made him look younger too, and virile, which wasn't a welcome impression just now. He pointed and said, "You take too many liberties."

So the old thoughts returned to me briefly: how difficult can it be to crack a skull? If he was terrible it would make it easier. Quietly,

I said, "If I vex poor Stalin he should shoot me. Shall I get out of the bed for him?"

"What have I done to you?" he interrupted, still angry, and that made me sit up myself and lean. I said, "And *that* you don't want to ask *me*, Comrade Stalin!" Which broke him up—small convulsions that he tried to keep his lips around, then a great wave of squinting laughter. I could feel a smile on my own lips as well, but I pushed him: both hands against his shoulders. He pushed me back, still laughing, and I pushed him back harder this time. Then he had his hands inside my collar. It was a low square collar with bunchruffle sleeves, his knuckles against my bones there. He yanked the dress down, a little tearing, a shot of pain when my nipples caught. He stopped laughing. He stared hard at my eyes, not my bosom. My arms were confined with the sleeves tight around my elbows. He sat still breathing. A door slammed in some distant part of the house—as if to remind me that the Germans were coming. Watching Stalin, I didn't think he was pleased with himself. This wasn't what he wanted, and he was still available to win back—I could see that. So finally I decided. I said, "Shall I take it off then?" Not solicitous—just a question.

His laugh was thin and through his nose. He was frowning, but he nodded yes.

He was a suckler, you know—like Sasha but not Father. Nothing like Beria. When you look down past your chin at such a man it's difficult not to take responsibility. All I had ever done with men was make myself available. Take what you need, was what I knew, although none of them had needed me yet. It wouldn't work with Stalin. He was so clumsy. Probably he had been with no one since his wife. I wasn't sure he would get past my bosom—stopping and starting, laying still while I touched his hair. What could be sadder than an old man's hair, and if I helped him who would know? Most things would be erased once the Germans arrived, and even if my dead were with me there was nothing they could do. I did think of

Father, in fact. I closed my eyes and there he was. *I'm not responsible*, I thought, crying, while Stalin huffed and breathed. *And where are you when I need you, anyway?*

●

HE WAS UP before me, whistling "Douglas the Dog" in the lavatory while he shaved. He poked his head around the corner when he heard me rustling. He was bare-chested with the morning male smells on him. "*Pod'yom*," he said. "We have a picnic to arrange." Look how cheerful I had made him.

It had taken a long time for me to fall asleep but then I had slept heavily. I said, "A picnic for breakfast?" From the lavatory he called, "It's almost noon."

The tear in my uniform was in the back. Not so bad, but it ripped more when I pulled it on. I said, "I need to change clothes."

Back around the corner comes his head—concerned this time, thinking, buttoning up an identical tunic. I said, "Make them bring my clothes to me," but he said, "No, I don't think so. Come," he said, decided now. He strode past me while I found my shoes. My underthings were on his lavatory floor.

Remarkably, Stepan was still on guard. He must have come and gone. Stalin looked at him with that combination of stern regard and trust that certain men can manage. Pointing at me, he said, "You're to escort her to her room, wait for her there, and escort her back to me. No stops for anyone—including Vlasik. Do you understand?" Stepan offered a military nod. I could think of no safe way to thwart the plan.

Only when Stalin was behind the door did Stepan face me—with a stare much too cruel for such a young man. Where did they find these boys? I stepped past him, and he spat on the floor before following me.

Apparently the despairing quiet had descended over the dacha again. We met no one all the way to my room. Stepan spoke over my shoulder in a hiss that began as a whisper but gained volume along the way. "You'd better have things to tell me, little *blyad*. Beria would have me kill you now. What does he say while he fucks you then? Hm? While the Nazis rape our sisters—what does he say? How does he like it while the tanks roll through our villages? Why don't you show me what you did for him—here." I closed the door. It had no lock so I propped a chair.

I expected pounding or shouts, but when there were none I slipped out of the uniform, noticing the rip in back, which must have dominated Stepan's attention. I scrubbed at the basin and brushed my hair. At first, out of habit, I picked a clean uniform from the closet, and I had it on before I realized it wasn't necessary. I changed into a pale blue dress from my first life, one of the three dresses I had carried with me this far into the next. It smelled of storage—cedar and dust—but it put someone else in the mirror before me, an image I doubted I could claim any longer.

When I was ready I listened at the door. Nothing. I opened it quietly and slipped out and closed it without a sound. Then I leapt because they were right there beside me: both Stepan and Vlasik. Vlasik was amused and red in the face. He said (in a stage whisper), "Sneaky little mouse. Is this your new uniform?" he asked. "Have your duties changed?"

They blocked the way. I had never seen Vlasik so happy—his florid face was bright. Looking at Stepan I said, "You heard his orders."

Which set him off like a dog, cursing.

But Vlasik held him away and said, "Katia dear. Ambitious little housekeeper."

He pushed Stepan back.

"We need to ask you just a few questions before we return you to your duties. We're concerned for Comrade Stalin, you see—just as you are, I'm sure." (He leaned in, Stepan behind him.) "You have a picnic planned—I know. We'll be sure to get you there safely.

But you see, Russia is falling into Nazi hands just now, while you take him on this picnic, so that has us worried. You can imagine. We wonder why *Stalin* isn't worried, you see."

He waited, as if for an answer. I was thinking how lucky it was that there was no one in my life they could threaten me with. I said, "I'll tell him you asked."

He had a quick fake laugh, bright and high. "No, you won't, Katia. No, you won't. You won't tell him about this conversation at all. It's our secret, the three of us. Tell me, please, do you care for Russia?"

"Get out of my way."

"Maybe you don't. Has she treated you poorly? Has Adolf Hitler been kinder?"

"He'll have you killed."

"Do you think? How long have you known him, Katia? What is it—fifteen, twenty hours maybe? I don't have a watch. Let's say a full day, yes? Do you know how long I have known him?" (He touched his chest, his eyebrows raised.) "How long I have been in his confidence? Even poor Stepan here—still a young man yet he's been with Comrade Stalin since he was a boy. I mean yes, Katia, granted: it's a *very* fine dress." (He touched me now—rubbed the fabric between two fingers.) "And you look well in it, yes. And you and Comrade Stalin have become close in all that time—I know. But do you think it will be enough when he hears about your friendship with Adolf? Were your duties similar there, Katia?" (He rubbed his knuckles up and down across my chest.) "Did you wear this nice dress for him too?"

I began to scream.

Immediately Vlasik said, "*Shut up*," but when I didn't he put a hand over my mouth. Valenchka, of all people, came running. "What's happening?" she shouted from the end of the corridor, as if we had failed to ask her permission. "Who do you have there?" she demanded, and Vlasik shouted back, "Shut up!"

Then came Stalin behind her. I hadn't seen him yet but I turned to look when Vlasik let go of me. Stalin appeared confused more than angry, standing behind Valenchka with his mouth open. After a long pause he said, "Keke! I'm waiting!" He held his hand out for me—stern and impatient in his paternal way, but not a glance for Stepan or Vlasik. What a strange man, I thought. I looked at the other two but their eyes were on Stalin and they were both terrified—for themselves maybe, but also for him. I walked past them and took his hand. When we rounded the corner I wrapped my other arm into his too and squeezed. I had been wrong to worry that he would shoot me. In fact, I was safe only when I was beside him. He might kill me still, but just by sending me away—leaving me to my fate, I thought. I leaned against him and he patted my cheek.

The cook had packed a great basket, which Stalin carried. Not until we were outside in the garden did he speak to me. "You dressed properly," he said quietly. "Good girl."

He led me across the terraces and into the trees behind, where the forest floor was cleared of brush and picked clean and mowed. There were crude cottages with deck chairs out front, but we walked past these to where the trees were closer and darker. When we settled I noticed that three guards had followed us from the dacha. They posted themselves in a triangle around us, politely distant. Stalin spread a gingham cloth. There was an oversized meal packed: cheese and salads and pickled beets. A wine from Georgia that Stalin was proud of. He collected some stones and built a fire within them and cooked shashlik. He was becoming himself again, I imagined: expansive and instructing. I thought, Just one night, true, but look what I've done for him. "What can I feed you?" he asked, and I said, "A black olive." We lingered over it a while, licking fingers. He was at ease with me now, his smile presumptuous.

There were some folders at the bottom of the basket and later on he opened them while I lay back on the gingham. A blotch of sun warmed my stomach and I meant to let him be, remembering everything Vlasik had said. But when I looked over he was intent and disposed, already beyond me. And everyone knows that they come at night when you're least expecting them—they knock on the door and take you with them. They might kill you that evening, or send you away, and everyone knows you don't get a last meal. "Misha?" I said. He said, "Hm?" still intent on the page. "What did you do to me last night?" I asked, my voice coy but a little desperate. "I can't remember now."

It worked, of course—of course it worked. He turned and smiled. And he seemed surprised by what he saw. His smile quickly drained away. Quietly he said, "You can't imagine how you look, Katia."

Which hurt very much. "Don't say my name."

"How sweet you are to me." He leaned and kissed. "What a good girl," he whispered.

·

MOLOTOV AND another man were waiting for him in the dining room. I thought they looked frightened, prepared to beg. Stalin said to me, "Wait in my room now. Finish your nap." He spoke quietly so they wouldn't hear and he had let my hand go before they saw us. I made it safely into his rooms. First I lay curled up in the bed a short time, but eventually I came to my senses. I went to the desk and turned on the lamp. I took a pin from my hair and bent it so and picked the lock on the bottom drawer. Start at the bottom. A man will think he has hidden something further from reach there. It was crammed full of envelopes—the Council of Ministers, the Defense Ministry. Most had not been opened, but the few that had contained money: thick packets of large notes. And receipts—they were his wages. I took a fat-bellied envelope from the bottom of the pile and left it out on the desk.

The drawer above this had two things in it: a strange telephone with no numbers on the front—just a plain black face—and a revolver loaded with three bullets. It was a heavy, gleaming gun, more substantial than the one at Lipki. I put the telephone on the desk. Carefully, I lifted the receiver. There was a conversation in progress on the line already, two men involved in an argument. Between the unfamiliar terms and the poor connection, I couldn't follow the conversation well. But it seemed to be about troops—artillery, divisions. The voices sounded antique on the line: hollowed out and distant, their urgency a little comic. I had held my palm over the speaking end, but now I said, "Boo!" My voice bounced back to me in a dead way, making no impression on their argument. I hung up and put the telephone away.

I was trained not to press my luck so I closed up and relocked the drawers. But I kept the revolver out along with the envelope and found a place to hide them, wedged between the headboard and the wall. I waited for a long time more. The proper thing would be to anticipate him now, though, gun in hand, perhaps in the narrow lavatory. I could call to him, and he would come to see if I had left the door open. He would round the corner hopeful and lascivious. Two bullets for him and one for me.

But when I had sat a little while on the cold tiles I realized I didn't want him dead. Not if he would come back to me, at least. If he would come and be good to me again I would trade that for revenge—my own and everyone else's too. I would let him keep me if he was sweet; I would make the bed and wait around for him. Be nice. Take care of me. Don't say no all the time.

I went to the last of his private rooms, where I could peek into the parlor. Approaching the door I heard music playing on the phonograph. It was the folk song "In This Tiny Village," which I had always known, and I wouldn't have believed this was his voice—singing out over the recorded tenor—if I hadn't seen him through the keyhole. It was a high, weak sound that his speaking voice would never have betrayed. His brow knit in a foolish way and his mouth bent into shapes. In my narrow view I could see Valenchka behind him and the cook—both watching with indulgent smiles—and just a shoulder past the cook, which was enough to know it was Vlasik.

That was as much of the room as I could see. But when the song ended there were applauds and "bravos" from the near side too. How proud and shy he looked in the lamplight. "Encore!" someone shouted—a girl. "Encore!" And when the needle was dropped and the song began to play again he laughed and turned to a part of the room not available through the keyhole. "Please, Setanka. Once was enough." But he was happy, ready to be budged, and his daughter began singing it herself to prompt him. Her voice fell away when he took it up again. He watched her this time—it was evident in his smile. He sang and watched her. It broke my heart. I turned away to the dark room and sat with my back against the door frame, listening. I had an image in my mind of my father and husband huddled together in the next dark room, their ears pressed at that door too, listening after me. And then more again in the room past them—a sequence of ghosts left out in dark rooms, listening after the next.

•

WHEN THE MEN woke me in the middle of the night I thought they were Nazis. Perhaps I'd been dreaming. They were impatient but gentle.

"We've packed your bags already," they whispered. "They're in the car. Hurry," they said, "Stalin is waiting." Which was a mean and unnecessary lie. I was perfectly pliant.

It was true about my bags though—they were there on the seat. While the driver pulled away I searched for the photo of Father—quickly, so that I could ask him to turn around if necessary. But there it was. I took it from the bag and sat with it in my lap. It was too dark to see. "Where are we going?" I asked. The driver said, "We won't be long."

He took me to the station and put me on a train. It was a very short train, just two cars: the engine and a good, clean passenger car, such as you seldom saw in Russia those days. A porter carried my bags. I carried the photo. There was no one in the car, though—only me and the porter. He picked a banquette toward the middle, identical to all those around it. "This one?" he asked. I frowned and stared into his eyes, but it was evident he didn't know any more than I did. "It will do." He got down from the train. I was left alone. When I had settled and looked out the window I saw the driver still there, leaning against his car. The whistle blew and I waved. We pulled away.

At the next station we picked up a string of regular cars—filthy and crowded—and the platform was full of passengers loading and others staying behind. They were women and old men and the crippled—no one fit for service. No one was loaded onto my car, and the old women watched me and pointed and whispered. When we pulled out again the sun was up. There was a water closet at one end of the car. I washed my face and combed my hair. I remembered the gun I had left hidden and the envelope of money and wondered if they would change my present destination, whatever it was, when Valenchka found them. I tried the door at the end of the car, but I wasn't surprised to find it locked. When I called out, the voices chattering in the next car grew quiet. They wouldn't answer, though. I resettled in my banquette and fell asleep.

I woke to more familiar landscape. We were traveling east. A porter came with a key and let an old man in who sold me tea and a sausage. He wouldn't speak—just held things out to show and then took my money with a little bow. We stopped again at Kazan, Sarapul, Yekaterinburg in the Urals. We passed my town but I won't name it. I got tired of looking at Father in the photo. I thought he wouldn't have recognized me now. Then Omsk and Novosibirsk, into Siberia. All the way I had the whole car to myself.

The third night the porter let a band in. I had heard them playing for the car before me. They shuffled up the aisle, wary, clanking with cymbals tied to their knees and bells attached to the tips of their shoes. They had the big flush smiles of old men from the steppe, and the bandore player had no teeth. I didn't know the song, but when it was through I leaned and clapped. They promptly stood and turned to go, but I said, "No, wait. Another please, one more!"

It was as if they couldn't hear me. "I can pay you," I said, willing to lie. This led the last man to touch his cap, but the porter freed them and locked the door behind.

They took me off the train at Tomsk—two officers from the camp. They were strangely polite, loading me into the car. They allowed me to bring my bags, though after that car ride I would never see them again. The Victorian homes of Tomsk sink a little further each year into the melting permafrost, and in some the ground-floor windows were not much above the sidewalks. They were painted bright colors, with turrets and spires, but past the last street the forest crouched above them. We drove to Kolpashevo on the Ob. Slabs of ice still lounged along the bank. It was a low building with a tin roof. They took my blue dress and my bags. The showers ran yellow—I don't know what. They gave me pants, a sweater, a vest, a quilted jacket, and felt boots and puttees. Special treatment—they'd been expecting me.

Then I cut timber. Because it was July when I arrived we still had black bread. We had turnips and goose feet for the broth. But by January it was cattle feed and meatless bones boiled for the marrow. Also groats—groats and groats. You rot from the inside, eating that way. Through the war I cut timber and afterward too, until Stalin was dead and I was old and homely. I made no friends at Kolpashevo. No one forgave me and I didn't want them to. One night I'm sitting by the stove, rolling a *papirosa*, when some Leningradka with the rings round her eyes and no hair left on her head says to me, "Did he touch you?"

She—*this woman,* if you could still call her that—*she* looks at me with disgust, repulsed by the very thought. Everyone waits for my answer.

I say to her, "He suckled like an infant." Staring through my smoke.

But she was good as dead, you know. What was I thinking? I didn't impress her. She looked at me the way Stepan had and Vlasik—a cruel look that no one would have thought to give me when I lived on Semya Street with Father and Sasha, before I was so desirable (as I never would be again). And though I should have been long past it by then, I thought I might cry under her withering gaze.

So I tapped my ash and said, "He loved me."

She stared and stared.

"I could have killed him a thousand times," I said.

TANNER AND JUN HEE

THEY ARE ASLEEP together when the phone rings. The early morning sun casts a bluish light through their curtains. Tanner reaches back to the end table for the receiver without rolling over. He recognizes the heavily accented voice of his father-in-law, though he hasn't heard it in a number of years. The line is thick with fuzz. "No," he says, "one moment." He hands the receiver to his wife, who is awake now, already concerned by the tone of his voice. Her hair swings out across her face. "Hello? Oh, hi. It's early here. No no. What's the matter?" Then he watches her hold her breath for a moment, rise to a kneeling position, listening, then lay, with some care, back down onto the pillow. "No," she says, speaking Korean now. "I don't know. No." She lies still with her palm pressed to her forehead. Tanner doesn't hear a voice from the telephone. In English, she says, "Dad, I'll call you back. Yes. Well, I'll call you later." She remains on the line, not speaking or moving. "I'm hanging up now." She hands the receiver back to Tanner. She watches him pick it up, roll half over, and return it to its cradle. When he rolls back she is watching him still, her hand still pressed to her forehead. She says, "My mother died," and Tanner raises his eyebrows—he can see himself. What shall he say? "Oh no," is what emerges. Jun Hee rolls half over, exposing her back. It's summertime—the windows are open. He leans against her shoulder and says, "That's terrible" and, a few moments later, "I'm so sorry, Love." After a few minutes more, he asks, "What happened?" She lays still. Then she pushes the sheets off, puts both feet onto the carpeted floor, steps out of bed. She hesitates between each movement just long enough for Tanner to think that she'll stop, but she doesn't. She stands and takes her robe from the hook by the dresser. She looks at herself in the mirror and sighs. This is a Thursday: the radio alarm by their bed clicks on.

•

IN THE SHOWER, Tanner tries to picture Jun Hee's mother. He hasn't seen her in almost three years, since the day she unexpectedly appeared at the house. He had answered the door in his bathrobe, wondering who it could be, early on a Sunday. "Good morning," he had said, smiling, not knowing who this was but worrying that he ought to know—someone Jun Hee had introduced him to. She said, "Is my daughter here?" It was enunciated as a statement rather than a question. Perhaps she had rehearsed the phrase. She didn't understand, or perhaps she pretended not to, when he invited her in. Her husband was seated in a rental car in the driveway, watching the exchange with what Tanner could only interpret as malevolence. Tanner went and found Jun Hee, and she dressed while her mother waited outside on the step. When Jun Hee emerged at last, they spoke for a moment without touching at all. Tanner had stood back in the hallway and watched. He couldn't hear them. His wife came back and stepped around him into the kitchen. She returned with her purse and kissed him. "I'll see you later," she whispered. As she left the house—her mother ahead of her, halfway back to the car already—she turned and offered him an ironic grin. He waved. She looked happy enough, he guessed, but also afraid, and Tanner felt as if she was being kidnapped.

He shuts the water off and opens the shower door, now. How

long that day had dragged. He had tried to occupy himself, but the longer she stayed out the more distracted he became—the more neglected he felt, and jealous. He hangs his towel and dripping washcloth. That evening he had marinated chicken and put off dinner, expecting the three of them at any moment, but eventually it was obvious she must be eating out with her parents and he made himself a sandwich. She came back alone, finally. He wouldn't be properly introduced, evidently. Business had brought her father to the States, she said. Her mother had come to see Jun Hee. The next day they had a flight back to Seoul out of Kennedy; they were staying down in the city. He fills the sink with hot water, opens the cabinet, and takes out shaving cream and a razor. The three of them had gone to the Litchfield Inn for brunch, then strolled through the shops across from the courthouse, then to dinner at Mai Pan's, staying until the restaurant closed, drinking tea and talking. Her parents had presumably been introduced to people—Alan in the bookstore and Gail or her daughter in the sweater shop, at least, possibly friends they would have bumped into on a Sunday. *Where's Tanner today?* someone may have asked, but he couldn't quite imagine what Jun Hee's answer would have been. He dunks the blade and pulls it through his beard, watching himself in the mirror. Jun Hee was vague about what they'd discussed.

At this moment his wife is in the kitchen, probably drinking coffee and watching the toaster. When he got out of bed he had suggested she take the day off—"naturally," he had said—but she either didn't hear him or disagreed, and she began to go through the steps of her morning. Here he is doing the same thing, wondering if she's also thinking of that day three years ago. The razor has caught in his beard. He tosses the dull blade into the trash.

He cuts his finger on the new blade—he's not paying attention. Is he permitted to be angry at his wife on the day her mother has died? Put that way, in his mind, he's embarrassed, and newly concerned for her. But he is also freshly remembering how she had volunteered so little information about their visit, answering his questions without elaborating until he had decided he didn't really care, or wasn't supposed to, at least. But why not come home for dinner, after all? Why not call? He could have met them at the restaurant. They would have had the whole day alone together by then. He should have told her these thoughts, so he wouldn't be thinking them still, but the fact that they had come to visit her at all was a significant step, and his reticence was partly just a response to her good mood. For weeks she seemed pleased and relieved, although she didn't talk about them. He had been happy for her.

In many ways, but particularly because of her parents' disapproval, his marriage to Jun Hee had been as much a separation from others as a tie between themselves. They had been together in college despite her parents' regrets. They had a small, formal ceremony that could not have been improved upon in his mind, but again it was without her parents. Then they lived together for four years—breakfast together if not always dinner, the paper on Sundays, a cottage on Block Island for two weeks in the summer—all as if she had no family. It was selfish of him to resent their sudden appearance. Rinsing the last of the lather from his face, he wonders if she'll want him to fly back with her now.

His own mother, just a few hours away in White River, had gotten fed up with them too—had sent a bitingly polite letter that enumerated the few times he called or visited during the first year of their marriage. Tanner's father had died when he was twelve. His wake and burial are still vivid in Tanner's memory, and ordinary: the clumsy condolences of adults he'd never spoken to, and playing games with their children in the backyard. The unappealing casseroles that lingered and the visiting parishioners, one by one, who leveled charges at Tanner on their way out: "Now take care of your mother," they said, and "You'll have to be the strong one now." There were new varieties of awkward conversation with his mother. Tanner blots his chin and cheeks with a towel. How *does* Jun Lee feel? he wants to know. What is the ceremony like in Korea?

•

WHEN HE comes into the kitchen, Jun Hee is at the table with a cup of coffee and the morning paper. She looks up and says, "You're going to be late," placing a crust of bread onto her plate full of crumbs. "I thought you might have drowned," she says, returning her attention to the paper.

Tanner rinses his cup in the sink. He takes a tea bag from the canister, pours the water, and replaces the pot. "You're not still planning on going in, are you?" He's hopeful because she isn't hurrying to follow him into the shower. She sips from her mug without answering. "Should we be calling a travel agent?" he asks.

She looks fine this morning, shiny and at ease. He would prefer some clear evidence of grief, or simply confusion. It's a busy time of the year, as they both know, but he tells her, "They'll make do without you. God knows you've got the time coming."

Jun Hee puts the mug down, and the paper, and looks at him. It's an extension of the look she gave him earlier, in bed—a little sharper now. "The one thing," she says, holding her palm up as if to push him away, "that I'd really appreciate is if you'd just be yourself, Tanner. That's it." Returning to the newspaper, she says, "Just be honest."

Tanner shrugs. "Do you think I've lied to you this morning?" he asks, then wonders what he's doing, needling his wife. Though he is angry, isn't he?

"Not yet," she says. She turns and pats a leaf of the newspaper with some emphasis. "Not yet, but you're worrying me. You didn't know her. If you did . . ."

But she doesn't finish. He sips his tea and burns his tongue. "So you're just going to work?" he asks.

"Right," she says, without looking up. "I'm going to work, you're going to work. Tonight Kim and Sung come to dinner and I'll still make tofu, probably." She scratches her arm without taking her eyes from the page. "I don't know about you but I haven't given my mother a thought for weeks. I don't—" She shrugs.

Tanner leans against the counter and watches her. She never looks up but he is nearly certain she's not really reading. *Jun Hee?* her father had said to Tanner, although even the poor connection could hardly have turned his hello into his wife's. Her father had sounded frightened, an emotion Tanner had never connected with the man.

"What did your father say?" he asks.

"I don't have to do anything," she says. Her voice is light and suddenly fragile, petulant. He wishes she would look at him. She says, "This will be easier if you don't pick on me."

•

HE HAD JUST stepped through the door when he was told that one of the SCR-packs on the Bromberg furnace had quit—the furnace that was three weeks behind on delivery already. Frank had taken a look but couldn't find the problem. A few minutes later the customer was on the phone again, as he had been all week. Tanner's morning retreated to the back of his mind for a few hours until he washed his hands on his way from the shop floor to the phone again and the sink and mirror reminded him. He had lunch with Frank and mentioned what had happened, realizing in the process how little he knew. How had she died? She wasn't very old—early fifties, perhaps. Frank's own mother had passed that spring, and he had taken two weeks off: one for the funeral and immediate arrangements, one more to be with his father through his first days alone in the house. Tanner felt a little foolish, sitting here in his ignorance, far from his wife. Why don't we head back to the office and call her? Frank suggested. They got the check and paid without finishing their meals.

An assistant at the lab said Jun Hee was still at lunch. Tanner went back to the furnace, where the problem had perhaps been narrowed down. In his office he called again and got his wife, and she said, "I'm all right, actually. I'm sorry, Tanner. A little better now."

"I'm glad," he said, "you sound better." They should probably cancel dinner with Kim and Sung, he suggested, but she said she was looking forward to the diversion. She had to run now, but he was sweet to call and to worry.

"I am worried," he told her. "I'm still worried, you know."

"Don't be. We'll talk tonight."

He hung up and sat back in his chair, still feeling misplaced and insufficient. Her father was a gruff and imperious man (at least in Jun Hee's stories), a successful financier with traditional notions and a wealthy man's pride. That morning he had sounded like no more than an old, bewildered man. When the phone rang again, now, Tanner was sure it was Jun Hee, and forgetting the secretaries he picked it up himself. But it was the customer calling from Bromberg. "Guess who?" he said.

•

WHEN TANNER pulls in, his wife's car is in the garage already. This seems like a good sign since she's seldom home before him. Maybe she has taken the afternoon off. He finds her in the kitchen, wrapped in an apron, chopping the tofu and vegetables. He puts the wine in the refrigerator and takes a hold of her from behind. She smiles and he asks, "How are you feeling, Love?"

Jun Hee nods and kisses his cheek, finishes with the carrots, and pushes the pile aside. Next are the leaves of bok choy. "Still up for this?" he asks.

"They'll be here any minute, actually. Maybe change first, would you, then set the table for me?" He holds her a moment longer, until she puts her damp hand against his cheek and kisses him again.

Sung Lee sits on the leather sofa in the living room, describing the addition he has begun to build off the south end of his house. His wife has drawn up the plans, he says, but refuses to get involved with the construction—all those messy details between design and completion. Tanner has been trying to pay attention and at the same time listen to Kim and Jun Hee in the kitchen. The Lees are a couple who still always manage to divide the pre-dinner conversation by gender. Tanner can hear Kim complaining about one of the doctors in the lab where they both work. His wife is agreeing politely. She hasn't mentioned her mother, and Tanner has resolved to follow her lead. Then Kim leans into the doorway, wiping her hands on a dishrag, and tells them to come and get it.

Tanner follows Sung to the round table at one end of the kitchen. The candles he had set earlier are lit and the overhead light is off. His wife looks perfectly well after all, as though she is sailing toward the end of a pleasant and uneventful day. While she tends to the stove and the Lees take their places at the table, Tanner fetches the wine from the fridge. Kim Lee shows Sung the silverware at her place—it's a pattern she likes, or she's being polite. Tanner uncorks the wine and fills each glass, and Kim asks Jun Hee if there is anything she can do.

"Is there anything I can do to help?" she asks.

Jun Hee stops what she is doing. She has a fat, floral pot-holder stuck on the hand she holds up by her lips now. She stands still a moment, and to the Lees she must look as if she's considering the offer, reviewing last steps for the meal. Her shoulders slump, though—her mood has changed. Tanner pours the wine and watches. "Yes," Sung says, undaunted, "what can we do? Everything smells so good."

She seems to come to, but her smile withers. She lifts the wok and slides the tofu into a serving bowl. "Nope," she says briskly, "nothing." After filling his own glass, Tanner takes a seat while she carries the bowl around the counter. She places it on the table, and speaking to no one in particular, she says, "It's too late anyway." Tanner is tempted to interrupt her.

She says, "I mean, what am I going to do now, right?" and laughs, unhappily.

Kim Lee smiles and raises her eyebrows. "It looks great," she ventures. Jun Hee turns back for the rice. She stops when she gets behind the counter, though, and faces them again from the half-darkness past the candlelight.

"I don't think I can do this," she says to Sung. He opens his mouth to speak. "Jun Hee," Tanner says. "No," she continues, "no no—I'm sorry. Never mind," she says, looking down now, pushing herself away from the counter, "never mind, never mind. Let's just . . . let's not do this, okay? Let's stop now." Her tone has shifted again, softening. "Why don't you guys go home," she suggests, matter-of-factly. "I'm sorry."

She takes the pot-holder from her hand and Tanner stands and goes to her—awfully late, he's thinking to himself; he has been late all day.

"Of course we were a *very* tight family," she's saying. Tanner wraps his arms around her and at the same time looks past her to the Lees. He shakes his head and holds up a finger—one minute, he means to promise. Just a minute longer and I'll explain. Jun Hee leans into him and laughs, at the edge of tears.

"Come on now," he says. "It's all right." Then a great and surprising wash of relief flows through him. It's more than relief, in fact. It's almost elation. How wonderful her capitulation feels, how wonderful to feel her lean against him softly! He has to keep from smiling. What a display they've put on, he thinks—what a show for the poor Lees—but that thought doesn't dent his elation.

"Good God," she is saying, tsking, beginning to cry. She shakes her head against his chest. Tanner rubs her back and takes another look at the Lees, offers one more reassuring and postponing smile. How very far away they appear, nervous and small at the candlelit table, ready to leave, of course, to be out of the room. (They aren't intimate friends, Tanner thinks—they aren't up to this—but then again, they are the best friends Tanner and Jun Hee can claim, lately. This thought doesn't bother him either.)

"Dinner is ruined," Jun Hee is saying.

•

THAT NIGHT when they are together in bed, Jun Hee lies flat on her back and Tanner lies against her with one leg and one arm bent over her warm skin. He has been telling her that they will both take a day off or a couple of days. She doesn't want to go to Seoul—she's convinced him that it's not practical or necessary—but they can still take the time off. Work can wait, he has been saying—they were foolish to go in today. And not to worry because Sung and Kim understand, probably as well as anyone. (Tanner had explained it to them in the garage, on their way out—whispering, for some reason, and absurdly cheerful, hoping it didn't show. They had said, *Oh dear* and *Tell her how sorry we are.* "Tell her to call me when she wants to," Kim had said. Perhaps, Tanner had thought, they'll become better friends.) She has been quiet for so long that when Jun Hee finally speaks, it startles him, though she speaks softly.

"There's this one day," she says, "and I just keep thinking about it. One of the days my father was away—I don't remember where. I was eight, maybe?"

Tanner turns his cheek from her shoulder. They both stare at the ceiling.

Jun Hee says, "I remember that night she asked me if I would sleep with her, to keep her company, you know? We lay back to back so her hair tickled my neck. I couldn't sleep at all. I finally woke her up, fidgeting around, and said I wanted to play a game. One game, that's it—to help me fall asleep. Are you awake?"

Tanner is feeling the vibrations of her voice, his fingers resting on the bones at the base of her neck. He is forming a picture of the scene in his mind as she speaks. Jun Hee is fat-cheeked and perpetually disapproving in childhood photos. "I'm listening," he says.

Jun Hee tells him, "I tried to think of a game, but nothing was going to work in the dark. So she asked me to pretend I was getting married the next day and tell her what my husband is like. This is my mother, Tanner—I'm eight."

He nods.

She shifts under the blanket and turns to face him. He keeps his eyes on the ceiling, on nothing in particular.

"The first thing I thought," she says, "was 'I'm never getting married to any boy.' I wanted to play the game though, so I started telling her. I said he'd be smart, but not smarter than me. And tall, and rich. And I wanted him to have a big nose for some reason. Then I said he would have blond hair. I'm just listing attributes for her—God knows where I got that from."

Jun Hee pauses and Tanner waits. She laughs once, not unhappily.

"So when I got to that part, she stopped me. 'Blond hair?' she said to me. 'What kind of man has blond hair?' Then she started laughing and I laughed too. I thought of how silly that was for me to say. What could I have been thinking? I wondered. She thought I was telling a joke."

Tanner can feel the shape of the bone in her shoulder and he's heard every word she's said, but his mind has trailed away nonetheless. He is thinking, This is my wife beside me and her mother has died though I never knew her. But I know my wife, he thinks, and here she is, right here beside me.

TANNER

HE WOKE LATER than he had meant to and immediately listened for his mother's call. It had taken only a week for the vigilance to become rote. He lay in the lumpy twin bed of his childhood. He had been in to turn her at one, and then again this morning at five. Now the house was silent. On the walls above him hung a poster of Catfish Hunter and two fly-rods crossed like sabers and a char-coal portrait of himself as an infant, done at the Rutland fair his first summer. The sun fell at a sharp angle across Catfish's leg-kick. It was the first morning he and his mother had slept in. There were cro-cuses suddenly open in the bed by the tennis court. He listened a moment longer, then got up and pulled on his pants.

The floorboards creaked in their predictable patterns down the hallway. When he knocked on her door, lightly, and received no answer, he began to worry more actively and specifically. In her room the window shades were pulled and it was still dark. "Mom?" She lay on her back in the center of her wide bed, just where he had left her, three layers of blankets covering everything up to her neck. "Mom?" he asked, less politely this time. His thoughts crabbed in two directions: a sordid relief that came with the selfish sense of things being placed right again, order restored, followed by the backward scramble of guilt. Her expression appeared pegged and clenched, with her down-turned mouth and dry lips, the halo of silver hair. Half of him anticipated fishing for her wrist beneath the covers; the other half was determined not to. He leaned down over her.

"Mom," he whispered.

Her eyes came open, blinking into the middle distance, then turning to him.

"Tanner," she replied, quietly, pleasantly.

His involuntary grunt was close to a laugh—he hoped it didn't sound mean. "You slept well."

•

AT THE card table in the kitchen, Tanner positioned his stool close to her wheelchair and set two cups of coffee and two bowls of oatmeal on the table.

"I hope you're hungry," he told her. "I made too much."

She was looking out the window at the brick pathway, the greenhouse, and the sun in the trees behind them. She had asked to be dressed in her blue robe over the nightgown. "It's clearing," she said of the day.

"Here." Tanner held a spoonful of oatmeal. His mother turned from the window to the spoon and made a sour face. "What's in it?"

"Prunes. Some of those prunes you had in the refrigerator."

She shook her head. "Those were old, Tanner."

"No, I tried one, they're fine."

"They've been in there for months."

"They're fine, Mom, I tried one. Here." He ate the spoonful himself. With wide eyes he said, "Mm mm."

He refilled the spoon and she watched it approach her with disgust before finally obliging.

"We were due for a change," he said, "something a little more exciting."

She chewed and swallowed deliberately, watching him, while he dipped into her bowl again. "Prunes," she said.

"Tell me it doesn't taste better."

She closed her lips on the spoon again as he slid it away, her eyes coolly cynical. "It tastes like prunes. It'll make me shit."

"Please . . . ,"Tanner laughed.

"That Mrs. Carlis won't think it's funny."

"Come on now," he said. "It's her job—it doesn't matter. How about if we change the subject? You want coffee?"

She didn't. She allowed him to guide another spoonful between her lips but her eyes had shifted to the yard again, the row of birches at the back of her property. "What's the matter?" he asked. She could recede so quickly since the stroke: in a flash her cheeks would go white and her eyes would deepen and water. "It's not a bad subject," she said in a toneless voice, turned away from him still. "It's just the way it is, Tanner."

He put the spoon down in the bowl. "You're right," he admitted. "I'm sorry."

"It's not revolting—it's not anyone's *job*."

He nodded. "I apologize." And shrugged.

•

HE TOOK his wife's phone call in his mother's bedroom, closing the door behind himself. Mrs. Carlis had arrived for the day so he could afford to escape and be alone with his wife for a few minutes. Jun Hee told him the fog that had lingered all week had finally burned away this morning; she said she would leave Connecticut by six and be with him by ten, providing the car didn't overheat. "Is it doing that again?"

"Once this week. It'll make it though."

"I'll look at it while you're here," he said, looking forward to the diversion. He and Jun Hee lapsed into a short, comfortable silence. Finally she asked, "So how is she?"

"Yes, the question of the week." Tanner slouched down into his mother's stiff-backed chair. Before him was her full closet: a crush of dresses, skirts, and blouses in a narrow span of colors, the styles modern and only vaguely conservative; an orgy of shoes trading partners on the closet floor. "I'm afraid you'll be surprised when you see her."

"What do you mean?"

"Well, you'll see. She looks defeated sometimes—these moments when she's decided to give up some ground."

He said, "But then she comes out of it. She can turn it on and off."

"Not surprising, I guess," Jun Hee replied. "She *did* lose some ground, of course? She lost a lot."

Tanner wasn't certain what exactly she had lost yet, or what she intended to live without. There was more to it than he knew how to explain to Jun Hee, but each time they talked he felt again that this was a manageable crisis, with a solution hidden in the midst of the details and a recovery in store for both his mother and himself. "It's just off-putting," he said. "You'll see. It's not what I would have expected from her. My father was like this, you know—a little dependent on pity. She was always the crutch, he was the armpit."

Jun Hee said, "You're surprised she's grown old like everyone else."

"But all at once. Doubles champ to this. You'll be surprised too." He thought of her sallow cheeks that morning at breakfast, the guilt she could suddenly induce so well, though that never had been her style. She was more inclined to direct coercion, demands, and ultimatums. "I don't know, Jun Hee. Maybe it's better the way you lost your mother," he said—he had woken up with this thought—"not so close up, and slow. Maybe the distance from here to Seoul wasn't entirely a disadvantage." There was no immediate reply. He could hear Mrs. Carlis holding forth in the kitchen. "I don't mean to say that that was easy for you—for either of you. But wait until you see her."

The pause stretched into a silence. Jun Hee said, "Your mother's not dead, Tanner. She's not even dying."

He sighed. "Yes." Closed his eyes and rubbed his forehead. "I know," he said. "That's not what I meant."

"She's had a stroke."

"I know. I've been here all week."

Jun Hee didn't answer, but when she did he knew that she would say she had to run. He would lose the calm pleasure of her voice, the temporary reach out of the dusty, medicated sunlight.

·

HE HAD been building a ramp over the front four stairs since she came home from the hospital. He resurrected the carpentry he had not used since summer jobs during college, since the last time he lived in this house. The day filled with the first real promise of summer, and soon he was sweating. When it was finished, he brought his mother out for a test run, and the nurse, Mrs. Carlis, stood in the sun beside the ramp and gestured. "Oh that's perfect," she said. "Would you look at that, please? Are you a carpenter, Tanner? I had no idea."

"Tanner can do anything," his mother said.

"But nothing well," he added.

"It's steep though, isn't it?" Mrs. Carlis amended. She watched him ease the chair down the slope, the wheels faintly clacking between the planks. "It's a little steep I suppose, after all. Don't you think?"

"Probably," Tanner agreed. It seemed fine to him, but of course it would be Mrs. Carlis wheeling his mother up and down each day. "We could get some momentum up," he told his mother. "Open the car door and let you go."

"My goodness," she whispered, "what a day."

Mrs. Carlis said, "You'll want a handrail of course." She was ignored but undaunted. "It's marvelous, Tanner, all it needs is a handrail. Your mother is lucky, I think."

In the afternoon the three of them sat together on the patio by the greenhouse. Tanner made lemonade. With an accordion straw his mother could drink for herself while he held the glass. She would need a table of some sort, attached to the rail of her chair. She would need a new, better chair. The phone rang and Mrs. Carlis delivered the standard message: Emma was doing well but was not presently inclined to receive calls; she herself would gladly pass along a brief message.

"It was the same Margaret," she announced when she returned to the patio, "and she said she's ready to help however she might. And I really, Emma, I truly think it's about time for visitors." Tanner's mother sighed while Tanner smiled and turned away. "I'm just the nurse," Mrs. Carlis said, backpedaling even as she pressed ahead, "what do I know? I've only seen a hundred clients do the same thing you're doing, always regretting it, and so much for me. But am I allowed to point out that you have a new ramp to show off—"

"Oh dear, it's not a question of—"

"—to show off as well," Mrs. Carlis continued, raising her voice and her hand. Tanner's mother laughed. "It's been a *week*, but la-di-da, and what do I know after all? Laugh if you like, I don't mind."

His mother said, "It is not feeling better or worse, or showing anything off, Mrs. Carlis—believe me. I'm not particularly proud of that ramp as the first thing to greet whoever comes to the door, despite how grateful I am to my handy son." She gave Tanner a sidelong glance. In the past, she might have clapped his knee beside hers, or mussed his hair—still, though he was past thirty. "It is simply a matter of . . ." She sighed and paused. "Lemonade?" she said to Tanner. He held the glass and turned the straw to her lips.

"Thank you." He took the glass away. "My problem is curiosity. A morbid sort of curiosity that I won't feed, if I can help it. It's a matter of . . ."

"Vanity?" Tanner provided, and the phone rang.

"I've got it," Mrs. Carlis sang, leaping to her feet.

"Whose side are you on?" his mother asked him. She said, "Take me to the greenhouse. Quick, while she's gone."

He pushed her down the brick path and in through the translucent door. "You don't really believe that, do you?" she asked.

He closed the door behind them. "Maybe not. A little vanity never hurt anyone."

She said, "Look at this—she's been watering it to death. Look at the dead buds, Tanner." She helped him tend to some of the plants, showing him leaves to trim and stakes to tie to. The humid greens and the smell of black soil were an aphrodisiac recovered from his teenage years. More than once he had hidden out here with a girl who should have been home already. When he was up on the stepladder checking the humidifier, she said to him, "I smell."

"Hm?"

"I don't smell good. Like a sick person. I need a bath before Jun Hee gets here."

He turned around and nodded. "Okay."

"I don't want Mrs. Carlis to give me another sponge bath. They don't work. I need a real bath, Tanner. Really."

He stepped down from the ladder. "That's fine. I'll do it."

"You're the only person I can ask. I'm sorry. I don't want her to do it. I have my nightgown on underneath—we can leave it."

"It's okay," Tanner said. "I'll do it."

"Before Jun Hee gets here."

"Of course." He put his hand across both of hers in her lap and tried to summon a confident look—unfazed. "Soon, you know, I won't be here all the time. Mrs. Carlis will have to do these things, or some other nurse if not her. I know you know that . . . ," he said.

Her expression turned in just the way it could now—fell away, it almost seemed, leaving a mask of sadness and weakness—and Tanner felt foolish. "Let's just make this easy?" she said.

"All right. I'm not trying to upset you."

•

HE CHECKED the temperature again but it never seemed right. When the tub was full he wheeled his mother into the bathroom. "How do you want to do this?" he asked.

"Leave the nightgown on," she told him, and he was grateful.

"Are you sure?" he asked. He stepped behind her and began to wrestle with the tiny buttons of her soft print dress. "I don't know what you want here," he said. "Let me know."

"I need a bath, that's all. I'm sorry to do this to you." Her voice was stern—had the schoolteacher's edge to it. "I don't want to see Jun Hee in this state."

"That's fine," he said. "I don't think she'd even notice, but I know what you mean."

"I'm sorry," she said. "I know it's not easy to touch me."

His throat clenched at this. "Nonsense."

He held her back away from the wheelchair to slide the dress down from one shoulder, then the other. He eased her into the chair again, then came in front and pulled the sleeves straight off, supporting each elbow in his palm. He leaned down over her and bent his left arm around her back and beneath her arms. He lifted her slightly from the chair and used his right hand, his free hand, to maneuver the dress down to her thighs. It caught here and there but he managed. When he lowered her into the chair again his cheek brushed against her nose. "Pardon me," he said. From the front of the chair he shimmied the dress beneath her thighs, off past her feet.

When she was wearing only the thin, sliplike nightgown, he put one arm behind her shoulder blades and the other beneath her legs and lifted her from the wheelchair. In the week he had become accustomed to her weight. He eased her into the water, as slowly as he could. "How's the temperature? Is it all right?" She didn't answer him and he lowered her still. "Is it okay, Mom? Hot? Cold?"

"It's fine."

When she had settled, her legs were bent at the knees and her arms lay straight along either side. Her head rested back on the porcelain lip of the tub. She had closed her eyes. "Okay?" he asked. She nodded her chin. She kept her eyes closed and lay still in the water. He wouldn't disturb her, then—it was clear she didn't want to talk. Her expression was difficult to interpret but it seemed to Tanner that she was content, possibly even relaxed.

He soaped the sponge—it smelled of lilac—and began across the sharp edges of her shoulders, then down her freckled arms. It was ridiculous, really, sponging her soaked nightgown. It clung to her torso like skin. It hung below her knees and behind her elbows. The veins on her wrists and ankles were prominent. The shapes of her small breasts and her ribs were clear. There was the wide pink of her aureoles. Was it that obvious, his fear of touching her—had it been that evident all week? He had half convinced himself he didn't feel it, and no longer hesitated that instinctual instant, as he knew he had the first day or two. He brushed the sponge along her arms, then across her legs. She kept her eyes closed and seemed to ignore him. There was no sound except the fall of the water. He wished she would say something, or open her eyes. "We'll wash this nightgown at the same time, I suppose." He spoke softly while he touched the sponge across one ear and along her neck. "Two birds . . . I guess."

Her expression was carved and set, and on closer examination Tanner saw that it was not serene as he had supposed—it was embarrassed. A look of shame and endurance. "Is it okay?" he whispered. "Tell me if the water is okay. Am I hurting you?"

She didn't open her eyes. She nodded, slowly, no. It occurred to Tanner that when this was over, he would have to take her nightgown off and change her into something dry. Only Mrs. Carlis had so far tended to his mother's change of clothes, and the nurse had left for the evening. There would be a moment when he would have to hold her empty body, naked, and this was his mother after all—how could it be a problem? He wondered if she was dwelling upon the same future.

•

WHEN JUN HEE was finally there, long after dinner, he kissed her in the doorway and hugged her and kissed her again. She smiled indulgently. Her eyes were dark and she looked tired. "How was the drive?"

"Long. I missed you, you know." He nodded and kissed her.

They sat together at the card table in the kitchen. His mother had asked to wear her yellow cotton dress, and the high collar and soft shade made her look younger. Very nearly herself. Tanner stood at the stove with a pot of raspberry tea, watching his wife and his mother together. He admired his wife's graceful questions, her nimble balance between concern and discretion.

"I hear you pretended to be asleep when you had visitors," Jun Hee said, her smile tilted toward mock disdain.

"Oh please." His mother closed her eyes and shook her head. Jun Hee laughed. "The parade of morbid tourists. Save it for the funeral is all I ask. They even wore black, Jun Hee—some of them did."

"How would you know?" Tanner said.

"I peeked."

When the tea was ready he brought three mugs, one with a straw. But his mother said, "No, thank you."

"You don't want tea?"

"No, thank you." Her tempered smile was final. "Have your own, go on."

Jun Hee told them about the strangely persistent fog that had blanketed their part of Connecticut for several days. The morning when it finally lifted, the sun through the windows felt almost excessive. The snow was gone—there had been so much this year—and already there were new spokes of green in odd patches through the lawn. Red buds on some of the trees. "It felt like a season change in a play, with the fog curtain dropped between acts." She sipped her tea. "I love New England."

Tanner's mother asked about spring in Korea. This was often her line of inquiry when Jun Hee spoke of something as distinctly American, or when she praised New England—a compliment that would extend to the old New Englander at hand, of course.

They talked about spring and summer in childhood—Jun Hee had left Korea when she was fourteen—and decided that the lure of long evening daylight translated well between cultures. While his mother told her again about Tanner's athletic boyhood—his father's awkward attempts to keep up—Tanner allowed himself to bow out. He went to the stove to refill the kettle. His mother seemed transformed by his wife's presence, though perhaps she'd only slipped into the host's demeanor she would have offered to any guest. There was an ease to her smile and to her replies, as if she were briefly unaware of her new condition.

The kettle whistled and Tanner poured more tea. He came back to the table and they were quiet together for a moment. He looked forward to putting his mother in bed and being alone with his wife.

Emma and Jun Hee began to speak at the same moment. "Go ahead," Jun Hee said, and Tanner noticed that his mother's eyes had turned the softer, uncertain shade. She said, "Well, listen, this is something I've thought about and I hope you won't mind me just telling you, dear. I hope you won't mind. Last summer, when your mother passed? I think you should have gone to the funeral. You should have," she said, nodding. "It's a long way, I know. You had your differences. But grudges should be buried before people—don't you think?"

Jun Hee breathed deeply and shrugged, and Tanner felt awkward, for both his wife and himself. She said, "You're probably right. We had a different relationship than you and Tanner, of course. But I did think I'd go back one day." There was an implied message for himself, of course, in what his mother had said. He wondered why the conversation had veered into this somber alley when they had been doing so well. "I thought I would have more time," Jun Hee said. "You know."

His mother closed her eyes and nodded. "I know, I know. I understand. It's just too bad."

Tanner asked, "What exactly brought this on, Mom?" They turned to him. "What is it we're talking about exactly?"

His mother didn't answer, and he held a hand up, inquiring, and asked, "Am I missing something?"

She stared for a long moment, then turned to his wife. "Have I upset you, Jun Hee? I didn't mean to upset you." She adopted the measured intonation of the fourth-grade teacher again, a tone never out of her reach.

"No," Jun Hee said, "of course not."

"It's something I've been meaning to tell her, Tanner. Something I've thought about—it's troubled me. If there's a reason to be sorry, then I am."

Tanner shrugged and waved his hand, relegated to the role of the classroom upstart. "Never mind." He fingered a crack in the table. "Apparently this is none of my business."

Jun Hee looked from one face to the other, then tried a smile and said, "You two are beginning to sound like you're related."

·

LATER ON, Tanner felt an expectant edge to his mother's gaze as he turned back the heavy covers and smoothed her wrinkled sheet. He avoided the question in her eyes and in her vague smile, stepped behind the wheelchair, and began to take off her dress. He was familiar now with the soft density of her inert body, but for a moment he imagined she was fighting him somehow, tensing these muscles she could no longer tense. When he came in front to pull the dress from her legs, she still watched him. He knelt down to her shoes and anticipated the question, whatever it was. But she kept quiet. He lifted her from the chair, in the different nightgown he had put on beneath her dress, and laid her down in the position she preferred to begin the night. He covered her to the neck, as she preferred, and successfully avoided her eyes.

When he turned to leave she said, "Good night, Tanner." He continued to the doorway. "Good night, Mom," he told her—it didn't emerge in as conciliatory a tone as he'd hoped—then put out the light and closed her door partway.

In the room at the end of the hall, Jun Hee had changed into her nightclothes. "The old twin bed," she said, patting the pillow beside her and raising an eyebrow. "We haven't slept in one of these in a while."

Tanner sank into the chair by his desk. "Well, tell me what you think." He leaned forward to untie his shoes. "Has she changed? You see what I mean now?"

Jun Hee shook her head. "Tanner," she said, and in the way she said it he had his answer already—she was on his mother's side. "She's confined to a wheelchair and can hardly feed herself. *Your* mother, of all people. Come on," she said, but gently.

He unbuttoned his shirt and hung it across the wicker chair. Jun Hee got into bed.

"You know, I had to give her a bath today. She's very conscious of your approval—I don't know if you realize that." He spoke quietly, just above a whisper. "She lay there, not moving or breathing even, with this look on her face as if I were hurting her."

"That must have been hard. To have to ask you to do that."

"I'm not fishing for pity." He sat down again in the chair and rubbed at one eye. "I don't mean to, anyway. But I'd like to know what that whole thing was tonight. I'd like to be told what grudges we have to bury, if that's the case."

Jun Hee shook her head no. "I don't think she was talking to you." He shrugged and she patted the covers. "Come here, would you?"

He tried to consider what part of this anger was only self-pity. "Come to bed," Jun Hee said, and he went and lay down beside her. She reached across him to turn out the light. She said, "I don't know, Tanner. Sometimes you have these ideas about the way things are. The way they should go. You always seem to think it should come out a certain way." She kissed his chest and whispered. "I don't know."

He lay on his back while his eyes adjusted to the dark.

"You've been here all week," she told him. "And she's your mother. I'm sure you're reading her better than I am. But she seems okay to me, all things considered. She'll get better, I think."

The pebbled white of his bedroom ceiling was a familiar landscape, a sort of hypnotist's wheel. He felt misplaced, young in only the least flattering ways here in his childhood bed (but this was almost a comfortably familiar feeling by now too—it too was a week old). He lay quietly with his wife laying against him, uncertain if she had fallen asleep. He remembered a night with his mother in a green dress and his father in black tie. The formality was more pronounced than usual, but not unheard-of. It was past his bedtime but they were just going out. His mother leaned in with a fragrant kiss. Then his father sat on the bed to take his turn, but behind him Emma brushed at something on his shoulders, distracting them both. "I'll tell you a secret," his father had said. "Before your mother came along I could take care of myself. Believe me?" he asked. Tanner shook his head no. There was a space opening behind his father now, a blank middle distance into which he would disappear soon. With his father it was always a parting scene.

•

IT WAS DARK but not quite too dark to see—gray shapes and outlines. He remembered where he was, listened without moving, then pushed the covers away and slid out from under Jun Hee. She hardly stirred. He stood still and listened; opened the door and listened again. The long hallway was darker than his room. Her door he'd left ajar. He stepped through quietly, into her bedroom, where her bed was a vague loaf of shadow in one corner. He went to her and bent close to the bed. Under the covers he found her cool hand and took hold of it. He listened to her crying, sat down beside her. "I'm sorry," he told her.

She cried quietly and to herself, but her whisper was cracked and fierce. "Don't you talk about me," she said. He could feel the small shaking of her head in the pillow. Her hand was cool and limp. "Don't you lie there together and talk about me," she said.

JUN HEE

WE SPOKE around the word "abortion" the day the test came back, when we were still in shock, but it was only a formality—an option too familiar and long-prepared to go unmentioned, yet easily crossed off in our excitement. "Jun Hee, you're pregnant," Tanner whispered, his smile broadening. I wondered about our decision, of course—I would feel worse now if I hadn't—especially in the mornings and early evenings during those four weeks when I was miserable and made sick by even the smell of toast. I wondered if we had thought things through well enough. I wondered what would happen to the comfortable isolation that Tanner and I had contrived. I felt the weight through my abdomen and into my thighs—of fear, I supposed, and not entirely welcome instincts. I did have questions, but each day they moved closer to being questions of how to do this right and further from the question of whether we should be doing it at all. Still, when the child was gone, she left plenty of guilt behind.

My mother came at night and took the child from me. I saw her in something like a dream. There were Tanner and I, up above everything, and the tidy oval of blanket in my arms. Be careful, Tanner said, and we were. There was the sense of accomplishment about us—we were quite pleased with ourselves (as usual). And then my mother was below us. Yoo-hoo, she called. Her bright tone frightened me because she was a serious, often dour person. I leaned out the window. She stood on the sidewalk in the burgundy dress that she had worn the last time I saw her. Come down, baby, she called with a smile. She spoke in Korean and waved to me, or perhaps to the child. The child was in front of me now. There was the small sound of traffic in my ears, then my mother: Fall down, baby. Come, come. The child was there in front of me, and though I did not give her up, I didn't reach to save her. She fell into my mother's arms; that's better, she whispered, bent over the child. When she looked up at me her face was red with tears and accusation.

I let the doctor provide her own explanation. This kind of thing happens, she said, more often than most people realize. There wasn't anything we could have done differently. She called it an "isolated tragedy" and said there was no reason to think that we couldn't try again and have a perfectly healthy baby. "I am sorry," she said, but too soon—there were others, still pregnant, in her waiting room.

I understood that the dream was something that belonged to both of us, but I didn't tell Tanner. I knew he wouldn't have accepted it. He would have resorted to medical explanations that he knew nothing about, pretending they required less of his faith. I was afraid he would want to talk me out of the dream, as if doing me a favor. I should have told him, but I didn't.

For Tanner the past was something that always led logically and fluidly into the present; he had a funny, secular belief in fate. What had happened was for the best, he decided. We had never wanted a child to begin with and had been too caught up in the excitement and surprise to remember that. He compared it to a couple who fall in love at first sight and catch a cab to city hall, unprepared for the trials and disappointments of a lifetime.

At night, Tanner and I would lie together, pretending to sleep. I wondered how the child had left my arms, and what Tanner had known or sensed when he warned me to be careful. I didn't like my mother's saying, "That's better." I didn't like her tears, as if she had done something she hated but felt obliged to do. Most of all, I was troubled by the instant in which I could have reached out and taken the baby back. I wondered if this was a test that Tanner and I had failed. I wondered if every woman was tested by her own mother before being allowed her pregnancy, and if most of them remembered passing or only felt it as a certain leveling of their consciences. A narrowing of intent. We never wished the child any harm, I told myself.

·

TANNER WAS in a minor accident on his way to work. He made a wide turn pulling into the driveway at his company while a woman tried to pass him on the right. That night he dramatized her crazy defensiveness for me, the way she flew out of her car. "I thought you were turning left," she had said. "I was looking, you started left!"

"I had my signal on," he had told her.

"You didn't have your signal on—I looked. I'm a perfectly good driver."

The insurance company she told him to call had dropped her earlier in the year and she was, in fact, uninsured. Tanner had had to speak to her again on the phone. She was recently divorced, and working for the first time in her life at the age of forty-seven—busing tables. The bottom line was that we would either break this woman's back or pay for the damage ourselves. I didn't know whether to be mad at her for allowing herself to be dependent on her former husband or sorry for her as she paid for that dependence. Telling the story, Tanner furrowed his brow and winced, as if carrying on his own debate. I smiled and finally asked, "What is it, Tanner?"

"Hm?" He looked up. "Oh, I don't know," he said, dismissively, then added, "You're laughing at me."

"I'm sorry. I'll stop."

"Do," he said, smiling. "No, it's just that—I'm driving along on a road I drive every day, a road I've driven for however many years, turning into a driveway I've turned into a thousand times. No idea what I was thinking about—I'm taking this turn without paying a bit of attention to where I am."

He sat back and shrugged. "I probably did make a wide turn. I probably do every morning. But then she barrels into me," he said, gesturing, "and suddenly, you know, I'm right there again. Back behind the wheel. There are traffic noises, and this desperate woman begging me to say it wasn't her fault. I'd even forgotten it was raining."

"Kiss me," I said. He leaned and obliged.

"'I'm a very good driver,'" he said, quoting the woman. "I didn't know what to tell her. 'I have kids,' she kept saying, as if to explain why it couldn't be her fault."

•

I CALLED my father in Seoul, catching him in the morning before he went to work. I had spoken to him only twice in the ten months since my mother's death, so I asked if he was lonely. First he said, "You should hear yourself, Jun Hee, your Korean is worse than ever." Then he answered my question. "No, your mother and I talk more now than we did when she was alive. She's becoming a nag."

"What do you mean?" I asked. "Where do you speak?" I heard the front door open and Tanner came in, home early and carrying a bag of groceries in one arm. I waved to him and attempted to look happily surprised.

"Where do you think?" my father replied. "Wherever she wants to. Sometimes she asks me questions at work, in front of people. Questions she knows will provoke me."

Tanner began to unload groceries into the refrigerator. I took the phone out to the porch. "Can't you just *think* back an answer? You don't really have to talk, do you?"

"No, Jun Hee. I talk. She talks to me, I talk back. It's a conversation."

"Forgive me—I'm not up on all of this."

"She said she's seen you," my father continued.

"No, don't tell me that," I said. After a moment I asked, "What else did she say about me?"

"She said she took your baby."

I sat down. "That's true." I kept my back to the kitchen and there was no sound behind me. "It was a terrible thing for her to do." I knew that he would disagree, that my father believed our fate lay in the hands of the dead. They weren't particularly capable of right or wrong, of good or bad judgments—they merely had whims and appetites. There was a low rattle across the phone line. He didn't have to answer me, but in his long silence there seemed an intentional cruelty. "Did she tell you why?" I asked, surprised to find myself crying.

"No." His voice was sad, yet resigned. My father maintained a self-control that exerted its presence on anyone near him. With a conscious depth in his voice, he said, "I know why, though. She told me something before she died." He waited again, and eventually said, "She told me she forgives you. She said, 'I've forgiven our Jun Hee and you will too. But her children never will. They'll never have America and they'll never have Korea either.'"

I wiped a hand across my face, angry at myself for crying. It put me at a disadvantage with him. "That isn't fair," I said. "You both knew that we had no plans for children." I whispered, not wanting Tanner to hear me. "She had no right to take it away, to decide for us."

"Don't argue with me—I'm telling you what she said. Besides, you know, children or not, the fact is you've brought the end of our family. It's not your mother's fault."

My head was swimming and I felt suddenly foolish for calling him. Could I have expected anything better than this? So I disconnected the line. I sat still a moment and wiped my eyes again. Then I went to the kitchen and hung up the phone. Tanner was out of sight. On the porch I sat in a frayed lawn chair. I wondered if my father was pleased with the phone call, or if he could still feel sorry for me. I knew the next time I talked to him, in a month or a year, there would be no reference to any of this. We would act as if it hadn't happened and resume our narrow roles. And wasn't that exactly the way I wanted it? Wasn't that particular distance what I had been so careful to maintain since leaving Korea?

When Tanner came out onto the porch he had changed into shorts and a T-shirt. His right hand was taped up and his pinkie was stiff with a splint. He sat down in the chair across from me, and I sniffled and leaned forward.

"Guess who got into an accident?" he said, smiling and holding the hand out. "Broke the finger in two places. I may have totaled the rental car."

He laughed and I did too. I wiped my eyes. "What happened?"

"I missed a dog and hit a tree in the process. My pinkie turned backward when the hand hit the dash."

"Tanner!" I sat beside him and he laughed again. "What should we do with you?"

He said, "I blacked out for a minute too. They took me to the hospital, but decided my head was fine. We didn't discuss my driving skills."

"You should have called me."

"Frank gave me a ride. I didn't think you'd be home yet."

I smiled and shook my head. "And you stopped for groceries?"

"No lunch. I'm famished."

•

I WENT to a Catholic church where two Korean families I knew worshipped. I didn't hope or expect to see either of them. It was just the only church in the area that I knew anything about. I picked a Thursday morning—I didn't want Tanner to know—and called the lab to say I'd be in late.

My mother never left the Buddhasasana, though she had to face a lot of teasing and worse from my father over the years. He'd had a Protestant "uncle" from Britain when he was young—a friend of his father's. He always proudly insisted that he was a Protestant, and he liked to tell me, often while angry, the story of Christ. It was a surprisingly flexible metaphor in his hands. Later, at the girl's school he sent me to here, I realized how little he really understood Christianity and how his Mahayana Buddhist upbringing had colored his sense of it.

I knew the connection to my mother was thin at best in this church, but I went for my own sake—maybe I would feel closer to her.

It was a new, squat building with white aluminum siding and very few windows—industrial-strength religion. The only sign of holiness from the outside was a small golden cross, perched at the front crown of the roof like a weather vane. I arrived at twenty after eight and the next mass was scheduled for nine, which didn't bother me at all. It was the first time I had been in a church in seven years, and the last time had been for our wedding. I found a pew far enough from the altar that I wouldn't feel intimidated but close enough to help me work up something like a prayer. I folded my hands in my lap. There was a ceramic figure of the Virgin Mary hanging by the altar, her eyes cast down on the congregation.

When I thought of the baby I pictured the bundle of blanket from the dream, but I knew my child had been little more than a fertilized egg and a lot of blood. There were the films I had seen in college charting the development of the fetus—the tight curl of the back; the odd, oversized head; the translucent hands and dark red fingers. The wrinkled blue of this Mary's ceramic gown was nicely done. She had wide shoulders and a small bosom. Eventually I asked to speak to my mother—trying to dismiss the image of a receptionist that had come to mind, a celestial waiting room. Despite what my father had said, I didn't speak aloud.

I closed my eyes and that helped me to concentrate, to see her in my memory. *I want to talk to you. About what you did to Tanner and me.* I pictured her hearing me and considering an answer—tempted to lecture, very likely. *I want to know why you did it. I deserve an explanation.* I tried to imagine the weight of perspective into her features—the confidence of ghosts, the thoughtfulness my father had mentioned. I wondered what she had done with my daughter, and I wanted to see the child too, but my imagination had limits.

I waited a bit, then opened my eyes. There was a yellow glow in the church from the candlelight and the morning sun through the clerestory windows. A clean smell, like varnish.

No one was close enough to overhear. I rested my chin on my folded hands, on the back of the pew before me. "I don't know if this church helps anything or not, for you," I whispered. "I mean it though. I'm not asking too much."

I waited a little longer, thinking about my mother in Korea: the shuffle of her slippers and the bags under her eyes. "You owe me this," I whispered, trying to sound matter-of-fact rather than bitter. Then I stood to go. I decided to make the sign of the cross—what could it hurt?

•

At work, Tanner left the power on while wiring a control box and gave himself a shock that could have been fatal. He managed a smile that evening, but he was no longer up to a laugh. "So what's the story?" I asked. "You're worrying me, you know."

He said, "I haven't felt this clumsy since puberty. I'm regressing."

We had a leisurely dinner that occupied most of the evening. When we had finished dessert and there was only the last of the wine and a litter of dirty dishes before us, he said, "You want to know a secret?"

"I live for secrets." I felt pleasantly drunk. We both slumped in our chairs. Tanner swallowed at length, and then his lips—the object of my attention—thinned into a vaguely ironic grin.

"The night before the miscarriage," he said, "I was laying there beside you, couldn't sleep. You'd been out cold for a while and at some point, I decided I would turn the spare room into a nursery. I started planning how to do it."

He turned the grin in my direction, then back to the wineglass that he held in both hands. He said, "So okay. Clear out the wallpaper, first thing. I was thinking I'd paint the walls a light blue, maybe strip and stain the top molding."

I nodded. "Even if it was a girl?"

"Sure. I think so. I was thinking of some baseboards all the way around," he said, tracing a circle with his finger, "a nice cherry stain. A good crib in place of the bed. Painted wicker is what I had in mind, but I suppose I might have checked with you."

"Thanks."

"We'd have a mobile, of course. And pull the dresser out—we'd replace it with a new one in matching wicker. The drawers should smell like cedar. It could have a cloth top for changing diapers. Where the desk is I've got a bassinet and a hamper. What did I forget?"

I shrugged.

"A clock on the wall with fat numbers and a mouse on the minute hand. When I looked at the alarm clock I'd been at it for two hours. Just imagining it and laying it out. I was still wide awake though, so I actually got out of bed and went down the hall and sat in the room for a little while, looked out the window. Thinking about the view in the morning."

I had been with the child and my mother that night, perhaps while Tanner was in the nursery. It seemed to me that the accumulation of seven years of marriage hadn't closed all the gaps I had thought it would.

Tanner turned to face me and his grin widened apologetically. "It's the coldest room in the house—I thought about it later. It's on that corner with just the one duct."

"We could have changed that," I said. "We install another."

"No, it's too far from our room. We might not have heard the baby at night."

"We would have," I said.

•

He hit himself on the thumb with a hammer—not a hard thing to do, really. Then he got a sleeve caught in a stand-up drill, though it only scratched his wrist and ripped the shirt.

But he decided we needed a little trip. We would drive up to New Hampshire and hike in the White Mountains, a "someday" he'd been talking about for quite a while. We could do two day-hikes, and find a bed and breakfast for the Saturday night between. Friday, on the way up, we would spend with his mother. We both had the vacation time coming, and we both knew the break was overdue. We simply decided to go the very next weekend, and packed.

The day before we left I got our checking statement in the mail. There were two checks written by Tanner to a Janet Holden, each for two hundred dollars. It took me a moment to remember that Janet Holden was the woman who had hit Tanner's car, the woman with no insurance. At first I felt simple jealousy, but then I wondered why he hadn't said anything—I was the one who balanced our checkbook, so paying with a check was as good as telling me. I wondered if she had asked for this, and how they had decided on the figure. I felt a little angry too—we already had more than one premium to cover from his string of accidents. How long did he intend to keep up his philanthropy? But of course we could afford it—it was only that he hadn't told me. I didn't feel like playing the role of the nagging wife, or giving him the part of the good-hearted husband, so I decided to let him come and explain it to me. I left the statement out on the desk.

That night he said nothing, though I was sure he'd seen it. Friday morning we packed up the car and left.

We took the back way, through the Berkshires on Route 7 and into Vermont. Tanner worried about seeing his mother again. It had been three months since her stroke, and he'd been to visit and care for her several times. She had a full-time nurse and refused to live anywhere but in her home—a fact that bothered Tanner but that went right along with everything I had admired in her since we'd first met.

The nurse, whose name was Mrs. Carlis, greeted us from the doorway. "There they are," she sang as we stepped out of the car. She had a way of drawing her greetings out, with a soaring inflection. "Right . . . on . . . time," she said. "Right on time!" She was a loud and smothering presence, the kind of woman who wore no makeup on principle and was sure to tell you so within an hour of meeting you. I liked her.

Tanner's mother was charming and affectionate, clearly pleased with our sudden visit. He kissed her cheek and took her folded hands from her lap. He squatted before her wheelchair and whispered something to her. I gazed out the window and waited. His mother said, "Oh, stop it. Get lost now, and let me talk to your wife."

We all sat through the last of the afternoon on her porch. Tanner blushed while listing his recent accidents, and his mother smiled with concern. Occasionally she asked Mrs. Carlis to cross or uncross her legs for her, then to find her sun hat. In the time since our last visit I had forgotten the stillness with which she listened to people now—her concentration was both flattering and intimidating. But Mrs. Carlis carried the burden of tsks and sighs and waved hands for both of them. "Oh, no," she said to Tanner. "Oh, that's terrible. My goodness, what you've been through."

His mother said, "Do you expect more damage, or is this it now?"

Tanner shrugged. "If I knew . . . I don't have any scheduled, though."

"That's good. Don't lose your confidence," she said. "Just the same, we'll go with plastic knives for dinner, I suppose."

In the evening Tanner went out for ice cream and Mrs. Carlis disappeared into her room. "One thing I'll give her," Tanner's mother whispered to me, "she's careful to allow me some privacy."

"That's important," I said.

"Yes. She's okay. She's better than you might think. Sometimes

I like her chatter—it keeps me preoccupied. And when I'm tired of her, I say so."

I nodded. She asked me about Tanner—what I thought was causing all of his accidents. I said I didn't know, but I couldn't believe it was just coincidence any longer. "No," she said, "I think he's expecting things to go wrong. There's something in the way he walks, I think. Or maybe the eyes—I'm not sure." Then she said what we were both really thinking, a talent of hers. "I believe it's his way of dealing with the miscarriage."

She waited for my reaction. I didn't like the word "miscarriage" and never had—I thought it seemed to lay the blame on me, as though I had mishandled my own uterus. I instantly felt the urge to tell her my dream though—to explain what had really happened and hear her advice.

When I was still quiet she said, "How about you? Any of your own self-punishment?" There was empathy in her voice, nothing accusing or patronizing. I had given up comparisons to my own mother a long time ago, but there were still moments of envy.

"I don't know," I said. "There's guilt. Sometimes I wonder how much we really wanted a baby."

"Yes."

I was tempted to tell her, but the truth was that I really didn't know this woman as well as she and I sometimes pretended. If she had the wrong reaction it would be disastrous, and I felt a little selfish about the dream by now too.

I said, "Tanner thinks it was all for the best, that maybe we weren't ready for her."

"It was a girl?"

"In my mind it was." We both heard Tanner's car come up the driveway.

She said, "I hope you won't feel I'm butting in if I tell you this: no one is ever ready, Jun Hee. You should try again." She nodded. "Tanner told me what the doctor said—that it was an isolated thing—and I do think the best way for both of you to get over it is to try again. You'll have a perfect child this time."

That night we slept in the twin bed that had been Tanner's since childhood. Strangely, there had never been a guest room in this spacious house—it seemed an odd sort of Yankee stinginess to me. Mrs. Carlis had been forced to make do with a back room that was still appointed as Tanner's father's study, though he had been dead two decades or so.

Each time we slept over, we both went through the shifting positions that I remembered from the nights we'd spent together in college: lying close and entangled at first, separating slowly as our limbs became numb and sleep began to feel more important than intimacy, finally dividing the narrow bed into halves.

Tonight I found myself unable to sleep. I lay with my back to Tanner and my cold feet tucked beneath his calves. I imagined I could see the waves of his even breath in the room, the way I could sometimes picture the landscape of music. It was comforting, but I still felt oddly lonely.

And distant too—at a remove from both Tanner and my family. I had been in this country for a long time—through high school and into college, with the phone calls and my mother weeping and the letters full of affection and guilt—before I understood that this distance was inside me, that it was native to me. She told me that when I was born she had an idea—or a premonition. It came to her during labor, she claimed, when little else could get through. She guessed that she was about to have a daughter, and then she saw the years of my life flip by, a quick film from birth to death. I was going to live a long time apparently, and age well, with a straight back. This must have been a consolation, given her disappointment that I wouldn't be a son.

My first birthdays I only know by the photos. They would dress me in a silk pants suit—royal blue, a new size each year. My parents were not yet wealthy when I was young, and this was an unusual extravagance. The suits always took up one end of my closet: all of them a nearly identical blue, each one shorter than the next, each worn only once.

In the earliest years that I can recall, when I was five and six, there was a lot of expectation and excitement attached to the photo session. Before dawn my mother would come to wake me with the new clothes folded over one arm and a wide smile—a rare gift from her. We never spoke above a whisper while getting me dressed. I followed her cues. Her hands would be busy straightening and creasing, turning me around and back again.

My father would have the camera ready on a pile of books on top of a table (only later did he own a tripod). They counted floorboards to be sure the distance was the same each year. I assumed, when I was young, that he was as invested as my mother in this idea, but at some point I recognized that he was just going along, indulging her. I stood in front of the screen that had come from a fisherman in my mother's village, some generations before her. It depicted a fantasy: the carp leapt from the river into boats and each tree held a moon. My shoulders back, arms by my sides, I stared into the lens.

When I was positioned, my father and my mother took their places out of the frame and together we waited for dawn. I had been born at dawn—apparently the timing was important. The window behind them faced east toward the mills, but they stood with their backs to it, their eyes set on me. I had to watch the camera, but I learned how wide peripheral vision could be. They stood together but never close, my father's hand on the camera, waiting for the signal, and my mother's nervous eyes inspecting for the first light to fall across my cheeks. Over the years this wait began to swallow up the rest of the ceremony in my mind, and I half dreaded my birthday. For quite a while though, I had thought it was customary, that everyone went through this. Later I was deeply embarrassed; I stopped telling friends, and pestered my mother until she hid the blue suits in a box under the bed.

In the photos the progression was clear: the shadings in my face, one year to the next, from pride to concentration to boredom and resentment. I did understand early that the photos belonged to my mother, that this was her ceremony and not particularly mine, but I have an image of my own for each year as well, and in them her progression is similar: from pride to sadness and disappointment. There is the morning, coming through the windows to surround her, and the particular stillness, the empty promise. Sometimes I flinched at the click of the camera, having almost forgotten that I was posing.

I listened to Tanner's deep breathing, then eased my legs out of the covers and tiptoed to the door. In the living room I fumbled until I found the phone. I dialed my father's number while counting the hours: he would be just home from work.

The connection was bad—pops and clicks, the muffled echo of a ring. It occurred to me that I had nothing to say to him, that he was only a way to her. I tried to think of some transition, from small talk back to my dream, but no one was answering. He wasn't home. I hung up and sat back on the couch. The nighttime was pale through the windows—a nearly full moon somewhere behind the clouds.

I concentrated. Then I reached my arms out and felt the small weight and warmth, supported in my hands. I lunged forward—in that instant I didn't have to think or decide, because she was falling. I reached out and took her from the air. I took her in and whispered to her, held her tightly against my chest.

•

It was only a drizzle on the drive north the next morning, and sometimes it dried up completely for a stretch. The sky was gray, though, with no sign of light. When we were almost there we stopped at a visitors' center to ask a forest ranger about trail conditions. The woman marched through a list of obviously well-rehearsed warnings: trails may be wet and footing slippery, step with care; temperatures can drop thirty degrees in a matter of hours, always pack prepared; conditions above tree line can change in minutes, keep an eye on the sky. We told her we were aiming for Mount Madison but she said, "No. No no, not today," and recommended a peak called Mount Hale instead. She sold us a map and pointed out the safest trails. Her brown uniform was starched and she never bent her back. "Enjoy your stay in the White Mountains," she commanded.

We drove the few miles to the trailhead, Tanner imitating her, and parked our car by the narrow opening through the trees. We checked the map once more, then started up the first trail to the Hale mountain cutoff. There were exposed roots and shallow puddles, but we were wearing sneakers and the footing wasn't really so bad. In the distance, whichever way you looked, the trees seemed to mesh with the low sky into a gauzy gray. Occasional branches stretched across the trail and showered us when we cleared the way.

Tanner was a little giddy, here at last. He decided the weather would clear when we were at the top and tomorrow would be a perfect day and we would probably see some deer or a moose. "A bear," I said. "I don't go back to Connecticut without a bear."

We crossed a fast river on a footbridge and the trail began to rise more sharply. The rain picked up a little, but we could hardly tell beyond the sound it made on the ceiling of leaves above us. Our breathing picked up as well, and I could feel the sweat run down my back and the insides of my arms. We began to take short breaks, to rest our calves and take the packs from our shoulders. At one point there was a rocky, exposed outcropping, and the valley below was lost in fog. The trees fell off into a green carpet and disappeared.

It happened slowly, but somewhere along the way the mountain became much steeper. We took breaks more often, but we didn't talk much—in a way, it didn't seem necessary. We smiled, though: we were together, both pleased.

I began to think about the woman with the car who had hit Tanner—I couldn't remember her name. I thought of asking him right then about the checks, but the trail switched-back along a sharp slope, and it just seemed like too much effort. Soon I decided that I wouldn't ask—that he had no right to play this silence game when he knew that I knew. It all reminded me unpleasantly of something my father might do.

Maybe we were both distracted by thoughts, but it suddenly seemed that the trees were much shorter and the fog was dense and cool. "We must be close to tree line," Tanner said, and in a few minutes we were there. The trees receded into tough, squat shrubs and we were literally in a cloud. It was fantastic. You could only see a short distance in any direction and the mist rolled and tumbled across the rocks and up the mountain. It wasn't really raining any longer, but the fog was so heavy that it turned into drops on our parkas. Almost immediately there were droplets sown through Tanner's hair and strung through his eyebrows and hanging from his lashes.

"This is strange," he said.

"It's amazing." The silence was fuzzy and hollow, as if it would swallow up even a scream. Tanner took my hand, and I realized how wonderfully alone we were. We hadn't come upon another hiker all day.

"What time do you think it is?" he asked. I looked at my watch; it was past twelve thirty.

"Well," he said, "what do you think?"

He was asking what we should do, and I couldn't believe it. I couldn't believe he would actually consider turning back. "We must be close," I said. "The weather's the same as it's been all day—it's not even raining, really. Where's the map? Let's see where we are."

We studied the contours but we didn't know how to tell how far we had come. It didn't show the tree line, and on the back it explained that the level varied across the mountain, depending on exposure.

"We can't be too far," I said. "I can't imagine giving up now."

"Okay."

"We can have lunch at the peak. Maybe it'll clear a little and we'll get a view."

"Okay," he said again.

"Tanner. Do you want to do this?"

"I do." He nodded, avoiding my eyes. When he looked at me, he said, "Yes, I do. Let's just keep an eye on the sky, as our friendly ranger advised."

It didn't take long for the shrubs to give way to bare rock, with stone cairns every now and then to mark the trail. At first we could see two or three cairns ahead, but eventually the fog revealed only one at a time. The cloud moved past us and straight up the mountain, and I imagined that it could carry us: that we could close our eyes and let ourselves be lifted to the peak, and right past it.

Just when we were beginning to lose some confidence (at least I was; Tanner's concerned expression was steady and hard to read) we came to a wooden sign knocked in between the rocks. It marked a separation of two trails. One way led down a half mile to a mountain hut, and the other a mile up to the peak of Mount Hale. We took the Hale fork, and for some time it was nearly a flat grade—even downhill in places—so we moved quickly. At one point Tanner made a small leap between rocks, but his foot slid when he landed. He skinned the palm of one hand and tore a hole in the knee of his jeans.

"Put some antibiotic on your hand," I said.

He shook his head. "I don't want any. I'm fine."

Soon the trail turned back uphill, as we knew it had to, and I began to wonder if our cloud wasn't getting darker. For the first time, the possibility of a thunderstorm occurred to me. I couldn't understand why we hadn't made the peak yet, and I kept looking ahead, past Tanner, for the leveling off that would signal the top of the mountain.

Then he stopped, unexpectedly. I sensed everything right away, so when he said, "I don't know where the trail went," I wasn't surprised. We looked around us for a cairn.

"Let's backtrack," I said, but we each had a different idea of the way we had come. For a few minutes I followed Tanner, but I knew he was going too directly downward—we had come up and across.

"This is wrong," I said. "I think the trail's to the right some." He kept walking ahead of me. I stopped. "Tanner. You already got us lost. You don't know where you're going." Now he stopped. He sat down heavily, dejectedly, and lay down against his pack. There was something unnatural and afraid in his face.

I knelt beside him. "We can't be far, really. Why don't we look at the map?"

He held his hands interlocked over his closed eyes, the palms outward. One was spotted with thin lines of blood from the fall. "What good is the map if we're not on a trail?" he said. "We don't even know how to read the fucking map."

I felt it all drain out of me—my energy, my confidence, my enthusiasm for this trip. I said, "When's the last time you remember seeing a cairn? How long ago?" He shook his head. "Tanner, what's the matter? Are you sick? You're acting strange."

I expected him to sit up and deny it, make an effort to reassure me that he was all right. But all he did was shake his head no. "You're scaring me," I said. Finally he opened his eyes. "Let's eat lunch," I suggested. I took my pack off and opened it. "Let's eat something and have some water and try to think about this without panicking. All right, Tanner?"

He closed his eyes again and nodded, then took his pack off.

"I don't know what I was thinking," he said, eventually. He bit into a sandwich and stared vacantly at the rocks and the fog. "I thought I could tell the trail by the smooth rocks and forgot about the cairns." A bit later he said, "All the rocks are smooth."

After we'd eaten, we cut straight across the mountain and I kept thinking I saw the vague form of a cairn emerging, but it never happened. I kept my watch out now—it was already close to three, and in this weather it would be dark well before eight. I began to lead and Tanner followed me with his head down, watching each step he took. I got angry. "Tanner, what are you doing? You're not even looking for the trail."

"I don't want to slip again," he said. He held his bloody palm up. "Let's stop a minute and put something on that. Please?"

We got out the first-aid kit and I rubbed antibiotic cream into his cuts. "I figure if we find the trail," I said, just thinking of it then, "we can follow it to that hut. It's not very far, and maybe we could spend the night there." It occurred to me that I was treating him like a child. "You lead," I said.

He seemed a little more attentive now, and I found my mind wandering. I imagined that if the sun burned through for just a minute or two we would see the cairns and the shape of the mountain around us. Maybe the trail would be right there, a few yards away. Then the name came to me, for no apparent reason: Janet Holden. I could see it written across the canceled checks. I told myself, We woke up this morning in Tanner's old bed in White River. Tonight we'll sleep in a lumpy motel bed, or in a sleeping bag at the warm hut. I promised myself that I'd be thankful.

Janet Holden, Janet Holden: it ran through my mind with each step I took. I couldn't get rid of it.

When it was almost five o'clock my shoulders were burning under the pack and my legs were rubber. I realized, at last, that Tanner had completely given up. He didn't seem to be concerned about where we were—he wasn't looking around at all. He was wandering ahead slowly with his head down. So this was the overdue end of a protracted collapse for him, I thought, and I was both sorry and angry. I was angry at the pity I felt too, and at the fact that he had been so reduced. But this wasn't really Tanner anymore, I told myself. For all intents and purposes I was alone.

At some point I began to cry, and I just sat down. Tanner lay back on the rock beside me, acting as though he couldn't hear me. I got so angry that I punched him hard on the arm. He jumped and glared at me.

"Oh, he lives!" I yelled. "He still feels pain—thank God for that."

He rubbed his arm. I was busy crying and didn't notice the change, but after a while he spoke. "We should go down," he said softly.

"What?"

"We should go *down*. Straight down. We'd have shelter in the trees. We might be able to find water."

I continued to cry, despite myself. I hugged him and leaned against him, though I wasn't any less angry yet. "You had no right to leave me alone," I said. "You can't do that—don't do that."

He did hug me back. When I was under control he stood and helped me up. He said, "Let's get to the cover of the trees at least," and started down. I watched him a minute, walking away. I had the feeling of some kind of ending—though not of our marriage or anything as easy as that. It was the same feeling I had had the morning I discovered I was pregnant.

The way down was steep, and the fog wrapped more thickly around us. I listened to my own breathing and imagined that I could let go, just let myself lean over and begin to fall. I would tumble down the long slope and land in the wet embrace of a lake—but comfortably, it seemed.

And then Tanner saw the sign to the hut. He pointed and said, "There it is," as casually as could be. It was the same wooden trail marker we had come to hours before. As a celebration, we ate the last of our sandwiches and a good part of our trail mix. We followed the trail down, and neither of us lost sight of the stone markers. In a few minutes, the eerie shape of the hut emerged from the muddy gray around it.

•

THERE WAS a couple from upstate New York who lent us sweatshirts and pants to wear while we dried our own by a kerosene heater. We had missed dinner, but one of the workers at the hut made us hot soup and coffee. At first she seemed to think I wouldn't understand English; she leaned in to me and spoke slowly. I decided not to be offended, and when I answered her question fluently she seemed to apologize with her gestures and her smile. "You're lucky," she said, pouring our soup. "There isn't always room at the inn."

A little later a thunderstorm swept through, distant and indistinct initially, then completely surrounding us. Lightning flashed across the mountain in sheets, and the shadows were quick and long. Tanner and I sat on a wooden bench with our backs against the wall—I had been reading a guidebook. He laid his head down in my lap and put his arms around my waist. There was a younger couple watching us from across the room. But I touched his hair and leaned across his back. I missed him a little, as if we were still apart. "I'm glad we're not sleeping in the woods," he said.

We slept in wooden bunks, Tanner above me, in borrowed sleeping bags. I could hear him slip into sleep immediately, and was surprised to find myself awake. When I closed my eyes I saw an endless pattern of rocks; I felt the stepping up and the stepping down still in my bones. I opened my eyes and listened to the sound of the rain against the roof and imagined Tanner and I out beneath the trees. In Korean, I recited one of the meditations I had learned as a child from my mother, the only one I could remember: I asked the bodhisattvas to help me to accept the world of *dukkha* and impermanence, to help me shed my desire to control. Maybe I felt better. Not much better.

We might well try to have another baby—not soon, I knew, but at some point we would. Until then it would be just the two of us, which was as much as I had wanted until recently. My mother had never been available in any way I could accommodate. The day she died, I had thought it would be hypocritical to mourn as someone else might, another daughter—or as I would have if I had stayed in Korea. I went through a couple of weeks at a distance from myself. My father asked me to come to the burial, but I refused.

But there in the hut I said to her, I know I gave my child up. I'm sorry I let you down.

I saw her this time. She was in a burial gown. I don't know why she lowered her eyes before her daughter. In this dream I told her, Take care of my baby. The clouds skimmed past us, across the stones. I had the familiar feeling—nothing worthwhile to offer her. I wanted to touch her skin, but she wouldn't let me. She raised her eyes. She looked impatient, and different—not wise, though, so much as disgusted, beyond sympathy or understanding for me, as I'd never seen her in life. Take care of my child, I said. But she said, Go home.

AËRONAUTS

4 January 1896
Grenna

Dear Mrs. Hamilton,

You will not remember me, I suppose, but one day in 1876, under the auspices of your dear and well-remembered uncle, you and I very nearly went aloft together from the town of Huntingdon. It was an Independence Day celebration in your country. The balloon, alas, was punctured, and could not be mended. We rode the train from and back to Philadelphia together. Do you recall?

I have been compelled by a Swedish newspaper to compile a bit of a remembrance article and thus I have been recounting my trip to America, among other experiences. In any event, I was told some time ago that you married and have borne lovely children. Two is the number I was given. My congratulations. I write to you today simply to say that, speaking as a man who has (you may be surprised to hear) gained some connections and a little stature in the world of modern day aëronautics, I may tell you that your uncle is still remembered and regarded indeed as an important pioneer. And you yourself are recalled as well, in your continuation of his achievements. But perhaps you know this already. If so, forgive me.

Will you extend my greeting and warmest regards to all your family? And if you remember me, will you write only to say how you are now and what the children's names are? If you do not remember me naturally do please pardon the intrusion and do not bother to reply.

> Yours in all best intentions,
> "Andrée" (Mr. Salomon August)

7 January 1896

Dear Mr. Robert Hamilton,

Perhaps if you have received a letter from myself recently with the date of 4 January and it has perplexed or troubled you with its impropriety will you forgive me please and ascribe the accident to the ill manners of a foreigner? My every apology. If you have not received such a letter then my additional apologies.

> Yours with respect,
> Mr. Salomon Andrée

•

COUNT C. A. EHRENSVÄRD (captain, Swedish support ship): We who would stay behind in safety felt very anxious that morning, but Andrée appeared, as he always did, quite calm and self-possessed, not a trace of emotion visible on his countenance. Nothing but an expression of firm resolution and indomitable will.

ANDRÉE: Strindberg! Fraenkel! Let's get in the car.

NILS STRINDBERG (aëronaut, Andrée's Polar Expedition, 1897): [*passing a letter*] See that this gets to Anna, will you?

ALEXIS MACHURON (aëronautical engineer): [*taking the letter*] I will, I will. Get aboard now.

KNUT FRAENKEL (aëronaut, Andrée's Polar Expedition, 1897): [*hums Swedish anthem; steps lightly into balloon car*]

ALEXIS MACHURON: [*testing the wind*] Give it a minute, everyone. Stay calm.

ANDRÉE: You must not expect to hear from us for a year. Possibly two.

COUNT C. A. EHRENSVÄRD: I said to him, "We shall hear from you much sooner than that!" But he was not listening to me.

LIEUT. G. V. E. SVEDENBORG: There were three strong men at the rope moorings tied to the gondola. They held their knives at the ready. Above us the balloon tugged and bobbed as if it was a chained beast. We all thought of the year before—our lack of wind. This time we would have a launch!

ALEXIS MACHURON: [*nods*] Okay.

ANDRÉE: Cut away everywhere!

LIEUT. G. V. E. SVEDENBORG: And off they went! Great shouts all round!

ANDRÉE: [*to engineers and friends below*] Greet Old Sweden!

ENGINEERS AND FRIENDS BELOW: Long Live Andrée!

·

DR. NILS GUSTAF EKHOLM (would-be-aëronaut, Andrée's Polar Expedition, 1896): I will tell you—it's not a secret—that I am certain Andrée himself knew the plan was misconceived. Therefore, why did he go? [*waits*] Can you tell me?

TATIANA FREIBORG (biographer): I don't know why.

DR. EKHOLM: Don't you?

TATIANA FREIBORG: No, sir. But I'd be curious to hear your theory.

DR. EKHOLM: [*shifts uneasily—leather sounds*] He took caution once, after all. [*gestures—open palms*] The summer before, as I am sure you know. When I was meant to be with him instead of this Fraenkel. [*looks out the window at the snow*] Yes, we did not get the wind. But I had convinced him the balloon was not safe in any case. It leaked! [*waits; eventually, with emphasis*] You see?

TATIANA FREIBORG: I think so, sir.

DR. EKHOLM: [*takes his glasses off; cleans them, patiently*]

TATIANA FREIBORG: Perhaps not.

DR. EKHOLM: It was the same balloon! The same balloon in 1897! [*a pause—he stares, affronted*] He took two men with him!

•

11 February 1896
Göteborg

Dear Mrs. Hamilton,

How very kind of you to reply and how very pleasant to hear from you and hear you are better than well—indeed, flourishing. Mary Beth and Benjamin sound like very fine names (exotic to this Scandinavian ear). I'm sure the children both have their mother's kindness and gentleness and sharpness of mind in addition to equally good qualities from their father. You will be surprised (evidently) to hear that I myself have not married. I must admit to being curious why you felt so certain I would have . . .

. . . I did see that play myself although I don't find time for the theatre often. It caused quite a sensation here too. Mr. Ibsen is not Swedish as a matter of fact but from Norway. Near enough, one might say. We have a famous play-writer as well, who is named Strindberg, but perhaps his plays are not translated into English . . .

9 March 1896
Stockholm

. . . So you have heard? I'm flattered to know the news has reached you there. Yes, the plans and preparations are rather furious now. We sail for Spitzbergen on or about the 1st day of June, go aloft from there. At this moment I am meant to be reviewing accounts—I could steal myself away and close the door of my office only with such an excuse. But how much more pleasant to answer your letter.

I remember it just as you do: the charm of that little train and the pleasant isolation of our berth, my persistent naïveté (as the French would say) and the many strong opinions I endeavored to impress you with. I do recall the great crowd in the square, and all those ribbons on hats flying from the heads of the ladies. I recall your uncle impressing the crowd with his explanations. I had thought he would play the seller (you have a word in English, I think?), but I was much impressed with his little lecture in aëronautics, and how he made the people see that anyone could go aloft. I was even disappointed at this, to be truthful. I had thought he would present us as dare-devils and I think I felt myself a dare-devil . . .

How sorry I am to hear that it has been so many years since you yourself have gone aloft, although, if you say I must, I will take you at your word that you don't miss it. I can be gallant that way you see.

By the way, I must clarify: Mr. Nils Strindberg, my companion, is not the play-writer himself, but his nephew.

•

August Strindberg (in a letter):

PLAN:

I begin by searching out the primal elements of the world and their transmutation into one another in the volcanoes. I descend into the depths of the ocean with the Deep Sea divers and observe the origin of life out of water. Ascend into the air with the Balloonists and use their observations to reach my conclusions about the atmosphere and the way in which the earth took shape, as well as its relationship to the firmament and the other worlds beyond our own ...

If I finally encounter God, perhaps you as a Pantheist won't want anything further to do with me, but we'll see about that when the time comes!

•

ANDRÉE: I often feel a thing has not happened to me yet, or at any rate it hasn't gained the full weight of truth, until I have written it down somewhere.

•

ANDRÉE: In the year 1876, when I was a young man of twenty-two, I collected together my meager savings and sailed for the port of New York, determined to get to Philadelphia and the Centennial Exposition. I had already at that time a powerful interest in science of all varieties. In my bag I had packed *Laws of the Winds*, by Professor C. F. E. Björling, and when we had left the land well behind I settled down in my cabin to read. I was transfixed. Björling's description of the trade winds and thermal currents reliably circling the globe, little understood and largely unremarked, and of the divisible strata of our atmosphere, made me feel I had been duped in some way or had at least settled for a set of hemmed-in ambitions. I read the whole volume through. Then I went up on deck and watched a gull sailing along above the steamer, and I began to recognize that there was an additional realm, enveloping ours, with its own rules and physical laws, its own avenues and neighborhoods, its remote deserts and great half-charted rivers. The idea took hold in me that I wished to be among the first to explore that realm.

Once in Philadelphia, it did not take me long to be in con-

tact with the great aëronaut, John Wise. He was a man who had
been building his own balloons for forty years, discovering their
faults and possibilities through perilous trial and error and thrill-
ing audiences with his launches, although he was ever a scientist
first and a showman only by necessity. He believed that inter-
city balloon post and trans-continental balloon coaches were
perfectly feasible and merely awaited proper funding and the
public's better understanding of aëronautical safety. To prove the
latter he had taken strangers and young ladies from his family
on flights and allowed them to operate the aërostat with a few
minutes' training. He had flown directly into lightning storms
and had intentionally exploded his balloon when five hundred
meters up, sailing safely to the ground on the parachute he'd
improvised from the remains of his bag. These exhibitions had
perhaps failed at their intended effect, but they had certainly
given the old man a reputation as a courageous individual.

•

JOHN WISE (aëronaut): Now, as we rise up in the atmosphere, there
are two causes acting in beautiful harmony upon the invalid
calculated to produce the most happy results. While the most
sublime grandeur is gradually opening to the eye and the mind
. . . the atmospheric pressure is also gradually diminishing upon
the muscular system, allowing it to expand, the lungs becoming more voluminous, taking in larger portions of air at each
inhalation, and these portions containing larger quantities of
caloric or electricity than those taken in on the earth, and the
invalid feels at once the new life pervading his system, physically
and mentally. The blood begins to course more freely when up
a mile or two with a balloon, the excretory vessels are more
freely opened, the gastric juice pours into the stomach more
rapidly, the liver, kidneys and heart work under expanded action
in a highly calorified atmosphere, the brain receives and gives
more exalted inspirations, the whole animal and mental system

becomes intensely quickened, and more of the chronic morbid matter is exhaled and thrown off in an hour or two while two miles up on a fine summer's day than the invalid can get rid of in a voyage from New York to Madeira by sea.

•

ANDRÉE: When I had come to know Mr. Wise well enough to ask if he might take me aloft, he immediately agreed and suggested I join his niece, who was scheduled to make an Independence Day ascension from the town of Huntingdon in western Pennsylvania. We boarded the train the evening of the third. Mr. Wise's niece—whose name I cannot recall now—spoke to me a great deal about what it was like to float above the earth. She was a very pretty young woman with a good if eccentric education, a little younger than I. She had been aloft several times and seemed to be her uncle's primary protégée. In the morning, when we arrived, I was entrusted with filling the balloon from the gas main. There was a crowd assembled early in the city square, and all day it grew and became further enlivened. I worried for the safety of the balloon, but the young woman informed me that this was the mood at every ascension. I was myself elated at the prospect of going aloft with her. But as it happened, this was not to be. Just when Mr. Wise was finishing his introductory remarks, and as my "niece" (for so she had been billed to the public, so that nothing should appear untoward in our confinement) was about to climb into the basket, a rogue breeze swept into the square, blowing the balloon down sideways toward the crowd. There was much merriment and a little panic. The silk must have found a hat pin or the end of a cigar, for the bag collapsed with a bang and a squeal. To mend the tear and refill would have taken too long, and thus we were obliged to return to Philadelphia disappointed. Mr. Wise salvaged the trip in characteristic fashion: by befriending the train engineer and gaining an all-night course in this man's profession. But thus ended my first attempt to penetrate the secret realm in the air. Eighteen years would pass before I found my next opportunity, yet once I had ascended at last, I would immediately dedicate all my energies to the science. So I often wonder how my life might have turned out differently had fate permitted me access to my passion when so young.

•

MISS MURIEL WISE (on the train to Huntingdon, July 3, 1876): It's very odd at first. You'll see.

ANDRÉE: However, is it a pleasant "odd"? Or an unpleasant "odd"?

MISS MURIEL WISE: Oh, not pleasant—at first. One feels quite out of control. And one can't help but think about falling out of the basket. It's an unnatural feeling, I would say.

ANDRÉE: I think I shall find it pleasant.

MISS MURIEL WISE: You'll soon see.

•

ANDRÉE: As soon as I feel a few "heart leaves" sprouting, I resolutely pull them up by the roots. That is the way I happen to be regarded as a man without romantic feelings. But I know that if I once let such a feeling live, it would become so strong that I dare not give in to it.

ANDRÉE'S MOTHER: From the very first moment he opened his eyes to the light of day he had been an uncommonly big and strong child, and as regards the development of his understanding, too, he was rather before than behind his age. His questions were frequently very difficult to answer, for he was never satisfied with the shell, but always did his best to find his way to the kernel.

ANDRÉE: My father died when I was just ten. He was a druggist and a kindly, ineffectual man. At my commencement from public school, which he survived by only a few weeks, I had been called to the stage so often that a clergyman in the next row in front of my folks was heard to say, "That boy will wear out his shoes going up for prizes," to which my father replied, "That he may, for it is my boy!"

ANDRÉE'S FRIENDS: He was an unpleasant companion at the opera, though, for he would sometimes interrupt the most sublime aria to lean across and whisper at one about how the stage lighting could really be improved, or how a mechanical prop might have been better engineered.

COUNT HUGO HAMILTON (chief of the Royal Patent Office): When I had to convince Andrée that he was wrong about something, I usually had to begin with the story of creation.

•

ANDRÉE: In 1894 I purchased my first balloon, for five thousand crowns. It was French-made, of double-layered pongee, well varnished, by a fine balloon-maker named L. Gabriel Yon, and I christened it *Svea*. I made nine flights in it, each given to aerial photographs and scientific observations: of winds and temperatures at different altitudes, humidity and the formation of precipitates, the vertical movement of sound, and the chemical composition of air. One of my flights became famous in my country, but only because I was lost for a day. I was to enter the clouds above Göteborg, on the west coast, for three or perhaps four hours in the early morning in order to take simple readings, which I did. I knew I was drifting east, but when I descended back down out of the clouds I discovered that I had been moving very quickly, across the whole width of Sweden, and that I had drifted over the Baltic Sea. In all directions I saw only water. Soon I spied a steamship to the south, and I tried to steer toward it using my sails, but the wind was too steadily against me. I determined to cut the ballast lines and rise again, and let this wind carry me to

Finland. The sun came and went between clouds, and the sea changed colors. By three o'clock in the afternoon I had lost altitude once more and I flew very low over the waves. Again there was nothing visible but empty water in all directions. Should the basket touch down and begin to drag, it would tip and fill and quickly sink. But I stayed just aloft, and when it was nearly dark my draglines struck upon rocks, and I saw that I was above a very small and unexpected island. I hung from the drag ropes and then jumped, abandoning my ship, which rose with the loss of weight and sailed away. My island was only a few bare rocks. It was dark and quiet. I saw a larger island not far to the east, and I swam to it, but it too was uninhabited, and also bare of trees. I had long ago eaten all the food that I had packed that morning, and drunk all the beer and Vichy water. Soon it began to rain, but there was no good shelter on the whole of this island. I had no overcoat with me, and only felt slippers over my ordinary town shoes. In short, I had in no way anticipated or provisioned myself for such a journey. Still, *Look at what is possible in a balloon*, I thought. Look at this god-forsaken place I have come to, in another sea, off a foreign shore, a place I could not have found on a map this morning. I could just make out yet another island past mine, with trees, too far away for a second swim. However, my balloon had sailed over it—I believed it would not take long for a rescue party to appear. But thus I sat for sixteen hours. All night! At eleven o'clock the next morning, a fisherman finally rowed to me in his little boat. When I asked him (perhaps ungratefully) why he had not come sooner, he told me that his wife had seen my balloon pass overhead at dusk and she had taken it as a clear sign that the Day of Judgment had come at last. She forbade him to leave the house until morning, when the sun did rise once more in its usual precinct. By the time I reached Helsinki I learned that my "disappearance" had gotten abroad already, and already they were saying, in Stockholm and Göteborg and Oslo, "Where is Andrée?"

·

ANDRÉE (at the Sixth International Geographical Congress, 1895): It is chiefly the central portion, i.e., the most inaccessible part, of the Polar Regions that it should be the main aim of the expedition to explore. Is it not more probable that we shall succeed in sailing to the Pole with a good balloon than that we shall be able to reach it with sledges as our means of transport or with vessels which are carried like erratic blocks, frozen fast to wandering masses of ice? It cannot be denied but that, by means of a single balloon journey, we shall be able to gain a greater knowledge of the geography of the Arctic regions than can be obtained in centuries in any other way.

DR. RAMEAU (French representative): What will you do, Monsieur Andrée, if your gondola descends into the freezing sea before you have time to assemble your boat?

ANDRÉE: Drown.

COLONEL WATSON (British representative): [*interrupting general bustle and laughter*] That the attempt will be attended with great risk is a foregone conclusion and no one knows this better than Herr Andrée. But many expeditions are worth undertaking which are attended with risk.

GENERAL A. W. GREELY (American representative; Arctic explorer): [*standing at back*] Let me tell you that a balloon is subject to a minimum loss each day of one percent of its gas. Hence, if the life of a balloon is to be six weeks, it will at the end of that time have lost about one half of its carrying power. If Herr Andrée has succeeded in obviating this, then all I can say is that I hope, before starting, he will take us into his confidence. It is more than a risky endeavor. It is foolhardy, and doomed, and I don't see that he will ever raise the funding for it from sensible men.

ANDRÉE: May I ask you, gentlemen, when something unexpected happened to your ships, how did you get back? [*a beat*] I risk three lives in what you call a foolhardy attempt, and you risked how many? A shipload. [*waits—rustling in the assembly*] He hopes [*pointing at General Greely*] I may succeed in trying to raise the money. [*pauses; raises his arm with a letter in hand*] Well, I haf got the money!

GREAT HALL: [*rings with cheers*]

•

ANDRÉE (on the train to Huntingdon, 1876): No, what I am saying—

MISS MURIEL WISE: I think I understand.

ANDRÉE: If you had a reliable wind—let us say a trade wind—

MISS MURIEL WISE: No.

ANDRÉE: Pardon me, madam, but do you understand trade winds at all? Do you know how they blow and never cease, no matter the day or the season?

MISS MURIEL WISE: I do know.

ANDRÉE: One may *map* them. They are the unused rivers . . .

MISS MURIEL WISE: But it isn't only wind. There's the sun to worry about—when you dip into a cloud, the hydrogen cools. Down you go. [*gestures*] Right down out of your trade wind. Not to mention the little cross breezes that spin you like a top. I understand the attraction—you've been reading Björling, I imagine. But trust me, Mr. Andrée. It isn't the leisurely ride you envision.

ANDRÉE: [*dazed*] Call me Andrée. Simply Andrée.

MISS MURIEL WISE: You musn't believe everything my uncle tells you, either. Andrée. I'm afraid neither of you will have many repeat passengers on your balloon coaches.

ANDRÉE: [*hesitating; smiling*] I'm so sorry, but would you tell me your name again?

•

ANDRÉE: The problem of balloon travel is that it is a sensation so forceful and so unlike any other as to be unforgettable to any-one who has ever experienced it, yet indescribable as well. It is not only the extraordinary overview of one's daily limits and grounded prospects—a version of that, albeit paler, may be had by scaling a mountain and looking out from a ledge. Nor is it merely the sensation of easily attained velocity, which some will know from sailing vessels. No, what laymen seldom understand is that one travels *with* the wind in a free balloon, so that one has almost no impression of it. There is no sound of wind blowing or rushing by, no feel of it on your skin. In a hydrogen balloon there is almost no sound at all. The sensation is of constant still-ness. The flags aboard hang limp. At first one may be certain that the balloon does not move or rise so much as the world falls away and spins. The patterns of cities and the shapes of rivers become evident. There is the sense of transparency, both visual and aural. I have sailed a mile above Sweden and heard a dog bark in a yard as if I stood beside him. I have found myself in the midst of a great cloud and thus been rendered unable to deter-mine where I was, whether I rose or fell, if I moved with great velocity or hardly at all, or even which direction I should face to look forward. I have fallen so swiftly in the grip of a down-draft that when I poured sand overboard it flew up and hit me in the face. Such speed, silently attained, makes one seem free of nearly every earthly burden and inhibition. At other times, when the wind stopped blowing entirely, I have sat in midair for more than an hour, perfectly still. One seems to be weightless, and materially insignificant. I think it may be only natural to spend such an hour questioning one's decisions and the state of one's grounded existence, in the broadest sense. I decided to go to the North Pole in that hour.

•

August Strindberg (in a letter): If I see my pillow assume human shapes those shapes are there, and if anyone says they are only (!) fashioned by my imagination, I reply:

You say 'only'?—What my inner eye sees means more to me! And what I see in my pillow, which is made of birds' feathers, that once were bearers of life, and of flax, which in its fibers has borne the power of life, is soul, the power to create forms, and it *is* real, since I can draw these figures and show them to others.

And I hear a sound in my pillow, sometimes like a cricket. The noise a grasshopper makes in the grass has always seemed magical to me. A kind of ventriloquism, for I have always fancied that the sound came from an empty hall beneath the earth. Supposing that grasshoppers have sung in the field of flax, don't you think Nature or the creator can fashion a phonograph from its fibers so that their song resonates in my inner ear, attuned as it is to hear so acutely through suffering, privation, and prayer? But this is where 'natural explanations' fall short, and I am abandoning them forthwith!

August Strindberg (in a letter): For mine, for yours, for the sake of all seekers, read the two articles I am sending you, and see that miracles do happen in our time.

The cyclone in Japan is a 'miracle' like the cyclone in the Jardin des Plantes the same day Andrée took off and balloons were hurled to the ground in and around Paris, and I fled to Dieppe.

•

ANDRÉE'S FRIENDS: He had a brown mustachio which he kept bushy, and a very round face, and he liked to wear that almost brimless cap which accentuated the roundness. When he became fascinated with the Arctic we called him "the Walrus." We all thought he should be in politics.

ANDRÉE: The conservatives are always more active in their own behalf than the liberals. The reason is that the liberals or progressives feel sure of the ultimate triumph of their cause because they know they are supported by the law of evolution, while the conservatives feel themselves constantly threatened and are therefore busy protecting themselves.

MRS. MURIEL HAMILTON: He was almost frail when I knew him. He hadn't the broad mustache one sees in the newspaper photographs. A much younger man, of course. Very pale. Very tall.

ANDRÉE: I am not supposed to "understand love"—this is what they say of me. But I have never yet seen a man love in the way I intend it, and I have the impression that women are quite easily satisfied in that respect.

ANDRÉE'S FRIENDS: We all believed he had been jilted, but there were no candidates in sight and of course he would never say.

·

On the evening train, July 4, 1876, Huntingdon back to Philadelphia. Darkness passing by the windows; the rocking and steady clatter. A suggestion of other passengers, some asleep, at the margins. All of this in whispers.

ANDRÉE: You will not come.

MISS MURIEL WISE: No.

ANDRÉE: Then I will stay.

MISS MURIEL WISE: [*pause*] But I don't know why you should.

ANDRÉE: I would renounce my homeland for you. Do you know that?

MISS MURIEL WISE: [*turns away; her window is grimy and empty*]

ANDRÉE: So you will stay and marry him, who cannot love you as I do and never will?

MISS MURIEL WISE: [*smiling wearily*] Andrée.

ANDRÉE: You volunteer? For no more than that?

MISS MURIEL WISE: You'll make me angry with you in a moment.

ANDRÉE: Do you know that one of two fates will be yours? Only two. Let me make this clear. One: he will be a brute in the way many husbands are brutes and he will stupidly forbid you to go aloft. Or B: he will allow it too freely and with equal stupidity, not knowing what is safe or what is not, and your uncle, dear man, will miscalculate and he will kill you one day.

MISS MURIEL WISE: [*looks into her lap*] Forgive me if I have less faith in your predictions than you do.

ANDRÉE: [*gestures*] Mark my words! [*a passenger walks past the berth; Andrée sits back*]

MISS MURIEL WISE: What do you know, Andrée? You've never met Robert.

ANDRÉE: I know my heart.

MISS MURIEL WISE: That I believe.

ANDRÉE: And I know ballooning.

MISS MURIEL WISE: You know what you want to know. What does your heart know? I would prefer to be left out of your predictions.

ANDRÉE: And I know what is brave and what is foolhardy—

MISS MURIEL WISE: [*looking at her hands in her lap; still whispering*]

You're the bully. You're the husband who would forbid this and that, I think.

ANDRÉE: And in addition I know that I love you and that I am a man made to love only one woman and I have waited for her and she was you. The life of my heart will now be finished. [*turns to watch another passenger—a shadow and a rustle of crinoline—pass by; quietly*] And you know this too.

MISS MURIEL WISE: [*puts her gloves on; shakes her head; smiles*] What do you know about ballooning? You've never even been aloft.

ANDRÉE: [*peevish*] You tell me who is the bully. Who among us.

MISS MURIEL WISE: [*turns back to the window*]

Much later, nearing the station.

ANDRÉE: [*kisses her hand*] Forgive me.

MISS MURIEL WISE: Is everyone in Sweden like you?

•

4 April 1896

. . . I don't know how to answer your question, now that you have seen through my thin excuse of the newspaper article (although it was quite true and it has been published; I have left your name out in consideration of your family's privacy). I think you may understand that a trip like the one I am about to embark on does promote self-reflection. This can't be surprising, I suppose? It isn't an accounting or last contact with people who have been important to me— I know better than anyone that we shall be perfectly safe and will surely return in due course (having successfully crossed the Pole— that I can only hope). But it is a queer feeling to be about to do what you have meant to do for many years. It makes one (should I say, it has made me) take the measure of one's progress in other endeavors, or at least other intentions. For instance, I had secretly stored great hopes in marriage. (This topic again. We also spoke about it on the train—do you recall?) But here I am still a family of one, or two counting my dear mother, who has just reached seventy years. By now I am much too on in years myself to marry, and the freedom of unmarried life has made me stubborn, prone to odd hours and informal meals, not to mention quite wrinkled, so who can imagine the sensible woman who would want me any longer? Nevertheless, some days it is a disappointment, for as a young man I felt that love would be the center pole my life might spin around . . .

7 May 1896

. . . I must have conveyed a false impression to you then—indeed, I seem to remember you drew forth from me some rather embarrassing sentiments on that train. I'm sure it was through no fault of your own, however (unless your exceeding charm can be called a fault) and in fact it may not have been you only but the combination of elements—Independence Day in a foreign land, the anticipation of my first flight. Yes, as you suggested, also youth. In any case, no, I may say that I have never lost my head that way again, thank heaven. But when you speak of your life now as a theatre production, and as if this meant it was confined or narrow (forgive me if I have misunderstood your meaning), I think I must tell you that my experience of the theatre may be the very opposite. I am not a great fan of it, frankly, because the people on stage seem to me to speak to the heart of things with too much honesty and unconcealed emotion. I never quite trust that anyone off the stage speaks so, even in the privacy of bedrooms. However, who am I to say, of course? And then there is the strange exception of my time with you, of our train trip, which I do find myself recalling exactly as if it took place on a stage—within some amplifying and transparent box—and yet I sometimes feel that was a day of real authenticity and significance such as I have not had again in my life until now.

20 May 1896

. . . the last letter until we've returned. I hope you received mine of the 7th? I cannot tell you how much pleasure it has given me to be in touch with you these few months. I shall carry our discussions to the Arctic and keep warm with them. It is very possible that we will be blown toward America—how magical it would be to stop in Philadelphia on my long way home and see you again. Also to meet your family at last . . . With great warmth . . .

8 November 1896

Forgive me, Mrs. Hamilton, for not replying to your kind letter much sooner. Between explanations, managing of the world's disappointment (or so it seems), and initiating the preparations for our next attempt, I have been . . . We never departed Spitzbergen for only two reasons: our wait for a strong, steady wind from the south was fruitless, and one of my companions proved frail-hearted. So we will try once more next summer without Dr. Ekholm, and this leaves us a crew member short. All of our tasks require the presence of three aëronauts, and our carrying capacity (not to mention the limits of space in the gondola) can allow for no more than three . . . Let me, then, delay no longer in coming out with it . . .

As I say, Mr. Strindberg is certain he shall try again, and a perfect companion. You will like him. We would arrange a meeting in America between all of us—your husband as well, of course—as soon as possible . . . The gondola will require adjustments to facilitate your privacy: a separate sleeping compartment (it will be very snug, not to say cramped) and special arrangements for daily necessity. My backers have offered to pay for the manufacture of a new and larger balloon in any case. I believe we have all the physical strength we can expect to require in Mr. Strindberg's (much younger) person and my own. You needn't worry that we will require you to drag a sledge.

What we *do* require is exactly what it is most difficult to find: an aëronaut with a good deal of experience aloft in variable and treacherous conditions and a nimble hand with the aërostat. I know of no one who fits that bill better than yourself, even if you are out of practice . . . You would need to be prepared for the cold. We Scandinavians are often blamed for under-estimating that hardship, but I think I can safely promise that our excellent supplies would keep you safe, if not always precisely comfortable . . . Please understand that my first choice would be to have both you and your husband join the expedition. We simply haven't the room for four. The risk to your family cannot be discounted and I would not dare to approach you if your children were younger, but I hope you will take the fact that I ask you at all as an indication of my confidence in our prospects.

I know it is a strange proposal. Some will say a foolish one. I know this so well that I have thus far shared the idea with no one. You are the first to hear of it. Understand that it isn't something so frivolous as the pleasure of your company which makes me seek your assistance. It is, very simply, your perfect suitability to the job. I cannot help but think of the wider significance—of how much it might mean to the Cause of Women, in your country as well as mine. Here in Scandinavia you might be a Nora such as no writer of plays should dare imagine. I also believe that your uncle would have admired your contribution and lent his support, but you can guess if this is true better than I. Still, I emphasize that all these are only secondary considerations. An expedition leader's responsibilities are to the safety and expediency of the campaign, and it is those considerations alone which have led me to you.

> Most sincerely, and with
> deepest professional regard,
> Andrée

•

ANDRÉE: But the attractions transcend the practical, I believe—
as love transcends its sustaining value for the species. To an
aëronaut, there is a net of unpredictable possibilities and alter-
natives always strung just above one's head, above the tree-
tops, only evident in the movement of the clouds. Anywhere
he may be he may look up with his trained eye at the mesh
of breezes and prevailing avenues and know that he could be
somewhere else entirely, regardless of earthly obstacles. The
aëronaut leads two lives, for this reason: one down here, stable
and directed, like anyone else, yet full of longing; the other up
there, satisfied, capricious, and invisible.

•

ANDRÉE: The saddest part in the drama that is constantly played
about us is the reckless waste of spiritual power. In boredom and
tedium and love affairs and regrets.

•

12 December 1896
Stockholm

Mr. Hamilton, Sir,

Your letter could not have been clearer or more sensibly reasoned
and I think it only leaves me to apologize for the very presumption
of the inquiry and to both officially and personally withdraw it. As I
made clear in my last letter, no one has been appraised of the request
except yourself and your wife, and you have my word that no one
shall ever hear of it from me. With all due respect, I feel compelled
to emphasize once more that while your wife was once, briefly, a
person I would have ventured to call a friend, my recent communication with her was merely professional, and in consideration of all

involved I would not let stand even the smallest public suggestion to the contrary. Thank you for your prompt reply and all best wishes.

Sincerely,
Salomon August Andrée

8 May 1897
Stockholm

Dear Madam,

I thank you for your sentiments although it troubles me to know that the news of my mother's death has crossed the Atlantic. Perhaps I am not as prepared for fame as I thought I was. Having discharged my duty to acknowledge your condolences, I must break off all communication with you. We sail for the north in a few days in any case, but regardless I am not the man to communicate with a married woman secretly via addresses not her own or to in any way involve myself in matters her husband might object to. If something in my prior letters or my character gave you the impression that I was such a man, I regret the misunderstanding. Now please excuse me.

•

COUNT C. A. EHRENSVÄRD (captain, Swedish support ship): The vessel was so large when it was in the balloon-house—one hundred feet tall with the gondola attached. It towered over you. But when it was loose in that landscape it became very small. You could see it was under no one's control. But it did appear bound and determined in the same direction as its crew. It was not very many minutes before they had sailed out of sight beyond the mountains of Danes Island. I remember I said aloud, "At that rate they shall make the North Pole in two days." Now it has been ten years. But who's to say? Perhaps they did make the Pole. Perhaps they were the first. And perhaps the next man to make it shall find them there.

•

M. Henri Lachambre (builder of Andrée's balloon): Me, I like to imagine they sailed for many days in that land, seeing new things no man had ever seen, discovering new islands, before they met their fate without regret. My son-in-law prefers to believe that they crossed the Pole and sailed all the way to the New World— perhaps even lived for a time with the Eskimos there. And my grandson believes with all his little heart that at the Pole they discovered M. Verne's volcano and fell down into it, where he cannot decide if they burned to a crisp or continued exploring. Choose your enchantment and cloak the dead. It is all the same, I expect.

•

Muriel Hamilton (in 1927): Of course I wonder how the polar flight might have turned out differently if I'd been with him. Not that I flatter myself. I mean in the way that different events naturally unravel out of single decisions turned one direction instead of another. But I never regret declining his offer. Things may not have ended as we all would have liked with your father, but if I imagine having accepted Andrée's proposal, then I must contemplate the loss of my life with both of you these twenty years, and never having known my grandchildren. In any case, it wasn't in my nature to take such a sudden leap out of all that I was accustomed to. I wasn't like Andrée in that way, and I doubt whether many people are.

No matter how many times it's discovered, the North Pole will always seem to me a silly, untrue place, and I will never understand why anyone would wish to go there. But doesn't it seem a place for a romantic, rather imprecise man like Andrée, in his balloon, rather than an Admiral Peary with his sleds and sys-

tems and great determination, or Mr. Byrd in his buzzing aëro-
plane, there and back in a matter of hours? I do wonder what
became of Andrée and his companions, naturally. Very often I
catch myself speculating still, and picturing the three men on an
iceberg. Even back then, I remember how, for perhaps as long
as a year or two, I thought that I might not hear of it when he'd
landed—he had presumed it may be in North America—and
then perhaps one day a knock would come, and I would simply
open the front door on a warm afternoon, and there he'd be.
Greatly aged, no doubt. Though by now, the man of that particular fantasy appears young again, to me. Isn't it strange how
we drift into old age and find our unfinished youth waiting for
us there, as if we've looped around our lives? This is why I've
begun writing all this down.

MURIEL HAMILTON (in 1928): I do regret that I never went aloft
once more—with someone else, if not with Robert or Andrée.
It was where I belonged, perhaps. Now it's too late. Those balloons are gone, and I wouldn't care for an airship, I think. Also,
I could have gone with them, you know. I wasn't afraid. I was
quite qualified—Andrée was right. I wasn't one to mind the
cold. I've often wondered since if a lady has ever been among
the first to see some undiscovered land, or if a lady's hand has
ever drawn and named an island or cape? There are sound and
precious reasons why we don't risk ourselves in such endeavors—some of the same reasons I stayed at home with you, of
course—and if we one day learn what became of those poor
gentlemen I'm certain I'll be all the more relieved I wasn't with
them. But this is why I do so admire Ms. Earhart.

MURIEL HAMILTON (in 1929): For instance, I remember he said on
the train back to Philadelphia that if we had gone aloft together
he wished we might have never come down. Many more things

of that nature which I only half recall. He spoke English quite well, even back then. His accent was rather dear. His only consistent difficulty was with his v's. He would pronounce them as f's, so that, for instance, "love" became "luf," and perhaps lost a little of its force.

AUTHOR'S NOTE

MANY PASSAGES from "Aëronauts" are adapted from Salomon August Andrée's biographical life. Others are entirely fictional. The following are quoted directly from memoirs, diaries, and letters, obtained from these sources:

pp. 194–95 August Strindberg, "Plan":
From Michael Robinson (editor and translator), *Strindberg's Letters, Volume II: 1892–1912*, Chicago: University of Chicago Press, 1992.

pp. 196–97 John Wise, the invalid aloft:
From John Wise, *Through the Air. A Narrative of Forty Years' Experience as an Aëronaut, Comprising a History of the Various Attempts in the Art of Flying by Artificial Means from the Earliest Period Down to the Present Time* . . ., Philadelphia: To-day publishing company, 1873.

p. 198 Andrée, "'heart leaves' sprouting":
From George Palmer Putnam, *Andrée: The Record of a Tragic Adventure*, New York: Brewer and Warren, 1930.

p. 198 Andrée's mother, "rather before than behind his age":
From Edward Adams-Ray (editor and translator), *The Andrée Diaries:*

Being the Diaries and Records of S. A. Andrée, Nils Strindberg and Knut Fraenkel Written during Their Balloon Expedition to the North Pole in 1897 and Discovered on White Island in 1930, Together with a Complete Record of the Expedition and Discovery, London: John Lane the Bodley Head, 1931.

p. 199   Count Hugo Hamilton, "the story of creation":
From Putnam, *Andrée*.

pp. 201–2   account of the debate, Sixth International Geographical Congress:
Adapted from Adams-Ray, *Andrée Diaries*, and from Putnam, *Andrée*.

p. 204   August Strindberg, "If I see my pillow assume human shapes":
From Robinson, *Strindberg's Letters*.

p. 204   August Strindberg, "miracles do happen in our time":
From Robinson, *Strindberg's Letters*.

p. 205   Andrée, the conservatives and the liberals:
From Putnam, *Andrée*.

p. 205   Andrée, "I am not supposed to 'understand love'":
From Putnam, *Andrée*.